Leabharlann Chontae Luimni
LIMERICK COUNTY LIBRARY

Acc. No. 00403475 **Class No.** AFW

Date of Return	Date of Return	Date of Return	Date of Return

LOVE IN THE PROVINCES

The Novels of Stanley Middleton

A Short Answer
Harris's Requiem
A Serious Woman
The Just Exchange
Two's Company
Him They Compelled
Terms of Reference
The Golden Evening
Wages of Virtue
Apple of the Eye
Brazen Prison
Cold Gradations
A Man Made of Smoke
Holiday
Distractions
Still Waters
Ends and Means
Two Brothers
In a Strange Land
The Other Side
Blind Understanding
Entry into Jerusalem
The Daysman
Valley of Decision
An After-Dinner's Sleep
After a Fashion
Recovery
Vacant Places
Changes and Chances
Beginning to End
A Place to Stand
Married Past Redemption
Catalysts
Toward the Sea
Live and Learn
Brief Hours
Against the Dark
Necessary Ends
Small Change

LOVE IN THE PROVINCES

Stanley Middleton

HUTCHINSON

London

First published in 2002 by Hutchinson

1 3 5 7 9 10 8 6 4 2

Copyright © Stanley Middleton 2002

Stanley Middleton has asserted his right under the Copyright, Designs
and Patents Act, 1988 to be identified as the author of this work

Hutchinson
The Random House Group Limited
20 Vauxhall Bridge Road, London SW1V 2SA

Random House Australia (Pty) Limited
20 Alfred Street, Milsons Point, Sydney
New South Wales 2061, Australia

Random House New Zealand Limited
18 Poland Road, Glenfield
Auckland 10, New Zealand

Random House (Pty) Limited
Endulini, 5a Jubilee Road
Parktown 2193, South Africa

The Random House Group Limited Reg. No. 954009

www.randomhouse.co.uk

A CIP catalogue record for this book is available from the British Library

Papers used by Random House are natural, recyclable products made from wood
grown in sustainable forests. The manufacturing processes conform to the
environmental regulations of the country of origin

Typeset by SX Composing DTP, Rayleigh, Essex
Printed and bound in Great Britain by
Creative Print and Design Group, Ebbw Vale, Wales

ISBN 0 09 179478 1

In mem. S.L., K.W.S. and C.J.G.S.

She walks in beauty, like the night
   Of cloudless climes and starry skies;
And all that's best of dark and bright
   Meet in her aspect and her eyes:
Thus mellowed to that tender light
   Which heaven to gaudy day denies.
Byron

I

The young man stopped, drew himself up, stared across the road. On this fine September evening traffic was relatively light, but a pedestrian careful for his own safety still needed sharp eyes and agility. On the other side another boy of his age, seventeen, dressed almost identically, had raised a hand in greeting. Timothy Hughes acknowledged the half-wave and neatly crossed the road. The second boy, Julian Bishop, consulted his wristwatch and muttered, 'Dead on time.' He tapped the glass with a fingernail to express his satisfaction.

His companion eyed him. Curly hair, neatly parted, fresh face, spotless white T-shirt, denim jeans and black regulation school shoes recently cleaned gave the impression of attempted formality and exactly matched Tim's own. Both grinned. They had followed instructions to the letter.

They looked about them.

'Where's Plunkett?' Julian asked.

Tim shrugged, blew out his lips, concentrated on the window of a house agent's, though at this distance he could not read the notices.

'Ah, I'm not too late, am I?'

Mr Plunkett, their English master, appeared from nowhere, a broad-shouldered man in his early forties, strongly built but nowhere approaching the height of his pupils. 'We've plenty of time,' he said. 'We need first to cross the road, if that's possible.'

He glanced about him, set off with determination. Any saloon car, Tim thought, would have bounced off the man. The boys followed. All arrived at exactly the spot where a minute or two earlier, Tim Hughes had waited. Plunkett looked them over, nodded approval. He himself wore an open-necked white shirt, grey flannels, a tweed jacket and brogues.

'"Let us go, then, you and I",' he instructed.

'The clouds are moving,' Julian said.

'So what?' Tim, comedian's stooge.

'The evening can hardly be said to be etherised. At least, if that means "unmoving".'

Plunkett moved off. He said nothing until he had taken two or three energetic steps when he growled, 'Very good,' presumably congratulating Bishop on his recognition of the quotation from Eliot, or the aptness of his comment. The boys followed the working shoulders up the slight incline.

At the crossroads at the entry to the castle Plunkett stopped and held up a finger for attention. Neither had seen him use this gesture in the classroom.

'I don't want to be too early,' he confided. 'Harald Meades is a stickler for time and if we say we're due to arrive at eight o'clock that means no earlier than five minutes to the hour. And certainly no more than two minutes past it.'

The boys made no comment.

'I think you won't find him immediately eccentric. Neither in appearance nor in manner.'

'But he is?' Julian supplied the question.

'Unusual. Perhaps eccentric was not exactly the right word. You will be able, I think, to talk to him as easily as you talk to me.'

Tim raised his eyebrows conically high, facing away from the master as he was, and Julian responded with a slow, judicial nod.

Plunkett, to his credit, smiled at their antics. 'Watch it,' he said. 'He's not blind.'

A week earlier, at the beginning of term, Mr Plunkett had stopped the two on the corridor at school. This was his usual method. He rarely sent for a pupil. This gave the suggestions, the propositions made at these meetings, an air of fortunate chance, or even favourable intervention from fate or some higher power.

'Ah, gentlemen.' Plunkett addressed members of the sixth, to which Hughes and Bishop had just been promoted, ironically thus, in public. 'I wondered if I could interest you in a small scheme, not without advantage to your good selves, in the Christmas vac.'

The master immediately descended into a more demotic form. A Mr Meades, an elderly, rather wealthy man, who lived in the Park, possessed a largish library. During the Christmas holiday he had made arrangements to have the room redecorated and he needed the assistance of two strong young men to remove then replace the books. He proposed to pay these labourers at something like four pounds an hour, the minimum wage. The job should take three or four days, with a break in the middle while the painter was at work. If they put in eight hours each working day that would mean something like a hundred pounds. 'Not to be sniffed at,' Plunkett concluded, 'even in these days of affluence. Are you interested?'

'Yes,' said Bishop. 'Are there any snags?'

'I'm glad you asked that. I've consulted the school calendar, and you will be able to complete the job between breaking up and Christmas Eve. That is, if you are prepared to work at the weekend.'

'Sundays?' Bishop pursued.

'I believe so. Mr Meades will need to meet you, informally, to judge whether he thinks you suitable. He owns some valuable books, and it may be there will be some small reorganisation of the library and perhaps a search or two. Interest and brain as well as brawn are required.'

Now, a week later, they were on their way this Friday evening to be scrutinised by Mr Meades. Plunkett had indicated exactly the clothes they were to wear. This surprised them. They would have appeared in any case in well-laundered clothes, and would have decided amongst themselves what their appearance was to be.

'If he's so fussy,' Bishop said afterwards, 'why didn't he insist on suits?' This would have caused no inconvenience, as fifth and sixth formers could discard blazers in favour of charcoal-grey jacket and trousers during school hours. Ties were obligatory during term.

'I don't know,' his friend answered, expecting immediate enlightenment.

'I wouldn't be surprised if Plunkett hasn't made all these rules up himself.'

'Why?'

'Honour of the school demonstrated in rational clothes chosen with matching common sense. Men of the world already.'

'Oh, hell.'

Now they set off again. Their road ran through a deep cutting into the sandstone and at one place was guarded with a wide iron gate, fortunately locked back at this minute.

'I believe they close these gates and all others into the Park once a year,' Plunkett said. 'On Boxing Day.'

'To preserve privacy?' Timothy asked.

'Presumably. I have a notion that the residents are themselves liable for the upkeep of the roads. It used to be so, at least,'

They passed a house with small gothic windows at ground-floor level. This lowest wall stood flush with the pavement.

'I don't suppose', Julian Bishop said, 'you get much through-traffic even these days.'

'Might be used for parking, though,' Tim answered.

'Not encouraged.'

'Can you stop it?'

'Gentlemanly vandalism.'

'I suppose you two are both interested in cars?' Plunkett enquired, to keep in with his charges. He stopped again and stared up into the branches of a huge lime tree. The leaves showed little sign of autumnal discoloration. 'Spring is said to be arriving a week or ten days earlier than was the case ten years ago.'

'How do you judge the arrival?' Julian asked.

'Appearance of buds.'

They walked rather more quickly as the road sloped downhill. Plunkett once more called a halt, drew attention to a mansion, three storeys and a tower.

'I believe Lord Belton lived there,' Plunkett said.

'But no longer?' Julian Bishop's voice did not disguise sarcasm.

'No, my young friend. He'll live on one of his estates. If he has a penchant for city life then he'll have a flat in London. Not that I know him.'

'Is he a young man?' Tim asked.

'About my years. Agèd.' Plunkett consulted his watch again. 'These houses are not exactly suited to modern convenience. Kitchens are well below dining-room level. Twelve steps up for every course.'

'It should be easy enough to fit a suitable modern kitchen into a place that size.'

'Yes, and that's been done, and to advantage, in some of them. But I suppose people don't see much edge in being here. The car has made an enormous difference. When these were built, their

4

owners had stables and employed coachmen and ostlers.'

Plunkett stood his ground.

'Some of these places are divided into flats; some have sold off their gardens and there's a rash of what they call town houses. That's brought cars into the streets, and noise.'

'Did the plebs never come and walk about here before that?' Tim asked. 'With those trees it would have been pleasant.'

'People certainly used their legs a great deal more before, let's say, the Second World War than we do. But whether they came here I don't know.'

'How many of these houses are occupied by one family only these days?' Julian Bishop demanded.

'Again I've no idea. Not many I should guess. No.'

'Except your Mr Meades.'

'Exactly.'

They made two more stops at both of which Plunkett spoke about the Duke of Newcastle's park, the course of the River Leen, the division of the city between Norman and Saxon. 'I guess old Plunkett's been mugging up the guidebook,' Bishop pronounced later. The last instructional pause took so long that they had to complete their journey at a very smart light infantry pace. They had no doubt of Mr Plunkett's fitness.

They arrived, not breathless but slightly excited by this last-minute rush.

'This is it,' Plunkett said.

'Not giving much away,' Julian muttered.

All they could see was a substantial brick wall, seven feet high, the whole length of the house and punctured, perhaps two-thirds of the way along, by an arched gate towards which they hurried.

'One minute to eight,' Plunkett said, leaning on the bell.

The gate was of black-painted stout wood almost to the top of the archway. The last foot consisted of wired glass. As they waited the chimes of the Council House clock signalled eight; it seemed to sound remarkably close. Nobody passed them in the darkening street.

'He's in no hurry,' Julian said.

'Patience,' Plunkett said. 'We haven't all the advantage of slim, lively, athletic limbs.' This was a gibe at Bishop, who made no secret of his disdain for compulsory games. He acknowledged the point with a nod and a grin at the master. Plunkett,

Oxford rugby blue, England trialsman, relished Bishop's independence of attitude.

The glass above the gate suddenly displayed a faint gleam. Tim Hughes, who had been humming, stopped.

' "Sometimes a light surprises",' Plunkett quoted, ' "A Christian while he sings." ' A reference to Hughes's second name.

A key rattled and a small rectangular door was opened just off the centre of the massive woodwork.

'Watch the bottom,' a quiet voice warned. Plunkett ushered them forward and the boys stepped over into a wide corridor. The path to the front door was completely enclosed, with walls half glass and half brick, the roof completely transparent. A small bar light illuminated the place from high on the underside of the ridge. Though in structure and materials the corridor resembled a greenhouse, not a plant was to be seen. The larger part of the front door of the house consisted of stained glass, though neither boy could make out its pattern.

'Mr Plunkett,' the soft voice said. 'And these are the young men?'

'Yes.'

'We'll delay introductions until we are indoors and I can see you all.'

The owner of the quiet voice led them into the foyer of the house. They made out his bald head, glasses and beard. Together the four shambled to the foot of the stairs, perhaps a dozen yards from the door.

'Up you go,' Mr Meades's gentle voice encouraged. 'The next floor. I'll follow you at my own speed.'

They gathered on the dim landing. Meades played shortly with a bank of old-fashioned switches, shaped gold and faded porcelain, with only a slight diminution of the faint light below.

'Lead us in, Mr Plunkett.' Meades pointed towards a double door which the schoolmaster bent to open. Brilliant light splashed immediately from a chandelier within. 'This is my library.'

The room was large, almost the street length of the house. A dividing partition between two major bedrooms must have been removed. The walls were shelved and filled with tight-packed books. Two further high sets of shelves were placed at right

6

angles to these walls forming three spacious alcoves. Curtains of brown velvet were drawn over the width of the windows and a small desk and chair, dwarfed by the proportions of the rest of the room, stood before an equally diminutive fireplace, over which on a beige wall hung a picture, perhaps two and a half feet by just over three. The party paused to examine the painting, a squarish khaki building rising amongst trees, apparently the upper part of a larger foundation on the slope below. Meades made no attempt to move them forward. No one questioned him. In the end, he inhaled deeply, as if in disappointment, and whispered, 'Cézanne.'

He waited again, but received no reply, but neither did the party attempt to move away. The frame, Timothy noticed, was modern, a kind of dull silver, utterly plain.

'It's called the *Château-Noir*. He attempted it in several versions.'

Again the silence as the boys moved their heads as if to obtain insights. Bishop plucked at his lower lip.

'Mont Sainte-Victoire is hidden behind.'

The information conveyed nothing to either boy.

'He wished, I believe, to buy the place, but the owners were unwilling to sell. They did, however, allow him to rent a small room there to keep his painting gear and gave him permission to work in the grounds.'

'He'd plenty of money, then?' Bishop asked.

'Yes, but not from painting. His father left him well-to-do.'

Meades ushered them forward into one of the alcoves bounded by cross shelves. There they seated themselves at a rectangular table covered with a dark-red, tasselled cloth. Meades, smiling now avuncularly, switched on a table light and nodded as if all was well. To Tim the party took on a conspiratorial air.

'Well, now,' Meades began, rubbing his hands. 'Do we all take coffee?'

Without rising he swept upwards from the floor a white tray with four cups and saucers. He completed the action in one movement, almost as if he had been practising to impress them. From his other side he produced spoons, a half-bottle of milk and the largest vacuum flask Tim had ever seen. With careful deliberation, a ritual act, Meades unscrewed the cap and began to pour into the cups he had set out.

'How many for milk?' he asked. All three visitors. He completed his hospitable task, leaving his own drink black. Returning the milk bottle to its cool bag, he lifted a basin of sugar lumps and tongs. 'Help yourself,' he ordered. Both boys did as they were told. 'Coffee,' Meades said, 'instant coffee, unlike tea, retains most of the virtues of its taste in a flask. And thus it saves me the time-wasting, at your expense, task of my running in and out to boil kettles or percolators.' He dipped again to the floor and brought up this time a biscuit barrel, which he placed by the lamp.

'Hand them round. Help yourself. Never mind crumbs. My treasure will run the vacuum cleaner over this floor tomorrow.'

Tim guessed, wrongly, that he'd serve either arrowroot or digestive biscuits. They each took a sweet biscuit with a perforated edge and sparkling with sugar.

Meades passed the barrel on. He had no time for sociable eating. He cleared his throat. 'We should introduce ourselves. We all know Mr Plunkett so he can listen. My name is Harald Meades. Harald is spelt with two "a"s, Scandinavian style. I am a retired schoolmaster and librarian and bookseller. In fact, some thirty-five years ago I taught at your school.'

The boys gave their names and the subjects they were studying for 'A' Level, English Literature, French and Latin.

'Not German?' Meades asked, rather aggressively.

They shook their heads.

'Which of you is the better Latinist?'

Tim awarded that palm, with a grin, to Julian Bishop.

'But no Greek?' Meades pursued.

'We both did it for GCSE,' Bishop said. 'We both had A-star grades.'

'Scholars,' Meades said. 'I beg your pardon.' He swung round towards Julian and asked, 'Can you tell me what books are immediately behind you?'

'Lord Byron,' Julian answered.

'You'd make a good policeman.' With approval. 'Have you read any Byron?' Meades now asked Tim.

'*Childe Harold*. We're doing it for "A" Level.'

'With Mr Plunkett?'

'No. Dr Moore.'

'And would you say that he admires Byron?'

8

'He'll make a favourable remark from time to time. I don't think he quite understands why Byron was so popular and significant in his own time. *Le byronisme.*'

'Do you?'

'Easily.'

Plunkett looked on with a satisfied expression rather like that of a circus ringmaster as his animals went faultlessly through their routines. He did not join in the conversation, adding nothing when Meades asked the boys to say why they thought Shakespeare a great poet. His own silence did not deter the boys who showed off, competing each with the other. Their host seemed to enjoy their answers, though he rarely raised his voice, or showed much facial animation.

'If from all the Shakespeare plays you've read you were allowed to act one character, who would it be?'

'Orsino in *Twelfth Night,*' Tim answered at once.

'He's not altogether a satisfactory person, is he?'

'No. The characters in Shakespeare usually have their faults.'

'Prospero,' Mr Plunkett mildly ejaculated.

'He's bad-tempered when he's crossed,' Tim answered, 'even with his daughter and with Ariel, who are both doing their best for him.'

'Like God in the Old Testament, don't you think?'

'I'm no expert, I'm afraid.'

'Don't you do Divinity at your school?'

'We do Greek New Testament, but that's only a matter of being able to translate it. We don't talk much about the implications of what was going on.'

'And should you have done?'

Tim shrugged.

Meades raised his eyebrows. 'It's more important to know Greek grammar than that Christ died for your sins?' Meades's voice barely reached a whisper.

'Is that what you believe, sir?' Julian interrupted. He made the question sound like a genuine enquiry.

'Well, I don't know that I do, though I rather wish it was so. Or should that be "were so"?'

' "Was",' Julian replied, rather loudly, cheerfully. 'Because the use of the subjunctive makes hardly any difference to the meaning.'

9

'Not a suspicion of, let's say, doubt or uncertainty.'

'That's implicit in the opening: "I rather wish." That suggests that you think it isn't so.'

'Good,' Meades said. 'Good.' He breathed deeply, held his breath. 'Who teaches you New Testament Greek?'

'Mr Barnett.'

'I taught him at one time. He was a good linguist. And now, young man,' to Julian, 'after the diversions which Shakespearean character would you choose to play?'

'Easy,' Julian said. 'Hamlet.'

'He dies young,' Plunkett interrupted.

'I don't mind dying on stage.'

They talked over a second cup of coffee, easily supplied from the flask, until past nine o'clock, when Mr Meades invited the boys to look round the library while he consulted Mr Plunkett. Tim found a signed copy of T. S. Eliot's 'Ash Wednesday'and wondered if Meades knew the poet. A short burst of mental arithmetic showed the unlikelihood of this unless the author had dropped the poem in the youthful Meades's pram. Out of sight Meades and Plunkett muttered together. Julian was not to be seen. The boy seemed sealed away from the world. The poem likewise made little sense to him. He could have paraphrased it, but that did nothing to clear the air. It appeared to make unimportant statements. 'I don't play snooker on Wednesday evenings because that's the time I go to the badminton club.' Information of no importance. 'I do not eat meat on Friday because of my religious beliefs' seemed nearer to what Eliot wanted but failed to achieve. Perhaps he was unfair to the poet. He looked again at the signature. Not very distinguished. Scribbled in a hurry. Julian at the far end of the library pulled a ferocious face and devilishly wiggled his fingers either side of his head.

'Are you there?' Plunkett called, hidden in the alcove.

They marched back to the presence of their elders.

Before they had chance to reseat themselves Meades was talking. 'I've greatly enjoyed your company,' he announced, 'and if you seriously consider coming in for four or five days in the Christmas vac to help straighten my library then I would entreat you for a further hour of your time a day or so before battle begins. What do you say?'

10

Both, without further consultation, nodded agreement.

Meades rose, shook the boys' hands, then Plunkett's, said hollowly, 'A very satisfactory evening's work.'

They were out of the library, on to the dim stairs, the foyer, the glazed corridor and through the heavy front gate and into the street inside two minutes.

'That's that,' Julian said. 'Phew.'

'What did you make of our Mr Meades?' Plunkett asked.

Julian answered first. 'His appearance is odd, pointed bald head, cherry nose, spade beard but otherwise he seemed quite conventional.'

'Tim?'

'Why didn't he leave the choice entirely to you?'

'He's the sort of man who thinks he ought to trust his own judgement, and so while he's quite willing to allow me to pick out two of my best pupils, he must make his own final choice.'

'He asked us about subjects we had studied or were studying at school. I suppose that was to find out if we were amenable to instruction.'

'He'd have done better to ask to feel our biceps,' Julian said, sniggering.

'Now, now. ' Tim, as if Plunkett wasn't there.

'Is he well off?' Julian demanded of his teacher.

'Yes. I should guess so.'

'He made schoolmastering pay?' Julian asked impudently.

'His father was a bookseller, as were two of his uncles. Both, the latter in London, both well known among bibliophiles. He inherited from all three. That's the origin of his library. His father, who had sold out and died before I came to this part of the world, had shops in several towns in the Midlands and a large warehouse in Derby.'

'But his son didn't take over?' Tim asked.

'No. Not at once.'

'Is he well educated?' Tim continued.

'He was at my college in Oxford. Before my time. That's how I first came into contact with him. At a reunion. He's sharp.' Plunkett stepping out, held up a hand to prevent further questions. 'And always on the lookout for something further, not altogether on the surface.'

11

'You interest us,' said Julian, camping it up.

'You've a dirty mind, Bishop. This is not the prefects' room.' He gave his pupil a push on the shoulder so powerful that the joker ended staggering somewhere near the middle of the road. When the boy had returned, still grinning if startled, Plunkett continued, 'I think you two made a favourable impression. He's decided he'd like to talk, he said, to exchange an idea or two as you move or dust his books.'

'What does he expect to learn from us?' Tim asked.

'He's an optimist and it's possible you'll come out with some bit or piece he'll be able to shape into something interesting for himself. Why, for instance, did you choose Orsino, a self-regarding failure in love? That would intrigue him. As it does me.' He turned to Bishop. 'You're very quiet, young man?'

'I'm not used to physical violence,' Julian said. 'Without provocation.'

'Did I hurt you? I'm sorry. And I made quite sure there was no traffic about.'

Julian Bishop did not answer, but walked on, head in air. The shove into the road had confirmed Plunkett as the enemy and Julian gave away no helpful information to the other side.

II

A week or two later Timothy Hughes walked round the Lace Market at seven thirty on a Sunday evening. He had spent most of the day on homework, an essay on 'Was Hamlet a civilised man?' and now he strolled along these narrow streets between the towering Victorian warehouses, lifting his eyes from ill-lit brickwork to the narrow stretches of sky and back, as the occasional well-wrought phrase from his recent writing sounded still in his head.

Somewhere near the main gate of St Mary's Church a figure approached, half-recognisable, broad-shouldered with something of a quarter-deck roll. Tim concentrated; the light from street lamps seemed hardly efficient here. Meades. Tim stared again. Mr Meades in a raincoat and scarf but with bald head naked to October's chill.

'Good evening,' Tim said. 'Mr Meades.'

The man stopped, looked enquiringly but without fear at the young man now in front of him.

'Tim Hughes. Two of us came to visit you with Mr Plunkett. From the High School. We're going to help you with your library.'

Tim delivered the information in short bursts, pausing between each.

Meades squinted the harder in the silences. At the end he spoke, but with a question. 'What was the name of the other of Plunkett's pupils?'

'Bishop. Julian Bishop.'

'Yes. That's right. You're the quieter one.' He moved with a sidestep as if he intended to force his way forward, but discontinued and shook his hands in front of him. 'I can hardly make out human features in this light.'

'Yes,' Tim said. 'They don't illuminate the streets very well up here.'

'No. But this is rather off your accustomed path, isn't it?'

'I've got a good pair of legs. And I spend quite a bit of my weekend on homework, and so I go out for a walk on Sunday night, especially when I haven't been running for the school or the county.'

'Is walking good practice for running?'

'I've never thought about it. I've never connected the two. I run seriously on Wednesday afternoons and twice a week at least I tear round the streets on other evenings. I could do more, I suppose, but that régime seems to suit my style.'

'If you ran on Sundays it would occupy so much of the evening.'

'This walk is for pleasure. It's thinking time.'

'What do you think about?'

'School work. Life. Money. Holidays.'

'Girls?' Meades asked.

'Yes. They have their place.' Tim would answer the fool according to his folly.

'At your age I thought of little else. I was obsessed.'

'And you regret it now?'

Meades started back at this question, did not speak immediately but signalled with both forefingers that an answer would be shortly given.

'It meant that I spent less time on my studies, both at school and at university, than my tutors might have recommended, but I was quite good at passing examinations and I was never intended as an academic, so that these extra-curricular activities in their fashion prepared me for my sort of life. You are wondering, I expect, what sort that was, aren't you?'

'Yes.'

'A dilettante. One who delights in an art rather than takes it seriously.'

'Isn't that the same?'

'A good point, my boy, but though the two often overlap, no.'

The pair stood together, used now to the darkness.

Meades pushed his hand down under his raincoat and into his trousers pocket to fish out a handful of change which he examined, his face not six inches above the coins, before thrusting them back. 'I guess I've got enough to buy us both a drink if you'd be good enough to join me.'

14

'I'm afraid I shan't be able to return your kindness. I'm carrying no money at all.'

'Very sensible. If muggers knock you down, they won't make much out of you.' He laughed, as if he'd already outwitted the criminals. They might fracture your skull or cut your throat, but they'll get nothing from your already emptied pockets. 'Let's try the Mitre, shall we?' They set off. 'Not on account of its quality but its proximity. It's only a few yards.'

On the way Meades asked, 'Do you know what a mitre is?'

'A bishop's headgear.'

'Do you know what it was in Greek?'

'No.'

'I'm not surprised. It was a fillet for women's hair.'

'I'm not sure that I know quite what a fillet is or was.'

'A band of cloth, in this case. If I'm not mistaken it comes from the Latin word for a thread. So presumably it would not be too wide.'

They entered the Mitre and found the bar they chose almost empty.

'What will you have?' Meades enquired. He seemed almost cheerful. 'Beer? Lager?'

'Beer, please.'

'Mansfield Ale?'

'Is that good?'

'I think so. Of course I don't know the taste of young people these days.'

The place was not well lit, but had a solidity about it. The tables, of dark wood, had seen long wear and were none the worse for it. Meades ordered two pints. When he had served them, the barman asked if they would like more lights.

'No, thank you. These will suit me.'

'As long as you can see your glass, eh?' The man polished a square foot of the surface in front of him with his apron before disappearing, all smiles.

Meades chose a table at which the two settled. An apparently married couple and a solitary drinker were the only other occupants. The man and woman seemed to be discussing an incident from a recent holiday. 'Yes, that's the thing I couldn't understand about him,' she said. The answer in her husband's deep voice made no sense to people at the other side of the room.

Meades raised his glass to his companion, who responded with reciprocal silence.

'Not very busy,' Tim ventured. He felt slightly uncomfortable, unsure that he'd done right to accept the invitation.

'No,' Meades answered. 'I guess it will be more crowded in the daytime when the offices are open and the courts in session, and parties of tourists are doing the rounds. It's something of an attraction these days. And many of these warehouses have been made into flats.'

'For what sort of people?'

'I'm no expert. I imagine there'll be a fair range from small student bedsitters to quite luxurious apartments.'

'I don't know anyone who lives here,' Tim offered.

'I must say I did go a few months back into a most glittering penthouse on the fourth floor of a former lace factory The man who lived there owned the building and had converted it. Floor by floor and quite magnificently. The view over the town was really spectacular.'

'But there'd be no garden,' Tim said.

The objection seemed to worry Meades for a moment, so that he sat stroking his chin before lifting his glass. 'Ah, no,' he said, sipping, 'a garden.' He sniffed the air. 'A garden these days is not always an advantage. Are your parents keen horticulturists?'

'Yes. My mother especially. She spends hours out there.'

'And your father?'

'He'll lend a hand.'

'Good for him.' That seemed a curious remark to the boy. Meades continued, 'They don't mind your being out on your own in the evening.'

'They'd complain if I was out every night, because they think I'd be neglecting my work. "'A' Level needs assiduity" is one of my father's often repeated apothegms.'

'Is that what he calls it?'

'At one time there was a bit of an argument. Not with me. He took both sides. Apothegm or Apophthegm. I'm not sure but I think both are pronounced in exactly the same way. I didn't know the word and that gave him a slight advantage. He didn't do Greek at school and was slightly envious that I did. So if he had a word I'd never come across he'd make a bit of a song and dance about it.'

'Maliciously?'

'No. Not at all. I think he hoped it would make me more careful not to leave gaps in my knowledge. He didn't like to be caught out himself and so he was preparing me to be a know-all.'

'A polymath?'

'Yes. He'd like that.'

Meades was unsure whether it was the idea or the word Mr Hughes appreciated. 'What is he? A schoolteacher?' he asked.

'No, a solicitor. Commercial law is his line. He doesn't talk about it much at home. My mother doesn't want to hear about it. He laughs at her, and says, "That's where the money comes from".'

'It's a well-paid branch of the law, or so I'm told.' Meades sipped. A small wart of froth showed on his lip until he extracted a large white handkerchief and dabbed it away. 'And is that the career you'll follow?'

'I'm not sure. I shan't apply to do law at university. English is what I'd like to do.'

'Has that much commercial value? In the hard world?'

'I'm not sure. A decent degree from a good university will get you started these days, don't you think? I know that nowadays there's a good deal of talk about the value of vocational training. We discuss it in General Studies. A doctor will spend most of his time studying medicine and I'm never sure that's altogether good.'

'Why do you say that?'

'Doctors have to deal with people who are desperately ill, or with bereaved relatives, or patients whose lives are about to be changed. One needs to know about life to handle these matters as well as about the medicine to treat the illness.'

Meades nodded cheerfully. Presumably he enjoyed hearing Tim Hughes pontificating, though ironically or not he could not quite decide for himself. They talked, fluently, until Tim had an inch left at the bottom of his beer glass, when he said he ought to be on his way.

'Will your parents be worried?'

'I doubt it. They're not at home. They're out to dinner. I guess they'll be back at about eleven thirty.'

'There's no hurry, then.'

'I have, afraid, one or two things to do.'

17

'Connected with school.'

'No. One of them is to listen to a CD of the Kreutzer Sonata. Another is to look up a passage in *Hamlet* that's worrying me. Last but not least is to have a quick squint at the *Observer* Review.'

'Thank you.'

Tim could not tell whether Meades spoke in sincerity or with sarcasm. They left the pub together as another party burst noisily in, and set off towards the centre of the town. They passed a newish façade, decorated with a line of small lanterns.

'That will be a nightclub, won't it?' Meades asked.

'Yes. Toby's.'

'You've been in?'

'Yes. Twice. For birthday bashes.'

'Your parents didn't mind?'

'No. Or they didn't say so. They worry about drugs and alcohol . . .'

'And AIDS?' The interruption sounded frantic.

'Yes. I suppose so. Not particularly with Toby's. It's pretty conservative and expensive. I can't afford to go regularly.'

'If you took me in, would I seem out of place?' Meades asked.

'I'm not an expert. I've been in this and one other.'

'There are others here in the Lace Market?'

'I know of three.'

'And if I appeared?' Meades sounded almost pathetically eager.

'You'd find, as you'd expect, a large majority of young people. Old people would not want to be sitting about drinking and listening to entertainment that wasn't directed at them until three in the morning. I have seen elderly people there. I remember last time I was in Toby's, some crowd had brought in an old couple, for a golden wedding anniversary.'

'Were they enjoying it?'

'I can't say. It's rather dark where they were sitting and certainly they didn't leap about. People kept toasting them and they'd raise their glasses in response. But it's hard to say. Some sit there with funereal faces, others talk quietly and other groups suddenly burst out with great, noisy howls and whoops of laughter.'

18

' "Set the table on a roar"?' Meades quoted.

'Alas, poor Yorick.'

They walked down a narrow alley, darkly lit, cobbled still.

Meades seemed not to have any trouble in keeping up with his companion.

'Are your parents strict?' he asked.

'Not really,' Tim answered. 'My father likes me to be conscientious about school work. He got his degree the hard way. He left grammar school where he was doing well at sixteen, after matriculation, went into a solicitor's office and qualified by taking the Law Society's exams. He also did an external degree in law, working in the evenings. He took the degree after he was a qualified solicitor, not the other way round. There was no need, but he felt the necessity to carry the letters LLB after his name. Later he took an LLM. It was hard work. My mother's told me how he'd sit up half the night studying.'

'I can understand that. How old is he?'

'Fifty-two last week. Though he doesn't look it. He thinks I'm doing it, or going to, the easy way and he doesn't want me to make a mess of it. So he's always keeping an eye on me.'

'And you tend to satisfy him?'

'I try.' The boy smiled. 'I'm fairly amenable and I'm studying subjects I like, so it's not difficult. I put work in. Sometimes he annoys me by advising me to do things that I know are useless or irrelevant, but I don't kick up a fuss. It's hardly worth it. He's by and large a sensible man, but I imagine all parents get across their offspring some time or other.'

They were walking now in well-lit streets towards the city square. On their side were shops with offices above while over the road towered great, many-windowed buildings with porticos and wide steps up from the street. These, Tim thought, were clubs, sober enough for the very well-to-do and, in one case, the headquarters of a multinational oil company. The impressive stone façades indicated success, both in commerce and then pleasure, the commanding size needed no neon lights to advertise itself. Here wealth breathed and bred.

The two had now emerged into the square before the Council House, which offered a quiet imitation of its daytime activity. Dark groups, coupled figures walked about as if they knew exactly where they were going, unlike the dawdling midday shoppers. Young people sat on the Council House steps, or stood expectantly by the stone lions awaiting lovers, friends, partners in pleasure, the future.

Meades looked round, nodded, fiercely in exasperation. 'Damn me,' he said.

Tim glanced over in surprise at the vehemence.

'They've started,' Meades began in explanation, 'to put up the Christmas decorations. In October. Don't you find that ridiculous?'

'If you like them at Christmas, won't the same be true of October?'

'Not of necessity. One tires, you know. And the objects themselves become shabby.'

'They must have a great number to put up and only a limited workforce.'

'Then they should start in the backstreets and finish here on the Council House when the Christmas tree goes up some time in December.'

Tim left it at that.

The two crossed the square and at the far corner they paused again.

'The parting of the ways,' Meades said. 'Are you catching a bus?'

'No, I'll walk. It's a fine night. I'll still be home well before my parents.'

Meades raised his left hand to his cheek as if petitioning for permission to speak. 'I'm glad you and your parents get on well together.'

'Yes,' Tim answered. It seemed the only thing to say.

'My parents', Meades spoke calmly, 'were both mad. Quite mad. In different ways. There was little I could do about it.' His illustrative chuckle seemed embarrassed. He thrust out a hand, which Tim grasped. They shook and, keeping silent, Meades turned and made for home.

Tim, legging it northwards, felt exhilaration. The west wind scattered spots of rain.

III

'Saw your Eric Plunkett in the street today,' Timothy Hughes's father informed him over their evening meal.

'What was he doing?' Mrs Hughes asked. She feared conversations would flag if she did not inject questions.

'Like me, going home. I was just walking round to the car park.'

'And did he say anything interesting?' she pursued.

'He just offered me a word or two about this Harald Meades man. The one Tim's going to help with his books. He asked me if I knew him.'

'And did you?'

'I knew the name. Thirty years ago an A. F. Meades had a large, the largest, second-hand bookshop in Beechnall. The whole family were, I understood, in the same business, but not together. One in London, another in Derby in a very big way. Our local man, your Meades's father, seemed in some form or other to have kept all three going during the war. One of the brothers was in the Army. At least, I remember him telling me this in the shop on one occasion. I was only a boy, Tim's age, but I suppose he knew my face; I was in the place often enough. He had had great difficulty he said, getting employees, but he'd managed with the help of two or three retired clerks and some women. Most young men were in the forces or in reserved occupations. He seemed quite proud of his efforts. I'd forgotten all about it until Plunkett raised the matter.'

'What was he like?' Tim asked, remembering Harald's description of his father.

'Small, bald, foxy-faced man who always wore a kind of khaki lab coat in the shop. The sort of thing greengrocers used to have.'

'Eccentric?'

'Not that I noticed. He retired soon after this time. He was pretty old then, getting on for his seventies, I guess. At least he looked it. His son, your man, was said to have taught at your school. I don't know why I remember that.'

'An interesting sort,' Melissa Hughes glossed in a bright voice.

'You could be right. He knew a great deal about books and my friend, Herbert Houldsworth, who worked with me then in the office at Pearl, Simmonds and Shaw, used to claim old Meades was very well-to-do. Both his brothers had died and their businesses sold up, and as neither had married they'd left him all their money. The London antiquarian man, the oldest, owned his valuable premises as well as some very rare books. Herbert always seemed to collect these intimate family details. Where he got them from I don't know. I think he's the present Meades's solicitor, if I'm not mistaken, but he'd no connection with them then. Or I think not. Though he'd been at the High School where perhaps your Meades taught him. I'd let all of this drop from my mind, until Plunkett reminded me this afternoon.'

'That was the father, wasn't it?' Melissa said. 'He's dead, isn't he?'

'I expect so.'

Mr Hughes now concentrated on his roast beef and Yorkshire pudding. After he had congratulated his wife on her cooking, he watched her and his son clear the plates and return with his favourite sherry trifle.

'We're triumphing tonight,' he said to Tim, reorganising his serviette.

'In what way?'

'Beef and trifle. Good strong food. Every mouthful counts.'

'Yes.' Tim wondered where his father had picked up these phrases. His family? Mrs Hughes now served the trifle. In spite of his father's praise the old man did not eat particularly large helpings. He watched his wife's spoon with care and would have ordered her to take back anything more than his considered share. He thought often of his health and waistline. He drank no wine.

'And how did you find your Mr Meades?' he asked, in no hurry to begin on his second course.

'Polite. Rather old-fashioned.'

'And his library is large?'

'Oh, yes. Several thousand volumes.'

'And well organised?'

'Yes; he mentioned a slightly reformed Dewey system.'

22

'With a card index?'

'Not that I saw. A computer.'

Mrs Hughes was now ready to begin on her pudding. Father picked up, brandished his spoon. Silence descended again. His mother served Tim with a second large helping before the father had finished his first.

'Can I tempt you, Charles?' she enquired.

'No, thank you. No. Admirable as it was. You've excelled yourself, m'dear.'

On evenings when she was certain that her husband would be home on time, she prepared what she called 'a Sunday meal'. On other nights, the meal would be as substantial, but not served on the special china, large plates with patterned blue edges, a huge meat dish, gravy boat, deep vegetable dishes, all matching. If, and it seemed possible, Charles Hughes had brought no work home with him, the meal would last longer by a few minutes, as if the participants were at a celebration, or observing a rite. After an unhurried cup of coffee, Mr Hughes would retire to the sitting room with his as yet unopened *Times* and some programme on BBC 2 or Radio 3.

Tim helped clear the table. 'I'll give you a hand with the washing-up,' he said.

'There's no need. You'll have work to do.'

'This won't take all night.'

She enjoyed her son's company; he knew she would not use the dishwasher unless they had guests.

'Dad taking a break?' the boy asked, once they'd begun.

'Yes. He's been very busy. On a particularly nasty case.'

'He hasn't said anything to me.'

'No. He wouldn't. It involved incest. And money.'

'The Drayton business. I've seen the reports in *The Times*.'

'The case hasn't opened yet. They're still pursuing enquiries. Your father says it's extremely complicated.'

'Where does he come in?'

'He's assisting John Drury, the QC who's appearing for the second wife and the daughter. They're about the same age, I believe. Late twenties.'

'It upsets him, does it?'

Mrs Hughes glanced towards the door in case her husband made a sudden entry. This was unlikely, but her husband's behaviour had a streak of unreliability in it that made her careful; she had been caught out before.

'He says it does, but I don't know. It's quite a feather in his cap to be part of the John Drury circus. He won't appear any old how and for any solicitor. And very well paid. Drury expects value for money and publicity in the right quarters, but I think Daddy's good at his job. He can winkle things out and he knows the law pretty well.' She shot another over-the-shoulder squint at the door. Mr Hughes did not appear. Tim showed no signs of apprehension. 'He says he doesn't like court work, but that's magistrates' court appearances, when you're never sure when you'll be called and you're likely to be hanging about in corridors.'

'I'd have thought you'd have wasted more time in the crown court.'

'I think you do, but you're being well paid for it. And people admire him that Drury and Carberry and others use him. Brings the firm kudos, so that they're never short of work.'

'Good.'

She lifted her head at the word, suspecting irony. 'And it gives him something to talk about.'

'You mean he boasts?'

'Well. Not exactly. Your father is one of the most reticent of men when it suits him. But he'll let out selected titbits, probably after court proceedings are over and done with. Some lunatic thing some judge has said, or some bit of scandal one of the London lawyers had let slip. They're like old women are the legal profession.'

Tim laughed, as did his mother. The boy enjoyed these conversations. He and his mother had talked together since he was quite small, but in this last month or so, now he had joined the sixth form, she had switched the tenor and topics of conversation. Now, every so often, though not invariably, she had spoken about her husband. Before, Daddy could do no wrong, took his Olympian decisions and was not to be questioned by lesser mortals, wife and child, but these days she'd suggest that Charles did not always act rationally, was guided by whim or habit. Though she spoke lightly, without rancour, she seemed to be testing out her son to see if he would make a suitable ally, if the need arose.

'Hasn't he any work tonight?' Tim asked.

'He arranges it. Every so often he'll tell me, "I'll be home on time tomorrow and have a quiet evening. Put my feet up."' She imitated him quite well. 'And I know what that means. A rather more formal meal, with the best china and cutlery, and flowers on the table. And I'll ask him what he'd like. Usually I make the choice. Tonight he chose the roast beef and Yorkshires, followed', she imitated him again, 'by trifle.'

'And why does he do this?'

'I guess he's demonstrating to himself that he's made the grade.' She ironically emphasised the rhyming words. 'He has arrived at a station in life where he can not only utterly please himself, but can order the meal.'

'Like a restaurant?'

'Well, yes, except this is at home. He's not at the beck and call of chefs or wine waiters, not that he'll drink wine. He's in complete control.'

'Odd,' Tim mused.

'He's had to work very hard to get where he has and still hasn't lost the habit. Most evenings he can't exactly say when he'll be home. He knows you and I eat at six whether he's here or not; he also knows I shall have a meal ready that can be slipped into the microwave or served cold, a salad or something of the sort, meat or salmon, in the summer. He won't starve.'

'He doesn't eat a great deal.'

'He's not a growing boy and he's quite proud of his trim appearance. It's another sign that he's reached the status, the way of life he's always aimed at.'

'How often does he order these rest evenings?'

'You ought to know, if you're anything like observant. I'd say once or twice a month.'

'On no set day?'

'No.'

'And do you ever get two of these feasts together?'

'No. He might take me out to some legal dinner on the following night and he always makes a point of telling me that the food is nothing like as good as I serve. "You don't need to disguise the taste" is his line in compliments.'

'Is that anywhere near the truth?'

'Yes. The butcher and the fishmonger do me well, and I buy my vegetables from Mrs Smithson's husband's allotment.'

'Funny man.'

'No, I don't think so. Your father knows what he likes. And he has strict limits. It's this early life of his. He was short of both money and time for study. It was often touch and go whether he could afford a cigarette or a half-pint of beer. So he put them out of his life. I'm glad he did as far as smoking's concerned.'

Tim continued with his tea towel, carefully polishing the crockery he had dried.

His mother set off again. 'Sometimes, not very often, he'll say that it's spoilt him for pleasure. A glass of wine gets in the way of his career.'

'Does it?' Tim tempted her into indiscretion.

'I doubt it. It doesn't get the chance. But he's quite possibly right that he's the man he is because of his abstemious youth. He thinks university students enjoy their lives. They learn, if they're serious about their subject, but they also have time to spread themselves, with sport or girls or some hobby, acting or music. There's leisure at university for these extra-curricular activities, and if you don't make use of them then you haven't made the best use of your time. He's often hinted that he envies me the years I spent at university.'

'And is that right?'

'I suppose so. There are students who spend all their time in study, but they're warped. Or at least that's what I think. Girls, on the whole, work harder than boys, but they always seem to be in love with somebody, or worried about their periods or their mothers.' Melissa Hughes laughed. She had cleared the sink and was drying her hands.

Tim, half grudgingly, could see she was an attractive woman. 'Was he', he asked, 'much the same when you first met him?'

'Oh, worse. He was a fully qualified solicitor and was starting to study for an LLM. Now he's senior partner, is respected, is on this committee and that, is consulted by this society or that notability. But since you've reached the sort of age he was when he first started to be serious about the law, I think it's brought some of the old traumas back. Is that the right plural?'

'Not in Greek. You're worse than he is.' Tim rolled down his shirtsleeves.

She touched him on the arm. 'That's why he's worried about you and this Meades man.'

'Worried! What's he afraid of?'

'Mr Meades is out of the ordinary run of acquaintances. Your friends, your teachers. Your father often thinks about a lawyer he knew, a very successful man, and helpful to your dad when he was beginning his career. And this man had a son, very gifted, I believe, but he got into the wrong company, took to drugs and committed suicide. He was in his early twenties. His father never recovered. He retired early, he could afford to, retired to some village in Leicestershire where he came from and dragged about all day; he's still alive, in scruffy clothes.'

'He fears I'll end up like that?'

'I don't think so. But he wonders what that father could have done differently in bringing up his son.'

'And I worry him, in the same way?'

'I wouldn't say that. Your father's a fairly rational man. But there is this dark streak in his nature, which leads him to think something dreadful might happen if he's not careful. He's glad you're doing well at school. It would have broken his heart if you'd thrown away your chances there.' Melissa Hughes straightened her hair in the kitchen mirror. 'He'd like to see you the all-round man. That's his expression. But he can't help thinking to achieve it you'll have to be into drink, drugs, tobacco, women.'

'Does he think old Meades will be providing these delights?'

Melissa aimed a playful clout at him. 'Of course he doesn't. But anything slightly out of the ordinary makes him suspicious. "There couldn't have been a more caring father than Daniel Tempest," he says, "nor a cleverer man. But somehow his son broke clear of his influence and there he was, dead by his own hand at the age of twenty-three".'

'Was the father strict?'

'Not unduly. Nor did he neglect him. He put in a great deal of time with the boy. As far as we can understand he did everything right, but look what happened.'

'Perhaps the son's failings were genetically based.'

'But where did he inherit those genes?'

The mother inspected her kitchen, found everything straight and to her liking. She moved towards her son, smiling up, then linked her arm in his. 'Come on,' she ordered, 'Let's go and see the ogre. He might need more coffee. A liberal second cup.'

'For the all-round man.'

She slapped him sharply across the buttocks, then kissed him and pushed him towards the door. Both giggled, but straightened their faces for father.

Mr Hughes sat with his legs out in front of an unlit gas-fire. 'Done all the work?' he enquired jovially.

'As always,' she answered. 'Would you like another cup of coffee?'

'I've not quite finished this.'

'It'll be stone cold.'

'But delicious. Do you know when I've had occasion to work in a tropical country I've often greatly enjoyed an iced coffee.'

This was father boasting, Tim thought. 'Don't write me off as a provincial, blinkered dunderhead. I've been sent abroad to Africa and India to pronounce on the law there.'

'Finish it off and I'll get you another.'

Charles Hughes did as he was ordered, but cheerfully. He surveyed himself, found himself lacking and sat up straighter before he addressed his son. 'Well, young man? Thanks for giving your mother a hand. What's the programme now?'

'Homework.'

'And that consists of?'

'Latin prose. Then a piece of a French novel to read.'

'Which do you enjoy more?'

'The Latin. It's a sort of crossword puzzle.'

'Are you allowed to look words up?'

'Yes. As long as I note them down somewhere, principal parts and all.' Tim smiled to himself. 'I imagine there is a further matter of style. I compare what I've written with such Cicero as I've read. Or I'm supposed to. And we go in for such sophistications as attracted subjunctives.'

'There's more use of the subjunctive, is there, in Latin than in English?'

'Oh, yes. It's pretty well disappeared altogether in English.'

'Does that mean that Latin is a more subtle language than English, can express more shades of meaning?'

'You'd think that would be so, but I doubt it.'

'Why is that?'

'We sometimes discuss this with Jack Barnett when he gets

28

tired of us and our attempts at Latin or New Testament. He says it's good for us to discuss the functions of language, and where better than in a foreign-language lesson. The Anglo-Saxons used the subjunctive more than we do, and yet we regard them as rather a plain, rough lot. Eskimos have dozens of words for snow in its differing forms and Sanskrit apparently has a whole host of synonyms for "lotus". That may be useful to Indian priests or poets but not to us. I understand that in some cultures there are special ways, specific vocabulary and so forth, for speaking, let's say, to royalty.'

'The peasants wouldn't know it?'

'No. Certainly not. But at some stage it seemed useful, just as doctors have their own jargon.'

'And lawyers.'

'And literary critics.'

'But it seems odd that people far back in time should have these complications of language that we don't seem to need.'

They talked for five minutes, both enjoying the exchanges. Tim was surprised to note how keen his father was to learn, to tackle new ideas. Melissa did not appear with the promised second cup of coffee so that Charles Hughes now kept glancing towards the door.

'Your mother's taking her time?' he asked, lips barely open.

'I expect she's spotted something that needs clearing up and she's set about it.'

'Yes. Perhaps so. Did you think your mother looked tired this evening?'

'She seemed very lively to me.'

'Did she? What were you talking about in the kitchen?'

'The usual. Me, you and her.'

'And had she any complaints?'

'No. She seemed contented, and lively, as I said. Satisfied.'

'I sometimes think she is too self-effacing, modest, altruistic for her own good. I often wonder if it's a sufficiently full life for a university graduate to be cooking meals, washing clothes, polishing furniture.'

'It would depend what was going on in her mind. She reads a fair amount and attends classes, and she gardens.'

'She hasn't many friends.'

'Oh, I don't know.'

29

The turning of the doorknob interrupted them. Melissa Hughes appeared with coffee. 'Sorry I've been so long. I had a phone call from Phyllis Gregory. She's organising a little bus trip out to Derbyshire next week. Buxton, Matlock. Early start, early return before it's too dark. Lunch at the Peacock.'

'How many are going?' Hughes asked.

'Twelve, now, with me.'

'And who's this Phyllis Gregory? I've never heard her name before.'

'She's not been here long. Lives next door to the Marshalls. You'd like her.'

Hughes, rather pompously, Tim thought, gave his approval to the expedition, not noticing his wife's expression. Tim left for his Latin prose and Melissa, pressed to stay, said she'd be back in half an hour when she'd written two short letters.

'On the word-processor?'

'Where else?'

Her husband picked up his scalding black coffee, blew on it, returned it to the table without one sip. He looked round the room, as if he were about to list the contents, sighed, picked up his *Times*, straightened it, then began to read. He folded the paper to the back page, took out a handsome gold biro and began on the Crossword. He solved two ingenious clues, certain that the setter's answers could be nothing other than his, and felt better about the world.

IV

'I've had a phone call from your Mr Meades,' Melissa Hughes told Tim as he arrived back from school. 'He says you and Julian Bishop aren't to go on Saturday afternoon.'

'Right. I'll pass the message on.'

'What was the idea of this visit?'

'I'm not sure. Just another check-up that he hadn't engaged a couple of louts to shift and dust his books.'

'Last night something happened,' she said.

'To Meades?'

'No. But the man next door. They had a robbery. In the early hours.'

'And why does that interfere with Saturday?'

'It means he has to go to see somebody, some relative of the neighbour on that day. Presumably to give his account. It's not very clear to me.'

'Why can't the neighbour tell his relatives?'

'He's away somewhere. On the Continent. The relative lives in Worksop but will send a car over for Mr Meades.'

'I see, as the blind man said.'

Melissa moved back to her kitchen to fetch her son a cup of tea and a still-warm rock cake. When she returned to the dining room, where Tim was hacking through the morning's paper, 'Not too many crumbs now,' she warned. 'And don't muddle your father's paper too much.'

'It's the Sports and Arts section. He'll never notice.'

'You never know.'

She seated herself at the table. 'Don't you want to hear about the robbery?' she said.

'Go on, then. I can see you're going to tell me.'

'It wasn't a next-door neighbour exactly, but somebody at the back of the house. It's some distance away. A hundred and fifty yards or perhaps more, with a substantial brick wall between the properties. But it would appear that the criminals made their entry through Meades's garden and over this wall.'

'Why?'

'He didn't know. He seemed to think it a long way round and he wondered if they, the robbers, weren't wandering about at the back of his house and others along his road on the lookout for a suitable place for a break-in. But', here Melissa's eyes danced mischievously, 'he has the impression that the whole thing was planned.'

'How come?'

'The man who was robbed was a Mr Malcolm Newman and he is said to have quite a valuable collection of paintings.'

'Who says so?'

'Ah, ah. The relative at Worksop. Mr Meades didn't know Newman, but the relative in Worksop knew him, and it's from him and the police that he's collected all these bits and pieces of information. But he wants you to telephone him, so he can apologise at first hand.'

Tim postponed the phone call until after the evening meal.

Meades seemed genuinely glad to hear him, even enthusiastic. 'I'm glad you could ring so quickly. I like to share my little bit of excitement.'

'Yes.'

'It would be about one thirty a.m. on Monday morning last, and I couldn't sleep. I pulled my dressing-gown on, went downstairs for a cup of Options, a chocolate drink I've recently become very fond of, and took it up to the library. I'd switched a small portable electric heater on and sat looking out of the window. Suddenly there was an almighty banging and ringing from this house just across from mine in Anglesey Avenue. There hadn't been a murmur, but now not only were the alarm bells clanging, but lights, something like camera flashes, perhaps that's what they were, all part of the defences against the intruders. I immediately picked the phone up and rang the police, and I must say it didn't take them long to come. I told them that the raid had only just started, so that it didn't seem an inordinate length of time before I saw the police searching the garden at the back. I finished my drink, hauled myself back to bed and had in fact dropped off to sleep when there was a young policeman banging away on my front door. He asked me for a statement, but of course I'd seen nothing.'

'What happened, then?'

'The policeman said they'd be round again in daylight for further investigation. We did, in fact, walk up the garden to the wall, but there's a shubbery with trees my side and it was a very dark night. The policeman said he thought he could make out footprints and though he had a powerful torch I couldn't see much. And if there were prints, they might well have been my gardener's who'd been about up there that afternoon. We went back in, at length. I've never seen anything so slow. He did everything at a drop-dead pace, especially the report. He read it out like a small child learning to read.'

'Was it in joined-up writing?'

'Eh? Oh, I didn't look at what he put down.'

'Had they taken much?'

'He said he wasn't sure, but he didn't think so. The burglar, burglars, had broken into the front of the house, into the hall, and immediately the alarm started, really hard, and lights came on and cameras were used. The intruder didn't expect that, panicked and dashed out.'

'Without taking anything?'

'Not quite, but that didn't emerge until the next day. Another pair of policemen came round at about eleven, talked to me for a few minutes, walked up with me to the library and saw the place I'd been sitting. One of them made a drawing The other commented on my books and said he was interested particularly in an historical novelist called Alfred Duggan. I had one or two, but they were not my style, though Evelyn Waugh praised him. He'd read the odd one when he was a child from his father's shelves. His father was a teacher. And he had come round, somehow, trying to collect them, he didn't know why. He enjoyed reading them, but he wanted first editions.'

'You felt better about him, then? Than the illiterate who interviewed you in the night?'

'Yes. I suppose I did. Each according to his talents. If the burglar had attacked me, I would have been pleased with that slow young man's presence. He'd have given a good account of himself with his fists. As he was leaving he said, "Many a good hiding I've had from some of these criminals, but I'll say this for myself, I've handed them back just a bit in return. We policemen

33

can only go so far. Not like them. But I have a time or two lost my wool, and set about 'em." '

'I see.' Tim's voice soothed and encouraged.

'Anyhow the morning pair took me up the garden. I hadn't gone myself because although I am curious, I didn't want to interfere with the evidence. They pushed about, the pair of them, in what seemed an efficient manner, and showed me where they judged the intruder had come over the wall into my garden and the way he'd climbed out. They went about it carefully and then, after a fair time poking about in the shrubs and ivy, they came up with a picture. It was a sporting cartoon with the glass and frame smashed as if the burglar had dropped it over the wall and then jumped on it. They packed it carefully away because it might have useful fingerprints. They didn't know whether Newman's cameras had snapped anything useful. They concluded, I don't know how, that the criminal had escaped by running down my path and climbing my wall out into the street.'

'And have they caught him yet?'

'No. But the next thing that happened was that I had a call that evening from a man I know quite well who lives near Worksop, who turned out to be the cousin of Newman. I'd no idea. He's the one who's coming Saturday and who is preventing me from seeing you.'

'Had the intruder done much damage?'

'I think not. The alarm, which was really loud, had gone off immediately the intruder had broken into the hall, and what with that and the flashing lights, he, or they, had snatched a thing or two and made for safety.'

'The police haven't given you any further report?'

'No. They promised that if there were any developments they would.'

'And you're all right, are you?'

The phone conversation was interrupted by a ring at Meades's door bell. It turned out to be a policeman who, having reported to Newman's and finding the house still empty, had called in at Meades's home. Two men, both known criminals, it appeared, were now under arrest and being questioned. The stolen property, such as it was, had been recovered.

Meades reported this in a second call to Tim, who in turn passed the news on to his parents.

34

'The police were pretty good this time,' Melissa Hughes guessed.

'Yes,' her husband answered. 'That was because this Newman had a very efficient alarm system. It would cost money, that. But it worked. I'd also imagine that his valuable pictures are each provided with a separate alarm.'

'Do they bolt them to the wall?'

'They may do, but that would only be the frame. They can't bolt the canvas. That's why thieves cut the canvas loose and roll it.'

'Wouldn't that damage it?'

'Very likely. But once the picture's found its illegal buyer, a restorer will easily set right any minor damage.'

'Have you ever been engaged in cases involving works of art?'

'Not really. Only as part of my more general haul.'

'Haul,' Mrs Hughes said. She smiled.

A week or so later she reported with some excitement to Tim that Mr Meades had again been on the phone to her.

'Did he want me?'

'No. It was me.' She smiled, holding back her information. 'He needed my advice.'

'Well, then.'

'He said I had sounded sensible to him and that there were very few women to whom he could turn for guidance.'

'All very mysterious. Or was it?' Tim sounded amused.

'No, all very straightforward. He has a son who lives in Beechnall, and this son has a wife and daughter. The son heard, not from his father, about the burglars and called in to check that his father wasn't in trouble. This, it appears, was unusual in that the pair of them don't get on too well. He stayed half an hour and as he was leaving announced that his marriage was not always equable.'

'He'd no idea there was difficulty there?'

'My impression, unless I completely misunderstood him, was that he had little to do with the family. He always sent the grand-daughter a card and a cheque on her birthday, and at Christmas, and duly received a thank-you letter, but that was as far as it went. They rarely met.'

Melissa Hughes, delighted with the opportunity to rehearse the story to her son before she retold it to her husband, held her hand up to stay any interruption. 'Then, what with the police and the man from Worksop, and his gloomy son, he began to think, and came to the conclusion that he ought to help his daughter-in-law. He said he had no idea why he began to think along those lines. Then he thought of me and told me the tale.'

'And what did you advise him to do?'

'Not to do anything in a rush. To find out, if he could, where the faults lay, if faults there were. And not to burden himself with unknown entanglements. Though he spoke very freely to me, I had the impression that he was acting out of character; I couldn't say why. Neither could he for that matter.'

'And what did you decide between the pair of you?'

'To put off any action, to think hard for a couple of days.'

'And this he did?'

'Yes. This morning he phoned me again. He had been in touch with Adelaide, his daughter-in-law.'

'An odd name. Have you ever known anybody else called that?'

'No. But that's not her fault. They talked a long time. She was very suspicious for a start, tarring him with the same brush as her husband. In the end he offered her and Harriet, the daughter, rooms at his house. The girl is doing GCSE this year, it seems.'

'And they accepted?'

'No. Not exactly. He explained her legal position to her and how much she would get out of her husband. He recommended a solicitor who would not let Henry, nasty Henry the son, put it over on her. He also asked me if you knew Harriet, the granddaughter.'

'Why should I?'

'She's about a year younger than you and at the Girls' High.'

'No. Never heard of her.'

That evening Melissa Hughes raised the matter with her husband and, to her surprise, he showed interest. His usual advice was to do or say one or two sensible things, and then dodge out of the way and stay there in the wings. This time he suggested that Meades be invited over to dinner. 'We can see what sort of man he is.' She arranged this, without difficulty. He would come round on Thursday in two days' time. Tim would not be at home, as he was involved in a school drama trip. He could not help

36

wondering whether that was the reason the adults had chosen the date.

Meades appeared, decently dressed in a dark suit, modest silk tie and white shirt, and driving an impressive old Daimler. He stood, neat, upright, with his fringes of hair well trimmed. His suit was well cut, not new, but nowhere near shabby. 'What did you expect,' Hughes asked afterwards, 'mothballs? Nobody's used mothballs since you were a child.' The visitor spoke easily, seemed well informed about cultural and political affairs, as well as local events. They expected a certain eccentricity, perhaps from Tim's description, but found none. He refused wine, on the grounds that he was driving, and thus saved Charles Hughes the disappointment of opening a bottle he would not share. He ate heartily and congratulated Melissa in an unexaggerated but seemly manner on her cooking. He also clearly knew what Charles Hughes did, and his reputation. When he came to talk of his books he interested them with his anecdotes, his discussion of the expense involved these days. He knew a great deal, mentioned without ostentation all sorts of facts they had never heard, but the total impression he left was that he liked books because of their content, what appeared between the covers. His comparison of Charles Morgan and Meredith, writers neither of the Hugheses had read, showed that he had not lost any of his considerable skills as a teacher. Here they entertained a pleasant guest.

Not until they reached the Stilton and biscuits, Hughes's favourite, did Meades raise his domestic difficulty. 'Your wife', he said to his host, 'was kind enough to advise me on a small matter that was out of my usual run of affairs. Did she mention it to you?'

'She did.'

'I am considering offering shelter to my daughter-in-law and her daughter. It appears they are thinking of quitting the family home.'

Hughes said nothing, waiting for the guest to commit himself further.

'Do you get on with them?' Melissa asked, slightly to her husband's annoyance.

'Yes. Not that I know her well and our meetings are rare. Henry, my son, chose to have little to do with me. Not that I was without fault. Adelaide, his wife, is, I would venture to say, an attractive woman in her late thirties who works in publicity She is always quietly polite but lively and affects not to understand why Henry has so little to do with me.'

'Is there a good reason for that?' Melissa pressed.

'No. It's a matter of personalities. We both want to go our own ways and not to be interrupted, or forced by circumstances to take up some unusual option. Perhaps that's good familiar practice, these days.'

'What does your son do?' Hughes now asked. 'For a living?'

'He works at the university. He's reader in the mathematics department.'

'Is he happy there? Well regarded?'

'I believe so. I don't exactly understand what his line is, but he has published three books and a great many articles.'

'He lets you have copies?' Melissa.

'He gave us the first one. In fact, it was dedicated to us: "To my father and in memory of my mother with gratitude". I couldn't make head or tail of it, but it's still in print and much used. So it's said. His second was a much larger affair.'

'You have a copy?'

'Yes, because I bought it. By that time he was married and taking a path that did not include much dealing with me. I was invited to the wedding and to the christening of Harriet, and now and then at Christmas when they were at home. I went once, I think.'

'Did you enjoy it?'

'Yes. In my grudging fashion. The others were mostly university people, scientists and mathematicians, pleasant enough.'

'They talked shop?' Melissa asked.

'Not to the best of my memory. I can't really recall. We ate and drank well. Adelaide did us splendidly there. She's an excellent cook and manager as far as I can make out.'

'You didn't meet otherwise?' Hughes.

'Not really. If anything happened Henry would call round to see me. As he did the other day after this burglary in Anglesey Crescent. Or phone. We hadn't quarrelled. It was just that Henry chose to get on with his life, and while I was fit and in my right mind to allow me to get on with mine.'

'And that suited you?'

'I suppose it did. I rarely entertained.'

'But Adelaide could have come in now and then for a cup of coffee?' Melissa objected.

'She could, but I guess she felt I was like her husband, too preoccupied and busy to need what you might call casual company.'

'We all need that,' Melissa said.

'Yes. But I less than most.'

'May I ask', Hughes, head back, spoke at his most solemn, 'about the cause of the breakdown of the marriage?'

'I'm not sure. We didn't go into that in any detail. I would suspect reciprocal boredom. I'm not sure how irrevocable the breakdown is.'

'But had they, either of them, looked about, er, for other distractions?'

'You mean other partners? There was no mention, but Adelaide was a little suspicious of my motives and not prepared to talk too freely.'

'But you gathered she was determined to leave home?'

'Well, yes.' That did not sound too confident.

'And take her daughter with her?'

'Yes.'

'Mightn't that have been disadvantageous to Harriet's education?'

'You might think so,' Meades said, 'but the subject was never raised.' Meades waved his arms about as if to quell further interruptions. 'I've given this some little thought and I decided to intervene, if intervention it is, on my granddaughter's account. If the break is to be made then I want it to be painless. I have plenty of spare room in my house. I am not short of money.'

'Is Adelaide?'

'I've no idea. I was in no position to ask intimate financial questions. I mentioned Menzies and Dodd as suitable legal advisers. They've often been praised to me for their matrimonial work and I know Lewis Dodd quite well. A decent man. Was I right?'

'Yes. A good, middle-of-the-road choice.'

'Middle-of-the-road?' Meades's eyebrows rose in aggressive query.

'People want all sorts of results from the settlement. They want

39

enough to live on, sure enough. But often they want revenge, to rub the other partner's nose in it. And some even want confrontational meetings. And there are feminist lawyers who are fighting to screw every penny out of errant husbands.'

'Wrongly?' Meades asked.

'It's not for me to say. Divorce with ordinary people is, on the whole, unpleasant, and my concern, not that I ever take on cases, would be to get it over as fairly and painlessly as possible. I have known bad cases made worse by the conduct of the lawyers.' Hughes coughed. 'Dodd, the man you suggested, has a great deal of experience and has, to the best of my knowledge, no axes to grind.'

They seated themselves for coffee in the drawing room and Meades left soon after nine thirty; he thanked them gracefully, said he would carefully consider what they had said. At the door, the last goodbyes and handshakes exchanged, Meades suddenly wheeled to face Charles Hughes and said, 'If you were in my position, what would you do?'

'I have a wife to consider.'

'Think yourself into my place. An elderly, selfish widower.'

'Then I guess I would make no further overtures to Adelaide. But you realise I don't know what she's like.'

'Thank you.'

Almost militarily Meades marched along the flagged path and out into the street. Hughes pulled sour faces and his wife took no notice.

V

During the next few days the Hughes parents spoke occasionally about Meades's problems, but rather less seriously than Melissa would have liked. Her husband refused to commit himself, because he knew so little of the protagonists, while she thought that Meades ought to make the generous gesture, take in his relatives, and then put himself out to make it work. 'No half measures' was her motto.

She was, however, disappointed that she received no message from Harald Meades. It seemed impolite and thus out of character, but she guessed that Adelaide was in no sort of mood for quick or irreversible decisions. Once or twice she considered phoning the old man, but she set aside her impatience. She was, therefore, surprised to receive a letter from Adelaide Meades.

The morning post which arrived after Charles's departure proved particularly cheering. She had been sending out poems now for a year or two. Eighteen months earlier she had been published in a booklet with five other people from the Midlands. *Six Voices* had been produced by the head of department at a teachers' training college in Leicestershire, a man whose evening sessions on creative writing she had attended in Beechnall. She had been delighted to be chosen to appear, proud to see her seven short poems in excellent print and an elegant format on good paper. How well the book had sold she had no idea, but Eric Plunkett, her son's teacher, had made complimentary remarks about one of the poems 'Angle-poise Lamp' to her son, and Charles had appeared gratified with his inscribed copy and once had, very aptly, quoted a line to her out of the blue.

Now she learned that the *TLS* had accepted two of her poems and some American academic publication, said by her tutor to be highly regarded, had taken three more. She could have danced about the house, but kept her rejoicing to quick, utilitarian walks to the compost heap at the top of the garden or upstairs to

41

straighten the beds. The third significant envelope – the rest contained bills or appeals – was small with the address in neat italics. The enclosed letter, in large, rather flamboyant hand-writing, was short.

Dear Mrs Hughes,
   Harald Meades has told me how kind you have been to him during my little upset and for that I'd like to say thanks rather than letting it go by default.
   I haven't made my mind up yet as to my next move. I would, however, like to meet you some time if that can be done without difficulty. Please let me know. With thanks,
   Yours sincerely,
      Adelaide Meades.

The short note took up the whole of a large sheet of paper, dwarfing the neatly printed address and telephone number.
   Melissa in her heightened mood immediately phoned Adelaide but no one was at home and no provision had been made to leave a message. Presumably Adelaide had gone off to work. She tried again, twice, and failed to make contact, and so posted a card, a Bonington, with her telephone number, inviting Adelaide to give her a call.
   She was well into her chores and about to take her coffee when Harald Meades rang. She did not quite make out what he wanted, but in her happiness – she had been singing all morning – immediately invited him round.
   'I'm in no fit state to be seen,' he protested.
   'Nobody will see you. It will take you ten minutes to get here by car. I'll have a cup of coffee ready in a quarter of an hour, sharp.'
   'Yes, ma'am.'
   He arrived five minutes late, but seemed utterly neat, shoes polished, hair, such as it was, well brushed. He wore a sporty shirt without a tie, grey trousers and an excellent, navy-blue widely knit pullover. The nautical air suited him.
   She sat him down, enquired after his health and showed him Adelaide's letter.
   He read it slowly, refolded it and carefully replaced it in the envelope. 'Yes,' he said. 'That's the snag just at the moment. She

42

is not exactly sure now whether she wants to leave the marital home.'

'What's changed her mind?'

'Perhaps Henry has promised to behave rather better than previously.'

'Is that likely?'

'Yes. He's been given a personal professorship. It was announced in *The Times*, Adelaide said, but I saw nothing of it.'

'And that would alter the situation?'

'I can't speak for him, but she is nowhere near as certain as she was.'

'There you are, then. Your offer still stands. If she decides she doesn't need your helping hand, you're at liberty again. Square one, back to old ways. Fancy free.'

He smiled broadly at her lightness of tone, her high spirits. 'Ah. But.' His voice had real depth on the two lengthened monosyllables.

'Go on, then,' she said. 'Outline the objections.'

He straightened his face, put his shoes together and tidied his collar. 'In three weeks' time,' he began, 'I shall reach seventy-two. Past the biblical three score years and ten.'

He waited for a comment, but received none. He took in a deep breath, rather noisily through his nose, dragged down with both hands the chest of his pullover in a series of short, nervous jerks before he started again, speaking this time in a slow, hesitant voice. 'In these last few years, I've gradually found myself distanced from the world. When I first retired from full-time work, and that's some twenty years ago, I felt comfortable with myself. My wife died a year or so later and I recovered from that rather better than I expected. I surprised myself, shocked myself even. I could manage and had no one else to please.'

'Did you not enjoy pleasing your wife?'

'I would have said so. We travelled, quite extensively in Europe and America, and once to China. I took care when I chose presents for her. The house I live in now was the one she decided on for us. She was the headmistress of a large girls' school. I encouraged her to retire, but she said the job fulfilled her.'

'Was it stressful for her?'

'To some extent, but that was part of the enjoyment. She was in charge and she liked power. Then she began to have heart trouble and they found some form of malfunction, probably inherited. I pressed her to stop work at once, but she was adamant. She would act circumspectly, but the last thing she wanted was to hang about the house an idle, unemployed invalid. Mrs Smith, the woman who looks after my house now, came in three or four times a week. My wife seemed to act sensibly, balancing her lifestyle between activity and rest. Then she had a really serious heart attack. I was away at a sale in London. Mrs Smith rang for an ambulance and Joan was put into the Royal. She seemed to show marked improvement and joked that she condemned herself as a fraud, lying in bed when she felt so well. The day before she was due home, another massive attack killed her.'

'So it was quite unexpected?'

'To me, it was. The hospital said such an attack was always possible.'

'Where was Henry?'

'Still at Cambridge, and by this time about to complete his Ph.D. because I thought, and it's stuck in my head, how disappointed Joan would be not to go to the graduation ceremony.'

'I see. And you?'

'It hit me harder than I thought it would. I was unprepared. Perhaps I expected her to be incapacitated, or maybe slower, less energetic, not so full of ideas, but then to think she sat there in bed, in the full flush of health you'd have said, and then the next day to die, snuffed out. I couldn't believe it. On my own, I'd weep and shout, and behave like a lunatic. In public I did my best to put on a stoical face.'

'You recovered in time?'

'One never recovers from something like that. I found plenty to do, to occupy myself. The face I showed to the world was cheerful enough. But I missed her. She was a dynamic character. A rushing, mighty wind. I hadn't realised until she was no longer there how much I'd tried to impress her, or wring a word of praise from her.'

'Were you afraid of her?'

'To some small extent, yes. She was full of ideas. And she didn't stop there; she took action. It was she who encouraged me to build up the library I have. She was a reader, of sorts, but reading was not her main occupation. She saw I had a con-

44

siderable knowledge of books and book collecting, and she pressed me hard to build up a library, not a mere haphazard collection. I did some of the cooking for the pair of us except on Sunday. Mrs Smith kept the house in shipshape order; Joan had organised that. In time, after she died, as I went on book collecting, I managed to do without her. But I tell you, even now I come across some bit of information or see something interesting and I think, "Joan would like to hear that." Odd. It's odd.'

'Yes,' Melissa said, chairman-like, 'yes. How does this tie up with Adelaide?'

'From the time I retired from teaching, I was fifty, I seemed out of touch with the world, the everyday world of newspapers and neighbours. I would look at the magazines that the Sunday broadsheets produced and they would be full of photographs of famous people I had never even heard of. My wife was almost as bad. We did not look at television much and these people all appeared on it; that's the reason they were famous. There was no Internet then to enlighten me. But it was the same with the subjects that I was supposed to know about. When I was young, just after the war, Britten and Walton and Vaughan Williams seemed to dominate the musical scene. Where are their equivalents now? I don't know them. Is there an equivalent of Graham Greene? Or Evelyn Waugh? It's easier with writers to come up with a name or two there. But people like Angus Wilson have just disappeared from the scene. The broadsheets have more in them about pop music than about classical. Why? Because, presumably, pop singers make inordinate amounts of money. When the Prime Minister throws a party at 10 Downing Street he invites members of pop groups, I hear, television personalities, sports people, rather than real musicians, poets, writers. We seem a country of popular culture, rubbish in my view, but that holds pride of place.'

'Oh, come on,' Melissa mocked. 'In the great days when you were a boy before the war, look at the cinema. Even small towns had two or three picture palaces, with a change of programme twice a week. And the film stars, who were no better as actors than those playing for next to nothing in the local theatres, were famous the world over, with their scandals and parties round swimming pools in all the newspapers, And though there was a

45

depression, and unemployment and short time, quite a lot of ordinary working men and women still found money for the pictures.'

'Yes,' he said, pleased by her objection, 'I suppose you're right. I didn't go much, but, yes, the newspapers were full of film gossip and the film critics in the heavy Sundays, people like C. A. Lejeune and Dilys Powell, were respectfully regarded, or as highly as the theatre critics at their first nights in the West End. Still, that doesn't solve my problems. Perhaps it's my age. I'm lost to the world because it seems so trivialised. Look at those Tate prizes. There's so little worth doing. Now I do blame myself. It is my fault. There must be hundreds, well, dozens, of good causes to be supported, good new books to read, plays to see, music to hear. But I have allowed myself to sink into apathy.'

'Have you been to consult the doctor?'

'Yes. He suffers from the same thing. He was sympathetic, but I didn't want his Prozac or his St John's Wort. I used to think about this and decide what I'd do when I was old. University of the Third Age, ballroom dancing classes, fund-raising, daily visits to the swimming bath. I didn't want to touch any of them when the time came. I'd allowed myself to succumb to inertia. So when I heard about Adelaide and Henry, I immediately rang her and made my offer. I did it because I'd done nothing else for years and because I guessed that it was a foolish move, with all sorts of consequences.'

'But you're glad now you did, aren't you?'

'No. I've been dreading what will happen if Adelaide and Harriet finally do decide to settle in with me.'

'But it was a generous gesture,' Melissa soothed.

'Generosity's no part of my nature these days. The redecorating of my library was to be the big change in my life, something over which I'd have control. And that was hardly necessary.'

'Aren't you adding to your library?'

'Yes. If I see something really worth having, I'll make an effort. But apathy rules, even there. I don't know why I'm telling you all this. Half of it I don't admit to myself. Perhaps I'm still likely to be misled by a sympathetic female face.'

'I'm the tempter, am I?' They laughed. 'I'll tell you what. It's time I had my lunch. I eat early so that I've a long afternoon. Now will you join me? It's utterly basic. Crusty bread, new this morning. Butter or margarine. Cheese, I'm not exactly sure what's on the cheeseboard. That's one of the drawbacks of having two men in the house. They'll help themselves. And a glass of red wine. What do you think?'

' "And thou beside me in the wilderness".'

The quotation seemed out of character, but his facial expression bespoke his pleasure.

'One glass only. You're driving,' she warned.

As they ate, he continued with his complaint, but now he spoke more warmly as if he'd begun to convince himself that he'd taken proper precautions against a hostile world.

After a final cup of coffee, as he helped her wash the few dishes – he handled the china neatly – Meades put a final question to her. 'Will you see Adelaide?' he asked.

'Yes.'

'And will you let me know what her intentions are?'

'If they're fit to be heard.'

He walked from the house cheerfully, waving. 'I'll leave you to those omnivorous men of yours.'

'Omnivorous,' she called back. 'They're as fussy as a pair of spoilt cats.'

Next day Adelaide called in by arrangement for coffee; she had dodged, she said, out of her office. She was allowed to do this, infrequently, as long as they weren't too busy and she left no important task undone. 'It's called shopping time and it's one of the MD's bright ideas for keeping the women employees happy.'

'Successful?'

'I don't know. It's been in place for six months and this is the first time I've taken advantage of it.'

Adelaide Meades was taller than Melissa had imagined, soberly dressed, in cream blouse and dark slacks, for office wear. She spoke quickly in a breathless soprano and her face seemed always mobile, on the change, in contrast with the scraped-back hair and utterly sedate clothes. She spoke in an easy, friendly manner. 'You know Mr Meades quite well?' she asked, fingers informally round her coffee mug.

'No. Hardly at all.' Melissa explained the circumstances of their acquaintance. 'You'll know him a lot better than I.'

'I hardly know him at all. Our meetings, few as they are, have almost always seemed stiff, formal. There was invariably this air of coolness between Henry and his father, and it put some sort of damper on our conversation. Not that he ever gave the appearance of very much interest in me as a person.'

'It's always said that fathers-in-law are in love with their sons' wives,' Melissa risked.

'If he was, he never showed it.'

'So this offer of his came out of the blue?'

'Yes. I was staggered. I took it to be an underhand means of getting at Henry.'

'Was he serious?' Melissa asked.

'I'd no means of telling. When I think about it now, I imagine he'll be pleased if he's not called upon to do anything about it. But he's made the offer and he'll stick by his word.'

'Do you like him?'

'Not particularly,' Adelaide said. 'He made no great attempt to please me when we visited him. He'd all sorts of interesting things in his house, objets d'art (his wife was something of a collector), but he never showed me round. Not even to boast. The charitable explanation is, I suppose, that he left me to talk about the subjects I was interested in. It was a form of politeness. I don't know. But it left me with the impression that entertaining me was not what he'd chose to do very regularly, given the option.'

Adelaide refused a second mug of coffee, saying she must soon be on her way. 'I mustn't abuse my employer's generosity, must I? Ha-ha.'

'I understand that matters are better between you and your husband?'

'That's just about the language I'd use.'

'I don't quite follow you.'

'"Matters", "better". Flattish everyday words. We're not at each other's throats. Last summer we were so furious that we could barely exchange a word.'

'Were there real differences between you?'

'There have always been real differences. But we had Harriet, and in our ways, inefficient and contradictory as both were, we tried to look after her.'

'Then was there a reason for your state of incompatibility coming to a head? If you don't mind my asking.'

48

'Mind? That's why I'm here. In the last year or two I'd thought to myself that we'd be better apart. Or I thought *I*'d be.'

'You didn't mention it to Henry?'

'I expect I did. When I felt particularly wild with him. He heard me, but I didn't get much response. He'd shrug and say nothing, or mutter, "You speak for yourself." I could shout and swear at him, but it didn't much alter his attitude. He's a bit like his father, tied tightly up with brown paper and string. He'd never let you see what he really thought. I don't know why this is so. Henry's mother and father were an odd couple, or so I hear. I didn't know her. She was dead before Henry and I met. And mathematics is a curious discipline. People who do well at the university, as Henry did, and then follow it studying some out-of-the way branch of his subject are not very likely to be human beings.'

'Why not?'

'First they spend so much time thinking about topics that aren't connected with everyday life. I'm told that some small corner of Henry's research or equations or whatever they are is now used in the higher reaches of economics, but . . .'

'Mathematicians have to live.'

'Really.'

'They need to eat and clean their teeth and pay their bills. And fall in love and get married and become parents. Your Henry has done so.'

'You may say that, but those seem small beer to him. I guess businessmen and, let's say, all-night jazz musicians spend most of their time concentrating on their work to the detriment of everything else.'

Adelaide glanced down at her watch. 'I must be off. Thanks very much for seeing me. I'd like to come round again if I may.'

'Yes, please,' Melissa answered. 'It's been a pleasure.'

As she left, Adelaide buttoning her coat turned, spoke without force. 'The reason for our last real quarrel was that Henry was baffled by some mathematical problem he'd set himself. He'd been struggling with it for six months, thinking time and again that he'd got it out only to find he hadn't. I didn't know enough about it to explain it to you. He never mentions such things to me. It might make me decide that he was no good at his job. Just over a week ago he told me he'd unravelled it, got it out. It was then that he explained what he'd been at for these last months. He even tried to make clear what it was he was trying to solve.'

'Could you understand it?'

'No. He soon lost me.'

'Was he pleased? I mean, did he show it?'

'Yes, he did. "It was cunning," he said, "the way it all hung finally together. It was quite, quite beautiful." He didn't dance about the room, but I could tell that he was on top of the world.'

'Is it important? The problem, the theorem or whatever it is?'

'He didn't say. I believe one can't tell, from what I've heard, what's going to be important or what's not.' She straightened her coat, kissed Melissa and shot out of the front door. 'I'll ring you.'

The house seemed duller once she was out of the way. Melissa rinsed the cups with downcast eyes.

VI

Harald Meades arranged a small supper party.

He invited his son, Professor Henry, Adelaide and her daughter, Harriet, the Hughes parents and Timothy with Julian Bishop. He did a fair amount of telephoning to make sure that all could attend. The reason for this unusual gathering was to allow his guests to look closely round the library a week or so before the redecoration began.

'This is the reformed, sociable Harald Meades,' he informed Melissa. 'I'm looking forward to the new-look library, but I'm not altogether sure of my ideas.'

'Are we supposed to make suggestions?' she asked.

'You may, if you so wish.'

'There won't be time for any major alterations to your plans, will there?'

'I don't know. It's a matter of three weeks before the young men come in to clear the books. And the shelves will not be moved. But you and that volatile daughter-in-law of mine may make small suggestions that will turn the solid goodness of my ideas into excellence.'

'You don't expect much, do you?'

The guests arrived at six o'clock on a Friday night and sat down to 'supper' at quarter past. The meal was simple but ample; superb tomato soup, bucolic Cumberland sausages and mash with broccoli, broad beans, boiled onions and a kind of apple sauce, with thick gravy, jam roly-poly under sweet white custard, cheeses, coffee and chocolates.

'I chose the meal with the young people in mind. I suppose that these days they are used to Italian or Greek or Thai restaurants, but I chose the sorts of food I would have chosen at their age.'

'Is this the sort of meal you had at home?' Adelaide asked.

'Never.'

'I can't remember when we last had sausage,' Melissa said.

51

'Nor I.'

Husbands looked on in genial silence. They had had no part in the planning of this meal. A firm of caterers had prepared and served the meal from the kitchen; their work was near perfection. Mrs Smith, presumably, had taken some supervisory role, but she joined the eight at the large dining-room table, disappearing only once between the main course and the pudding. No wine was served, as Meades had warned beforehand. 'You'll all come in cars, and I don't want you driving about the streets with your brains and veins awash with alcohol.' Only Julian Bishop (and that privately at school next week) expressed disappointment about this. Iced water and jugs of fruit juices kept thirst at bay.

The young men ate with vigour, though the rest found the meal rather heavy.

'In the comic papers of my youth,' Meades said, 'grateful housewives always rewarded heroes with a plateful of "sos and mash", a huge hill of potatoes with the sausages stuck in the pile at all angles. You couldn't see any green vegetables. The virtue was in the quantity. I take it that the readers of these comics often went hungry themselves and stodge filled an empty belly.'

'Delicious stodge, this,' Charles Hughes complimented the host. He had taken only very small portions when serving himself.

'It's reported', Meades said, 'that Benjamin Britten preferred prep school food of this kind.'

'So we'll all go away and compose symphonies tonight,' Adelaide said.

'We had tapioca at my prep school,' Henry Meades told them cheerfully. 'We called it frogspawn.'

After the meal they retired to the library, where they were invited to look round. Henry Meades and Charles Hughes sat down at once, hands clasped over stomachs, to conduct their inspection in comfort. The womenfolk walked round together, Adelaide lively, Melissa searching for ideas, Harriet bored. The boys took books from the shelf, Julian Bishop a miniature volume of Byron's *Childe Harold*, Tim Hughes a first edition of D. H. Lawrence's *The Virgin and the Gypsy*, neat and brown with an apology that this had not been revised by the author: 1930, the year Lawrence died.

Meades attached himself to the women. They had approved his choice of the colour of the walls, a rich cream, and were now considering whether the shelves should be darkened.

'No,' Adelaide said. 'Lighter if anything.'

'Thank you. Melissa?'

'I agree. The books will provide contrast.'

'And Miss Harriet? What's your view?'

'I'm not sure. When we came in I thought this room was almost perfect. It's the most attractive library I've ever seen.'

Everyone, fathers included, looked up to hear the child's opinion. Adelaide seemed specially gratified.

'Then, in your view,' Meades said humbly, 'I'm doing wrong in making alterations at all?'

Harriet, now aware of the universal attention to her considered answer, blushed. She was, Tim thought, pale and pretty with dark hair in two plaits which made her look younger than her sixteen years, but old-fashioned. Her bosom was small and well-shaped, high, and she stood well, straight-backed, head still, contradicting the shyness of her voice. She made them wait for her answer. 'No,' she said. 'My opinion is hardly worth bothering with. This is the first time I've seen the library. You will be in it every day of your life. It's what you like that matters.'

There was a barely heard murmur of approval from the audience.

Julian Bishop spoke. 'Isn't it the books which are important?' he asked. 'And the library is secondary, not drawing attention to itself, merely making the books readily accessible.'

'No,' said Harriet, quite loudly. The others wanted the reasons for her denial, but got nothing.

'There. I'm answered,' Julian Bishop said.

'Yes,' Meades said, voice deep. 'Yes.' He ushered his party in front of the Cézanne *Château-Noir*. 'Now,' he concentrated their attention on him, 'now. This is my main dilemma.'

They all waited.

The old man seemed to enjoy his moment at the centre of affairs. He stood, as if he was about to deliver a lecture, his right arm extended, fingers pointing. 'This is a great picture. It's not the original of course.' He inspected them all to see that his disclaimer had been noticed. 'I still enjoy it. But I could relish', he smacked his lips at his word, 'a change. Now what do you suggest?'

'I think something rather larger than the Cézanne,' Adelaide said.

'Good,' Meades answered. 'But what? What would you suggest, Adelaide?' He pronounced the name into five syllables, as if to excuse his familiarity.

'Don't ask me. I'd go for an English landscape. Rex Whistler, perhaps?'

'Yes. Any other suggestions.'

'Why not a Picasso?' Julian Bishop spoke confidently.

'But which?' Harriet, in a supportive contradiction.

'*Rape of the Sabine Woman*,' Bishop said.

'Ugh,' Professor Meades from his armchair.

'*Les Demoiselles d'Avignon.*' Bishop's French accent was carefully pronounced.

'Too big,' said the professor. 'It's nearly eight feet square.'

'There speaks the mathematician,' said his father in a sarcastic voice. 'What do you suggest, Melissa?'

'I'd have a Vermeer.'

'There'd be a lot of space, bare wall, round it.'

'Yes,' Adelaide broke in, 'but worth it.'

Tim noticed that his father's eyes had closed. Perhaps he had fallen asleep. Suggestions for painting were offered: Turner, Modigliani, another Cézanne, Freud, Poussin, Titian, Raphael, a random list without much confidence. Clearly the decision would not be made on this night. Professor Meades and Charles Hughes were now talking pacifically to each other, chair by chair. They did not speak loudly enough to be overheard. Meades noticed them and called out, quite roughly, 'Is he telling you how much he missed his sushi, Mr Hughes? Or lemon sole?'

'No,' Charles Hughes answered soothingly. 'We were just remarking on the comfort of these chairs.'

'So don't throw them out,' Adelaide comically warned.

'This is a library for reading, not sleeping.'

'That's one thing you won't find my husband doing. You provide him with a pad of paper, a biro, a table and he's off. With his equations.'

Henry Meades signalled crossly to her with his hand that she had said enough. Adelaide stuck out the tip of her tongue in his direction. Both grinned like children. Harriet, blushing again, grinned with them. Julian Bishop had now deserted Byron and

54

stood shoulder to shoulder with Harriet who did not seem to resent the move. They were soon talking with some animation. Adelaide watched the pair. Mrs Smith passed round more golden-wrapped chocolates. Adelaide crossed over to Tim, demanding to know what he was reading. Melissa and Mr Meades walked the length of the library together, talking quietly, occasionally gently stopping and looking about them. They were discussing the alterations, or so it seemed to Tim. In the armchairs the fathers concentrated on their chocolate wrappings.

At about nine fifteen Meades senior said it was time to draw the proceedings to a close. He thanked them for their company: they had brightened his evening, but the young people had better make for home, not, he believed, for their beds but to spend a further energetic hour or two on their studies. He spoke pleasantly, so that there seemed nothing unusual or lacking in grace in their dismissal. Mrs Smith stood by the door to usher the guests through the corridor and out into the street. Meades seemed to fade into the background, perfunctorily shaking hands. Julian Bishop and Harriet held a short, private conversation in the street before the young man set off in the direction of his car, parked further along the road.

Professor Meades expressed his pleasure at meeting all the Hughes family. He said drily, to Melissa, 'You've nearly managed to make a human being out of the old man.'

Melissa smiled and said she hoped the three of them would come over for a meal one evening. Henry Meades accepted and his wife sketched in her delight with élan. Harriet waved to Julian Bishop as he drove past, tooting his horn.

Melissa talked all the way home. Had Tim enjoyed the meal?

'It was not the sort of food you provide us with.'

'No, but did you like it?'

'Yes. It filled you up. The old chap said so. It's years since I've had sausage. It's on the menu for school dinners, but I don't eat it.'

'Did you like it, though?'

'Yes. It was delicious. He'd had a very good chef in.'

'It seemed a bit of a miscalculation to me,' grumbled Charles Hughes, driving, 'to employ a first-rate chef and then order him to provide sausage and mash.'

'Didn't you like it, then?' his wife asked.

'Of course, but there are other things I'd have liked better. Sausages are not ideal for cordon bleu cooking. They're what I'd call extempore food, outdoor, barbecue grub.'

'What did you think of Harriet?' Melissa asked Tim.

'Impressive. She spoke up according to her size.'

'And sensibly,' father said.

'She was pretty, don't you think?'

'Yes,' said Tim, 'though I'm not much in favour of plaits.'

'Your Julian Bishop seemed quite attracted to her,' Melissa said.

'He's attracted to anything in skirts.'

When Charles Hughes came into the kitchen having put his car into the garage, his wife had a cup of coffee ready for him. Tim had disappeared upstairs.

'More like it,' Charles said, sipping.

'Instant. Straight out of the jar.'

'Suits me better than that pretentious stuff from percolators,' he said. He sounded not exactly comfortable. She admired his suit. He had been the best-dressed man at the supper. Now he clasped his chin hard in his left hand. 'So we saw the famous, infamous Mrs Smith.'

'Oh?'

'What did you think of her?'

'I hadn't given her a great deal of thought, but, since you ask, she looked quite handsome, nicely dressed, younger than I thought.'

'How old did you make her, then?'

'Fifty or thereabouts.'

'That would be more or less right. I've been asking a few questions about Beatrice Smith in these last few days.'

'Why?'

'Curiosity.' Charles took another sip, squinting at his wife over the top of his cup. 'It's rumoured that she is more than his housekeeper.'

'His mistress, do you mean?'

'That's what I do mean. For the past twenty-five, thirty years.'

'His wife would have been alive? During part of that time?'

'Yes. That would be so.' He nodded his head solemnly, as if pleased at his wife's acuity.

'Didn't she mind?'

'My informant offered me no clues there.'

'Are they still sexually active?'

'Again I must plead ignorance.'

They sat without speaking, giving Melissa time to digest these rumours.

Charles replaced his cup, wiped his lips and spoke again. 'Harald Meades married young while still at Oxford, I believe. His wife, Joan, was three or four years older than he was. Henry, their son, was born some years after. Something over forty years ago they moved into his present house. Joan wanted something rather more substantial and chose the place. It would appear that she was rather a forceful figure. Soon after Henry started school, locally, she was inveigled back into teaching. There was a shortage of teachers at the lower end of the range, it appears.'

'But Mrs Smith wouldn't be old enough to work for them at that time. She'd still be a schoolgirl.'

'I suspect you're right. She appeared later. Meades employed her mother, amongst others, but then the daughter replaced her. She would not have left school long. She married young, at eighteen, but continued at the Meades' house. Or so I'm told.'

'Who's this informant of yours, who's provided you with so much information?'

'I should have been more accurate if I had said "informants", plural. I picked up odd things here and there. I ran into my old fellow student, Herbert Houldsworth, and he always seems to know more than anyone else.'

'Accurately?'

'Ah. He'll distinguish for you what he knows for certain and what's hearsay. He has had connections with the family.'

Melissa took in a deep breath. 'Why is it that you're so interested in Mr Meades's wrongdoings?'

'Mere nosiness.' He used the vulgar word with effect. 'We've just come across the man, through our son, and he seems to have chosen you as a confidante, and now we've made contact socially with him a time or two. He's a well-to-do, retired schoolmaster; he plays little or no part in public life; he is said to be slightly eccentric, but whenever I've raised his name with anybody who knows him, before we've had two minutes I'm told about his adulterous relations with his housekeeper.'

'Perhaps that's the most interesting thing about him,' Melissa said.

'It's not what I'd have expected, certainly. And you?'

'No. I don't find him very attractive. At least, not in that way. But how did people know? Was there a scandal when, let's say, his wife threatened to divorce him?'

'Not as far as I know. Houldsworth would have known about that for sure.'

'Who let it out, then?'

'His wife doesn't seem the sort of tattling woman who'd take untrustworthy people into her confidence. Nor does he look the sort who'd boast about his conquest. As to Beatrice, Trixie, Smith, I know absolutely nothing about her.'

'It's quite possible there's not a grain of truth in the story.'

'Possible. And the unlikelihood of the tale makes people the more prone to repeat it?'

'Yes. Is that why you raised the story to me?' she asked.

'Perhaps. I'm not sure. I guessed you'd be interested. Are you?'

'Mildly. I do wonder, though, why you've repeated all this.'

'I'm not sure.' Charles had the grace to look slightly ashamed.

'I've no objection to tittle-tattle. Makes the world more interesting. Is there a Mr Smith still about?'

'No. He died some years ago on a continental holiday. Costa Brava, I think.'

'Was his wife there?'

'No. They had separated. He had a heart attack. In the hotel, I think.'

'Was it unexpected?'

'There was a history of cardiac trouble. So I hear. They had no children. Trixie kept their flat when he went off, but let it out and moved in with Meades. That would be twenty-odd years ago at least.'

'And was the move satisfactory?' Melissa asked. 'Are they happy? She and Meades?'

'I've no idea. He keeps her well dressed. And when he went to the States for a holiday a year or two ago she went with him. It's said that she did some amateur acting at one time. I thought tonight that she had a beautiful voice.'

'I didn't notice. She hardly said a word.'

'No. She was tactful, laconic, the whole evening. As was Meades for that matter. I guess she'd have spent a little time in the kitchen showing the caterers where things were to be found. They fetched her out just once during the meal.'

'Yes. I noticed. She spoke like an educated woman.'

'No local accent, you mean. Well, she's lived long enough under the Meadeses' roof. And if she has a good ear, her time on the stage would alter her pronunciation. I didn't notice the content of anything she said as of very much interest. She didn't make any suggestions about the picture, for instance.'

'She'd have plenty of time for that when she had Meades on his own.'

'I suppose so. Did you find Meades an interesting talker?' Charles asked.

'Yes, I did. He was rather shy, at first. But that's been so each time I've spoken to him, both face to face or on the phone. I thought that was because he'd lived so long by himself. Now what you say puts a different complexion on it.'

Charles Hughes frowned as if he'd heard bad news.

VII

On the next Saturday and Sunday in December Tim Hughes and Julian Bishop began to unload the books from the shelves of Meades's library. A careful plan of campaign had been thought out and written down. Each shelf had been numbered, and a place reserved exactly in two large rooms on the same floor, which were completely devoid of furniture, and the wide landing outside the doors. It was doubtful, the employer said, whether this would provide enough space. 'Books taken from their proper places seem to expand.' If this proved the case they would have to clear another room, but that would not prove beyond their capabilities.

Meades was insistent that they were not to rush, not to try to carry too many volumes at once. 'Dropping books causes damage and some of these are very valuable.' He provided them with gloves, dust coats and felt slippers, and showed them how he wanted each book cleaned, and how to deal with the shelves and carpets. 'Again, it's better to do it slowly and properly. I know how many books a careful worker can move in an hour and I shall judge you against that.' He watched the beginnings of their labour, said he would be downstairs if any query arose. They were to make a precise note of anything they were uncertain about, or anything they noticed of interest.

Shifting books is boring, and tiring, and dusty, but they had been warned by Meades to concentrate on their task; they were warned not to think up pastimes or start conversations which would take their minds from their work. Their employer watched them, made one or two small suggestions, and left after half an hour saying this was his busiest day, but he'd be reading below and would hear any appeal for help or advice. 'I shall also hear if you drop anything,' he said, not without menace.

At eleven fifteen Mrs Smith called them down for coffee. They were given clean gloves and sent back after twenty minutes.

Meades was not to be seen. At one fifteen Mrs Smith appeared again, led them downstairs to delicious beef and pickle sandwiches followed by fresh fruit and cream. 'Your time's your own until two o'clock. You can walk out into the garden if it's not too cold. If, for any reason, you want to walk out into the street you'll have to ring for me and I'll let you through.' She presented them with a packet of mint imperials.

'These sandwiches are good,' Julian Bishop said.

'Home-made bread and prime English beef.'

'How do you know it's English?'

'I don't. I just chose words to suit the taste.'

They sat in the kitchen until two when they donned their clean gloves and returned to work.

'Where's his nibs?' Julian asked. 'I thought he was going to be about in case we ran across some snag.'

'He knew we wouldn't.'

Julian had found two small books hidden behind the lines, both out of place: *The Vicar of Wakefield* and *Poems of Henry Kirke White*. 'I thought I'd stumbled on to his erotica,' he grumbled.

'He'll have that locked away.'

'Do you think he has any?'

'I don't know how you could tell. But all his family were in the book trade, so some pornography must have come his way.'

Julian made a meticulous note of the position of the booklets. Not half an hour later, in a copy of Henry Green's *Loving*, he found a letter. Two sides long, not in its envelope, dated merely 'Thursday', it was addressed to 'Dear Joan' and described briefly a concert by the Amadeus Quartet. Joan had missed a treat. The next concert was on the third of the next month and was by Dame Myra Hess. She hoped her friend would be able to manage this. The last paragraph, a mere two lines, hoped that Harald was acting more reasonably these last few days. Sincerely, Eileen.

'Interesting,' Tim said.

'Lesbian lovers?' Julian queried.

'Doubt it. Harald's our Mr Meades. I wonder what he was so unreasonable about.'

'Going out at night to concerts. Joan, whoever she was, Mrs Meades, presumably, used it as a book mark. Not altogether tactful when you consider the sentiments in the last paragraph.

Unless she wanted him to find it. Or knew he'd sworn an oath never to open a book by Henry Green. Ah, the mysteries.'

Julian made a note: 'Letter found p. 138 *Loving* by Henry Green. Shelf G 4'. 'I wonder', he mused as he carted the small pile out, 'why he has never found it before.'

'He didn't work as carefully as we did.'

Tim had barely finished when Meades appeared silently, as if by magic, at the door of the library. He marched smartly in without speaking and examined the empty shelves and the carpet below them. 'Good,' he said. He picked up Julian's notes, grunted. He unfolded the letter, read it, then tapped the paper hard with the fingernails of his right hand, attracting the boys' attention. 'Eileen?' he said. 'Eileen? I can't remember her surname. A colleague of my wife's. Another headmistress. I don't think my wife liked her much. "I hope Harald is acting more reasonably." If my wife didn't want to go to a concert with this woman, she always blamed me. Said I insisted on her preparing a special dinner that night or accompanying her and Henry on some sort of outing.'

'Did she tell you about this?' Julian asked.

'She may have done. I can't remember. I doubt it.'

'What was wrong with this Eileen?' Julian pressed.

'She was lonely. A spinster. She knew something about music. I'll give her that. Quite a good pianist. My wife would have gone to the concerts, but Eileen proposed always without fail, to use a musical metaphor, a coda or two. To go back to her flat for coffee and cakes, and hang about talking until midnight.'

Meades looked closely at them. 'My wife was conscientious about her own work. She'd often sit up until late preparing something or other. But she could see no sense in drinking coffee that would keep her awake and listening to Eileen Stockwell (Stockwell that was her name) muttering on about what the Director of Education had said to her about some other head as if it were the word of God.'

'No,' said Julian pacifically.

'Oh, I was a schoolmaster at one time. It distorts your vision of ordinary life.'

He made his way out of the room and along the landing to the prepared room where they were piling the books. He examined the carefully laid rows and the cards indicating shelves. Now he seemed satisfied.

'Good,' he said again. 'You're doing well. You'll have it finished tomorrow. Mark you, that's as well. The painter comes in on Tuesday. Or at least he says he will. He's on an inside job, so he won't be able to blame the weather. They're good, though, these people with excuses. Get plenty of practice.' He stood on the landing. 'Call it a day at five. Mrs Smith will let you out. Keep your eyes open for eccentricities of filing or books out of place or hidden bits, like *The Vicar of Wakefield*. Do you know, I haven't the faintest idea where that came from or to whom it belongs. You won't find many serendipities here, I'm afraid. Do you know what the word means?'

'Chance finds, mainly fortunate,' Julian said.

'Horace Walpole coined the word from the title of a fairy tale,' Tim added.

'Ah, scholars. And gentlemen.'

He stumped away, as if annoyed by their knowledge. When he was out of sight, Julian spread his arms and made a ferocious face, swore violently, shrugged off his disdain and turned his attention to the books once more.

On the next morning, Sunday, they reported in Timothy's mother's car, promptly at nine o'clock. There seemed few vehicles or pedestrians about in the low, frosty sunlight.

'You can see the streets,' Julian said.

'Are they worth seeing?'

'For the present. I expect I'd soon get tired of them. This is not the world's most attractive town.'

Mrs Smith let them in. 'You're very prompt,' she said. 'It's a cold morning. Did you have any trouble turning out of bed?'

'Infinite,' Julian answered, pretending to yawn. 'It does not bear thinking about.'

'What time do you usually get up at the weekend?'

'Depends what's on, what's to be done.'

She led them to the library, untouched since yesterday. 'There you are, then. You know what to do. Coffee round about ten forty-five.' She turned her back, then wheeled again. 'Mr Meades is still in bed.'

'So we're to be quiet?'

'You won't disturb him. Nothing could do that.'

'What confidence,' Julian said.

They beavered away, achieving more because of the expertise

acquired yesterday. At the coffee break Meades still put in no appearance, though Mrs Smith sat with them and made quite genial conversation. She said she thought they were doing a first-rate job. It was her idea to employ sixth formers. 'You're clever, strong, energetic and short of money.' They all laughed. 'He's been worrying himself about the library for a year or two now, saying it needed refurbishing. It's his pride and joy, you know.'

'Does he spend a lot of time in there?' Tim asked.

'Yes. But not so much as he did. One thing is he now has a little IT room, two computers, printer, Internet and he plays about in there. I tell him he's wasting his time and he agrees. He likes something new. The other side of the argument is that his eyes aren't as good as they were, and so he can't read as easily as he could.'

'Is he in there now?' Julian enquired.

'No, he's out. Special mission. You remember the picture in the library that was to replace the Cézanne? Well, he went to an auction a week ago in Newark and bought what might be the new one. Sunday was the only free day.'

'A real painting?' Tim asked.

'Yes. An eighteenth-century oil painting.'

'Of what?'

'Ah. He wouldn't tell me that. He loves a little secret now and then. He's worse than a child. "Guess, Trixie," he says to me. All I could think of was a general with a white wig and a red coat.'

'General Wolfe before Quebec,' Julian guessed, flamboyantly adopting an antique military pose.

'And was it?'

'I might learn today, but more likely he'll wait until all the books are back and that will be the crowning glory, put in place at the last. It won't be marvellously expensive or it would have been on sale in London or even New York.'

'So it will be a disappointment?' Julian asked.

'I'm not saying that. The Cézanne was only a print, though a good one. And he's very smart at picking out something he likes and will continue to like. He'll have decided how much he'd be prepared to pay. If the bids went above that, he'd stop.'

'And you don't know what he'll pay?'

'Oh, no. He won't tell me.'

At lunch, smoked salmon this time, Mr Meades did not put in

64

an appearance and Mrs Smith, having served them, left to work elsewhere. She asked them if they were likely to finish and said she'd see them before they left. They were to shout because she'd be somewhere about the house when they were ready to leave.

The afternoon's work did not produce any remarkable finds. One account of a Russian teacher and educationist called Makarenko had fallen into a corner behind a waste-paper basket. A hard-backed notebook had been kept behind a row of Shakespeare plays, Arden editions, new and old. Into the book had been stuck cuttings not of news items but of poems. Julian flicked through but said he did not know any of them, they were all modern. He knew the names, he said, in a disgruntled way, of one or two of the poets.

'If we took this home we could judge his taste and so find out something about him,' Julian claimed.

'Do you think so?'

'Well, we might.' Julian sounded deflated, but a moment or two later let out a whoop. 'Hi, come and look at this.' He pointed excitedly.

Tim came across. On rather better paper than the rest and almost the last to be included, was 'Magnolia', a poem by Melissa Hughes.

'Your ma.'

'Yes. I've seen it before.'

'Quite good,' Julian declared after reading. 'He must be an admirer of her work. Will you tell her?'

'If I remember, yes.'

'Bloody hell.'

They went back to their work, a slight embarrassment between them.

Just before five they finished, called down to Mrs Smith. She appeared, made a cursory inspection of the empty library, expressed her satisfaction and handed out to each a plain, unaddressed envelope. 'Here we are,' she said. 'I've written cheques rather than cash. I hope that's all right with you. It's more convenient for me.' They thanked her. 'He's not back yet. I don't know where he's got to. But we're ready for the decorator now.' She showed them out.

Once in the car they opened the envelopes. They had been paid from nine to five each day. The cheques were made out to J. Bishop Esq. and T. Hughes Esq. and signed B. E. Smith.

'I like the "Esquire",' Julian said. 'Perhaps she thinks it will so flatter us that we won't cash the cheques.'

'Had it crossed your mind?' Tim asked.

'No. Sixty-four pounds is sixty-four pounds.'

'Don't spend it all on drink and women,' Tim warned.

'Had that crossed your tiny mind?'

'Yes.'

'Next Friday,' Julian began, 'the beauteous Harriet has invited me to a disco at their school. A mind-shattering rave. Starts seven o'clock, over at nine thirty sharp.'

'Is this the first time?' Tim queried.

'With Harriet? Yes. I'd invited her out, but so far she said "No". I had the impression that her parents did not allow her out on week nights, but on this occasion, an official entertainment sanctioned and supervised by the school, I was thought worthy by parents and the young lady herself to accompany her.'

'You've not been out with her before?'

'No. I've taken her home once in the car. I happened to pass her.'

'By chance?'

'You could say so. I've tried the route every day I've had the limo, but only once has my luck been in.'

'What's she like?'

'I hardly know. She blushes, and wriggles, but sometimes lectures me like a grown-up of about seventy. I'd guess she was clever. But Friday will reveal all.'

A pang of jealousy troubled Tim, to his surprise. Julian, the man of action, had beaten him to it again. 'I met a friend of my dad's,' he said, 'who'd done maths at the univ and I asked him what Professor Meades was like. He said he was a good teacher, very clear, could understand their difficulties. But his own work was a bit of a mystery. The sort of maths he did wasn't taught to them. Some keen herbert got him to lecture to the Math. Soc. about his work, but this chap didn't go, because he had 'flu. His friends said he'd not missed much. Only one of them claimed he could follow what was going on, and one or two of the staff confessed that they were baffled, or seemed so.'

'A mad genius, eh? Just my luck to fall for his daughter.'

66

'That's not my impression.'

At home over supper, Tim gave his parents an account of their two days' work and Meades's absence on the second day.

Charles Hughes listened and then delivered judgement. 'A good employer,' he pronounced with finality.

'"Thy exquisite reason, dear knight",' his wife mocked.

'Ah, yes. First he makes sure that you know exactly what it is you are to do, and he spends some time checking that you have understood and are carrying out his orders exactly. Presumably he had another inspection on the first evening after you'd gone. Satisfied, he felt he could leave you to complete the job. He left instructions with Mrs Smith that if you'd given satisfaction you were to be paid. A good employer is one who knows when to delegate.'

'He delegated the job of paying to Mrs Smith, and out of her own pocket,' Melissa argued.

'Perhaps he'd expected to be back earlier. But he knew she could afford it.'

'Will he pay her back?'

'I've no doubt he will, as soon as he returns. Unless you two boys have done some damage or stolen some books.'

'Then he won't?' asked Tim, interested now.

'Then he won't, no. He won't. That was his insurance. She was in a position of responsibility and she insured that charge with her own money.'

'She'll have much less than ever he has,' Melissa objected.

'Very likely. She will therefore be more careful.'

'You seem to think very highly of Mr Meades,' Melissa grumbled.

'I'm not giving him a general commendation for every aspect of his character,' Charles Hughes said. His wife pulled a small sour face at her husband's pomposity. He did not seem to notice. 'All I'm saying is he appears to know his way around as an employer. He paid these boys pretty generously for unskilled labour.'

'They were handling valuable goods,' Melissa said.

'We worked hard, and carefully, and did just as we were instructed. I felt tired, I can tell you.'

'I don't deny any of that,' Hughes said. 'All I'm saying is that Meades had a job to be done, and he arranged to have it done

67

properly, without having to superintend every minute of it. That's the mark of a good employer, because at the end of the day all sides go away satisfied.'

'Even Mrs Smith?' Melissa queried. 'One hundred and twenty-eight pounds down on her account.'

'Melissa.' The father shook his head. He rarely called his wife by her first name. 'I'm sure he'll find it as important to keep his housekeeper happy as his casual labourers.'

Later, Melissa said to her son, 'Your father seems very impressed by Mr Meades. Now why is that?'

'He seems to approve of the well-to-do. If they're honest.'

'And what's your opinion of the man?'

'Neutral. He was invariably polite to us. He knows what he wants. I thought when he invited me into the Mitre for a drink that he was either lonely or up to no good. Now we discover his housekeeper lives in, and as regards the other he's not put a foot wrong.'

'You mean, I take it, homosexual advances?'

'Yes. So you liked him?'

'Not really. Not one way or the other. He spoke to us, as I say, as human beings, but what he'd have been like if we'd done something wrong, I don't know.'

'What did Julian say?'

'I think he took against him slightly. "He should wear a wig," he said. But Jules is one who loves attention and perhaps Mr Meades fell short.'

'Is he clever?'

'Who? Meades or Julian? Jules is, for sure, and very confident. Meades didn't give much away. I haven't the slightest idea what sort of impression we made on him.'

'And that worries you?'

'No. Should it? You and dad seem fascinated, as if he was Head of MI5 or something.'

'But not you?'

'No.'

VIII

On Saturday morning Tim dawdled over the breakfast table. His father had left for the office and his mother rushed stealthily round at her chores. She answered the phone while her son read the letters page of Charles's *Times*. He could vaguely hear her voice; she seemed to be answering, but he could make nothing of her end of the conversation. The phone was replaced after a few minutes and then there followed silence. His mother had presumably returned to whatever it was she had been engaged on.

A moment or two later he was startled as the door of the dining room clicked open. Melissa stepped inside.

Tim glanced idly up from his newspaper, expecting some banal message. His mother shut the door behind her, but did not come any nearer. Her face seemed white, pasty, and her lips trembled, as if from violent cold. A tear disfigured one cheek.

'That was bad news,' she said. Her voice sounded faintly hoarse; she had difficulty in digging the words out. The boy sat up; a shudder raked his back. His mother advanced towards him now, stood at the other side of the table. 'It's Julian,' she said, 'he's had an accident.'

'At home?' He did not know why he asked the question.

'No. In his car.'

'Is it serious?'

'He's in hospital.' His mother gathered her strength. 'That was Mrs Bishop, his mother. It seemed that last night he took Harriet Meades to a function at her school. Her parents had given orders that she was to be home early. They were holding the Christmas Fifth Form Disco and they came out before it finished and he took her for a little spin. "Early" they understood to be "ten o'clock".' Melissa stopped, seemed to drag her attention back from elsewhere. 'Is he a capable driver?'

'Yes. I've always found him so.'

'Not reckless, mad-headed? Exceeding the speed limit?'

'No more than anyone else. His car's no Grand Prix model.'

Again Melissa Hughes stopped, supported herself at the table. She rubbed the cloth uncertainly with the tips of the fingers of her right hand. 'He's unconscious, or was, in the early hours.'

'Is he badly injured?'

'Broken arm and a damaged leg, injuries and bruising and contusions. The doctors were worried that he was unconscious for so long. He must have knocked his head somewhere, quite violently.'

'How did it happen?'

'They were on the M1, in the slow lane, and a big speeding lorry cut across and hit the car. That knocked it off the road and on to the hard shoulder, where Julian managed to stop. He seemed uninjured, Harriet said.'

'Is she hurt?'

'No. Not really. Jules was able to point out to her his mobile phone and asked her to ring the police. Then suddenly he keeled over. Two other motorists had stopped and they rang for an ambulance. Harriet phoned her parents and then his. She seems to have acted in a really unflurried way. The police and the ambulance men were very good. And two of the people who stopped had witnessed this lorry nudging them off the motorway. They hadn't got the number but remembered the name of the firm. The lorry had been racing round them in a wild sort of way for some time.'

'Mrs Bishop told you all this?'

'Yes. They were just about to go back to hospital; he's conscious now, but she wanted you to know in case Mr Meades needed you both for his library.'

'I see. And Harriet?'

'Harriet did go to hospital. Just briefly. She seemed unhurt, but the paramedics suggested it would be wise. Her parents, who had arrived, took her along and then presumably back home. The Meadeses saw the Bishops in hospital. Fortunately they weren't very busy in the Casualty Department yesterday evening. The Bishops saw them leave. Harriet was walking and looked not too shaken. It must have been dreadful for her, but they said she kept her wits about her all the time. She'll probably feel something of the shock today.'

'Is there anything we can do?'

70

'I asked Mrs Bishop that. She thought not. What they need is leaving alone for a few days. They've been up all last night, apart from the worry. But she wanted you to know so that if Mr Meades needed the two of you, you could make Julian's excuses.'

'Wouldn't he know from Harriet's parents?'

'She'd know nothing about that.'

'Should I ring Harriet's parents to see how things are?'

'No. Not yet. Give them a day or two to get over it.'

On Monday, back at school, Tim was surprised to meet Julian, who seemed cocky as ever though he had a black eye and an arm in plaster. His car was a write-off, but they had traced the lorry with the help of the witnesses. The business would be in the hands of the insurance companies inside the week. He had heard nothing from Harriet, but this did not surprise him. He had rung her at home three times yesterday but nobody had been in, and there appeared to be no answering machine available.

'You're lucky,' Tim said.

'Don't tell me. This bloody great swaying lorry swinging right high above us and then clipping us one. It's a marvel the car didn't somersault over. By this time, and I seemed to be shouting, I had the brakes on and we stopped, and I don't remember anything more. They say I must have banged my head and you can see I scraped my face, though I don't know on what.'

'Did your life flash before you?'

'No. I was too bloody busy hanging like grim death on to that steering wheel. It's hard to remember exactly. I was conscious until we stopped. Perhaps that's when I banged my head.'

'How did you get here?'

'My mother. She'll collect me.'

Julian hobbled away, waving, not displeased with himself.

In the middle of the week Tim, to his surprise, received a phone call from Harriet. In reply to his enquiries she said she was bruised, felt some slight pain, but could get about moderately well, and had been at school, though they weren't doing very much at the end of term. The reason why she rang was to ask about Julian. Tim described his friend's difficulties, said that in his opinion he'd be better off staying at home, but that would bore him to death. When he'd finished this account, she paused and then began, in a rather frightened voice. 'Tim.' Again a stoppage. He could hear her breathing. 'They won't allow me to get in touch with Julian.'

'They?' he asked.

'My mother. She said he'd no right to take me joyriding on the motorway. She was very angry. I've never known her so cross. Usually she's a humorous sort in a quiet way, but she was shouting and crying. I thought she was going to hit me once.'

'When was this?'

'On Monday evening when I got back from school. I spent a good part of Saturday in bed and just lazed about on Sunday, and she seemed normal. Kept asking me how I felt and that sort of thing. But it was when I got back on Monday. She seemed all right at first, gave me a cup of tea, asked me how I'd done and all the rest of it. Then, half an hour later, she came up to my room. I could see she'd been crying.'

'And she showed no signs of distress first of all, when you came home?'

'No. But upstairs, she rapped on my door in a wild, furious way, hard and fast with her knuckles; she just taps usually. Then she burst out crying, and said, shouted really, that she couldn't trust me any more. How could I be so disobedient as to come out of the dance and go off in the car with Julian? She thought I should have more sense. I knew what boys of that age were like, showing off in their cars. And why go on the motorway? I must have lost my reason. She was bawling me out and sobbing all the time. She kept on with the same things over and over again. It was as if she'd gone off her head, and couldn't think of anything else to say but just kept repeating these few things over and over.'

'What did you do? Couldn't you argue or apologise or something?' Tim felt bound to intervene. The girl sounded almost as deranged as her mother, except that her voice was low.

'No. I was so shocked. And then she began to swear at me. She never swears. Well, hardly at all. And she tossed her head. I said as firmly as I could, I could barely get the words out, that I was sorry I had been so thoughtless and silly and had caused her so much distress. It was then I thought she was going to hit me. She came towards me, both fists up in the air, and screamed out, "You fucking little hypocrite." Then she dragged her breath in, and I thought she was going to fall over.

'I said, "If that's what you think I'd better go elsewhere. I see

I'm not wanted here." Her eyes rolled. I'd never seen anything like it before. I stood up, and she set off again saying they'd always done their best for me and this is how I treated them. I said, "I'm sorry. I've told you so." '

Harriet ceased speaking. Tim, taken aback, ransacked his brain for something to say. He ought to have dredged out a word of comfort, from somewhere, but it was not forthcoming. 'I'm sorry about this, Harriet, I really am.'

'That's all right.' The girl's voice had rested, restored itself, sounded normal. 'My mother must have been very agitated to act as she did. On those first two days, the Saturday and Sunday, she must have bottled it all up and it came boiling out on Monday. I've never seen her like this before. Screaming and swearing and crying. I knew she had a temper, but usually it soon blows over.'

'How has she been since?'

Harriet did not hurry with her answer. 'Quiet. Subdued. We don't talk much. We say what has to be said. I think she knows she went too far and is ashamed. I don't know whether it has anything to do with it, but she went that Monday while I was at school to see my grandpa Meades. He was furious with Julian.'

'Did your mother tell you this?'

'No. The old man rang me up next day. He was very bitter against Julian. Said he'd no right to take me out in the car, that he'd no sense or judgement but was a show-off and an idiot. He didn't rave like my mother. He spoke quietly and deliberately. I won't say he was spitting, but he dripped acid in every word. He told me to keep away from Julian. He wasn't going to allow him to finish off his library.'

'Did that apply to me as well?'

'No. You weren't mentioned. But he was certainly very angry. "You are precious to us, Harriet, to your mother and me." That surprised me; he hardly has anything to do with us, me especially. I don't know whether my mother broke down with him and it upset him. He seems to want to keep out of the way of everything unpleasant.'

'And what did your father say?'

'Nothing to me, except to ask if I'm in any discomfort. But I heard them talking together and I guess it was about me. And she must have told him how distressed Grandpa Meades was, and he

73

said, in a queer voice, "Don't base your behaviour on that of that old fool." And my mother slammed the door.'

'He'd let you go out with Julian again?'

'I doubt it. But he'd say so quietly. And give his reasons. If he had any.'

'And what's the total position now?' he asked.

'"Total position"? That's an odd phrase. No, I didn't mean it. We're back to a usual sort of life. My mother's quieter and my father's watchful, but I don't know which of us he's keeping an eye on.'

'And how do you feel about them?'

'Shocked. Shaken. It's done me good to talk to you. Having to put it into words has made it seem not quite as serious as perhaps I thought it was. It's come as a surprise that my mother sets so much store by me.'

'You're an only child.'

'So what? So are you.'

'I guess', Tim said, 'that as long as things go along in the family without any snags my parents don't stir the waters. If I stepped too far out of line, my father would soon be interfering to put me right.'

'And your mother?'

'She's more sensible, exhibits a touch of humour from time to time.'

'I don't know. What shall I do?'

'Do? If you ask me, and I don't think I've any right to say this, it's just to remember that you were very nearly killed.'

'Is that what Julian says?'

'Not to me. He's quiet about it, doesn't like being questioned. What you called "subdued". For him. Besides that, he's in considerable pain, I guess, and can barely drag himself about the school. He'd be better off at home, resting. But I think he's trying to diminish the accident, make it out to himself as something not too important. If he can get back to the classroom without too much bother, then the accident will appear minor.'

'Have you made that up?'

'Of course I have. He doesn't say anything to me. Not now. He did just hint on the first day that he was lucky to escape comparatively easily in an accident like that. A yard this way or that and you could easily be dead.'

'Do you drive?'

'Yes. My mother's wagon when she doesn't want it.'

'Do you go on the motorway?'

'I've not much call to do so. I have driven on it when we've gone out as a family and they've allowed me.'

'Are you particularly careful?' Harriet asked.

'No, but I'm not a Mad Harry.'

'A Jehu.'

'I beg your pardon.'

'A biblical character. Book of Kings. He was a furious driver.'

'We don't study the Old Testament at our establishment. But no. I don't say I never exceed the speed limit, but so does everybody else. Julian, of course, has his own car. I haven't. His is an old banger. My father wouldn't allow me to buy or drive a crate like that.'

'Yes. I think I'd better ring off.'

'Shall I ring you?'

'I don't know quite how to answer that. Perhaps not just yet. Give my mother the chance to settle down. They're both out now. That's why I could phone. Thanks for listening. I didn't know whether I should, but I had to speak to somebody. I was afraid', she slowed down, marking a pause between each word, 'you'd think I was cracked, making a mountain out of a molehill.'

'No. Nothing like that.'

'Thanks. I've got it off my chest. I'd have said before this week that I knew my mother better than anybody else in the world. But now I'm not so sure. She's shaken me up.'

'You must be pleased that she thinks so much of you.'

'Oh. Or blame the menopause, mid-life crisis. Women are said to be very vulnerable then. So our biology mistress tells me. She's about that age.'

'Yes. Are you sure I'm not to ring you?'

'No, I think not. Boys, any boys, are not the flavour of the month in this house. I'll perhaps call you some time while they're out. And you're in. Thanks again, Tim, for listening to me. I was a bit desperate, but I feel quieter now.'

She put down the phone before he had any chance to say more. He sat by the table, stroking his cheeks trying, to appear wise. To whom? Himself? There was no mirror available in which he could practise the necessary facial alterations. He mulled over

Harriet's sentences and felt old, though comfortable with himself, proud that she had taken him into her confidence. It seemed unwise to him; he would have advised against it. The girl did not know him well enough to speak so frankly. He might easily be a blabbermouth, but she was so harassed she might have blurted it out to the milkman, had his face been kind enough, or a passing policewoman. The quiet, composed Harriet clearly had, like her mother, a breaking point and then, worse perhaps, a need to confess, whatever the consequences. Tim was proud that she had chosen him, but warned himself that it was not on his merits. He happened to be there. He had no evidence that she had tried elsewhere, that she had tried to contact anyone else. One of her classmates? That was likely. It was one of the myths amongst sixth-form boys that equivalent girl students spilled gushing, blush-making confessions to each other. He had no idea whether this was true. Harriet had appeared to him, at her grandfather's house, as a thoroughly self-contained, confident person, almost a woman, with views of her own, which she expressed clearly and without exaggeration, as he couldn't. And yet she had confided in him as he could not in her. He sat in the conservatory where he'd taken the call, in half-darkness.

His mother bustled in, rushed out to the conservatory, carrying a couple of Christmas cacti. She switched on the lights, saw her son. 'Hello,' she called. 'What are you doing here?' She unburdened herself of the plants. 'Sitting in the dark?'

'I've just taken a phone call. This was the nearest.' He pointed at the instrument on the cane table at his side. His mother would want to know from whom, in view of its effect on him. She did not ask, pottered about with the new plants. She had passed the test. 'It was from Harriet Meades,' he said, strong-voiced.

'Oh. Is she all right?'

'Yes. Seemed so. She wanted to know how Julian was. Her mother's so angry with him that she won't allow her to phone him to find out. Seems a bit unreasonable.'

'I understand it,' Melissa said. She paused, then continued, 'She might well have been killed.'

'It was the lorry driver's fault.'

'He had no right to take her on the motorway. Even if he was the safest driver in the world, and his car the most up to date. I'm not surprised that Harriet's mother was so cross.'

76

'But apparently she acted like a mad woman. Would you expect that?'

'She seems excitable now and then. I'd agree with that. Besides, we don't know what other things she has on her mind.'

'What things?'

'I've just said I don't know.' She stroked back a strand of hair from her forehead. 'She's like me, has a quiet husband. I'm just about managing to teach your father to talk to people and not cross-examine them. He'd be just as happy if people said nothing to him and he had no obligation to reply. And I guess Professor Meades is another such with enough of interest going on in his head to keep him fully occupied.'

'Did you like him, Professor Meades?'

'I hardly spoke a word to him. He seemed very polite.'

'He and Dad got on pretty well. They sat there, the pair of them, happy as kings.'

'Like birds in the wilderness?' she laughed. 'No, your father said he took to Meades because he didn't intrude.'

'Is he busy? Dad, I mean.'

'Yes. The London end call on him regularly.'

'I thought it was the other way about, that solicitors employed or chose barristers.'

'That's so. But in some cases, John Drury insists that your father briefs him. It means more expense for the client, but, if they can afford Drury, expense is usually no object.'

'Is my dad so very good, then? At some things? Or are the solicitors not up to it?'

'I asked him that once and do you know what he said? It really surprised me.' Melissa Hughes looked at her son, her head attractively tilted to the right. ' "He looks on me as a lucky mascot." John Drury started in these parts, before somebody headhunted him up to London. And they had worked together. And Drury found two great advantages: one, if there was any tricky point of law, your father would have it sorted out, and two, he'd get out of their client a great deal of information.'

'Could Drury not do these things, then?'

'Yes, he could. Charles says he's one of the cleverest men he's met, but now he's so highly paid, it saves the client money if your father does the preliminary work, and Drury can trust that it's been properly and thoroughly covered.'

'Interesting.'

'Drury will always discuss the case as it's running with your father. Often the client's solicitor is just as good as he is, your father claims, though I doubt that. Drury's nobody's fool. But there they are.'

'My dad knows the law well?'

'Oh, yes. And if he doesn't know it, he beavers away until he does. Even judges have been known to question your father on some out-of-the-way point and I believe that's rather unusual.'

'You admire him, don't you?' Tim asked eagerly.

'I do. He's not without faults, but, yes, I do.'

She twinkled fingers at him as she walked away to her kitchen. He was never sure when she was pulling his leg.

IX

Tim Hughes had a call to help replace the books on the shelves of Meades's library. The room looked cleaner, smelt of polish but was not much different from when he had last seen it. The space above the fireplace stood empty; Meades had either not made up his mind, or was holding back the hanging of his new picture to the last. The man himself was not at home and Mrs Smith took charge. Tim carried books in; she dusted and put them on the shelves. He found Mrs Smith energetic without being over-cheerful. She issued orders politely enough, thanked him from time to time, but at least during the first morning made no real attempt at conversation. She seemed happy enough, singing to herself in a pleasant, clear soprano, as if he was not in the room.

Her dress, he noticed, was rather short, for a woman of her age, so that when she mounted the stepladder she treated him to the sight of long shapely legs in tights. There seemed neither provocation nor carelessness on her part. He stared, delighted if taken aback. Neither made any comment. They drank coffee in the kitchen, she running round concerned with her domestic duties.

Back in the library they worked as before, but now she addressed him as Tim. When he called her 'Mrs Smith', she said, 'You call me Trixie. My name is Beatrice, really, but that's what people call me.'

'Mr Meades?'

'Eh?'

'Does Mr Meades call you Trixie?'

'Yes. He was the one who started it. It seemed a daft name, really. Like a fairy. My mum and dad called me 'Beat'. But I was young then.'

'And your name wouldn't be Smith.'

'Oh, yes, it was. I married early.'

Later she opened up conversation again. 'Mr Meades is in

79

London today, you know. He's gone up for some sort of book-sellers' convention or conference or whatever it is you call it.'

'I thought he had retired.'

'He still keeps up his membership. He's interested. And he still buys books, and occasionally sells. So he likes to hear what people in the trade are up to. I'm not sure, but I think he still has a financial interest in the London shop.'

These conversations were broken. As soon as a pile of books was cleaned, examined and shelved the two would break off from the talk, and resume it when Tim brought in the next volumes, if either thought fit.

'Was Mrs Meades interested?'

'In books? Yes, she read as much as he did. And she insisted on a desk in the library, for her work.'

'What was that?'

'She was a headmistress, and she always brought papers and forms home. I don't think he liked that. But her desk was always tidy. Squared heaps of pamphlets and letters, and all in the right trays.'

'Why didn't he like it?'

'He has odd ideas. A library was a place for study, or for leisurely reading, not for filling in returns about how many had been vaccinated or had had scarlet fever or mumps or measles.'

'Did he tell her so?'

'Oh, yes. Often enough. And in my hearing.'

'But she wouldn't budge?'

'No. She was a strong-minded sort and could keep her end up.'

'They quarrelled?'

'Not exactly. He'd tell her plainly what he thought and then she'd answer him. They might argue a bit, but without shouting or blows.'

He hurried away for his next pile, eager to return for more questions and answers. It seemed to give Mrs Smith pleasure to talk about her employer.

'What about the son? Henry?' Tim asked.

'He was away at boarding school when I first arrived. Winchester, I think. And three or four years later he went to Cambridge. His mother died while he was there. Trinity College. She used to go there to visit him about once a term. I went with the two of them once or twice. He had a very nice room, but had to walk quite a way for a bath, they said.'

'Was he much the same as he is now?' Tim enquired.

'What's he like now, then?' she asked brusquely.

'He seems very quiet, withdrawn almost. It's as if he's got such a lot of important matters on his mind that he can't be bothered with ordinary everyday talk.'

'He's always been like that. And they didn't chat much to him, as I do with you, or my mother used to to me. They'd tell him things, as if they were educating him all the time. And he'd answer. I remember once he said, "No, father. You're wrong there."'

'Did Mr Meades mind?'

'No. He listened to what the boy had to say. They knew he was very clever. I don't think, from what they said, they understood what he was studying. Mathematics. He sat some special exam while he was at Cambridge and did very well, and then he took a doctorate.'

Next call, Tim learnt more of Henry's career. He'd taught at Cambridge, but when a full-time, salaried job came up at the University of Beechnall he'd applied and was, so his father claimed, by far the best of the candidates. Mr Meades was delighted. It would be company for him, he decided, now that his wife had died. Henry had stayed with his father for something over a year, but then he took a flat at the university, as a deputy warden in one of the halls of residence. That had caused trouble between father and son. They had argued every time they met. Mr Meades said his son was a fool; here he had free lodgings, where he could get on with research in quietness, not being bothered by daft, drunken students every hour of the day. Henry said he owed the university some little loyalty.

'Don't you owe me that?' the father had asked.

'Yes. But in a different sense. I can do you no good, whereas I can help the university out a bit.'

'Who was right?' Tim asked Mrs Smith.

'Who knows? Mr Meades went out quite a lot at that time, twenty years or so ago, so they didn't exactly fall over one another. I had to see to their evening meal, but more often than not it was only one of them. They were both at home on Sunday when the main meal was at midday. Mr Meades used to drag me into the argument.'

81

'Were you living in?'

'Yes, from the time of Mrs Meades's last illness. I'd bought a nice flat but when my husband died I let it out.'

'And what did he want you to do?'

'Talk to Henry and convince him how much more convenient and comfortable it would be to stay with his father.'

'And would it have been?'

'I guess so. But Henry was the last sort to bother about comfort. He was always neat and tidy. In everything. He folded his clothes and hung them away. He put his laundry out exactly when I said. He cleaned his shoes every morning. He made his bed as neatly as I could.'

'You liked him.'

'I'd barely say "liked". He didn't give me any trouble. But he seemed a cold fish. If I took a part in one of the Arts Theatre's productions, he'd never come. Now Mr Meades would. So I think I sided, if I sided at all, with the father. Henry should have stayed with his father if it pleased the old man. But no, he must go his own way. I sometimes wondered whether, if Mr Meades had made less fuss, he might have won the argument.'

This last piece of conversation took place at five o'clock when they finished for the day. As they washed their hands at the kitchen sink Tim asked if Meades would be back that evening.

'No. If he goes to London, it's for a day or two. He meets people. He hopes it'll cheer him up. He gets very depressed sometimes.'

'Clinically?'

'What does that mean?'

'We're all sad if something unpleasant happens to us, like bereavement or loss of money or our job, but some people are depressed not on those accounts but because of some malfunction of chemicals in the brain.'

'Is that so?' She sounded sceptical. 'Are you going to be a doctor, then?'

'No, I'm on the wrong side at school.'

She saw him quickly and efficiently through the door, but in the outside corridor she helped him on his way with a slap across his left buttock. This surprised him, but he said nothing.

'Nine o'clock tomorrow morning,' she said. 'Have you enjoyed it today?'

'Yes, thank you.'

'So have I.'

He could not quite fathom Mrs Smith. Her accent was not local, but the change, he guessed, would be the result of her theatricals. Occasionally she used a plebeian expression. She talked to him as to an equal, who was entitled to learn something of their employer and his background. He wondered what Meades would say if he knew she discussed his depression with schoolboys.

Next morning she was waiting, ready for him. 'We'll get it finished today,' she said. 'Easily. Unless there's some real snag.'

'That's not likely, is it?' he asked, hanging his coat and scarf away.

'Harriet phoned to say she might look in to give us a hand.'

'Did she think we needed it?'

'I don't know what she thought. She rang her grandad up, and that was unusual, last night, and when she found he was out talked to me. I told her what you and I were doing, and she asked if she might come along. I said she could. Then she said she'd need her parents' permission. I expect she's lonely. She'd be glad to see you, I guess.'

'Her parents won't let her have anything to do with Julian.'

'I know. Mr Meades told me. I was taken aback by the angry way he talked. He said Julian was crazy to drive the girl skittling down the motorway. He clearly thought highly of Harriet. I'd have said he hardly knew her. To be truthful I used to wonder why he didn't make more attempt to get in touch with his granddaughter. I mean, it's not the child's fault if he doesn't get on with her parents. Now he's talking as if she's the light of his life.'

'Perhaps he's lonely.'

'If he is, which he isn't, it's his own fault.'

'And you tell him all this? To his face?'

'Oh, yes. Often.'

'And he doesn't mind?'

'Sometimes he does and sometimes he doesn't. He's down in the mouth one day and cheerful the next. He takes offence one minute over something that's not anything. It's what all old people are like for all I know. They're children again, with not much control over themselves or their environment, and make it up to themselves by being unpleasant to people round about them.'

'Is that so?' he said.

'Yes, young man,' she answered, 'it is.'

They worked hard. She assured him that he'd be paid for the full day even if they finished early. Today she wore trousers so that her legs were not exposed. In the same newly modest way she said little about her employer from whom she had heard nothing. 'He won't bother to inform me of what he's up to. He knows he can trust me to keep the house clean and warm, and get the books on the library shelves. With your help, of course.'

When they broke for coffee she said, 'No Harriet yet. She probably doesn't get up very early. Her mother will be away at work. And her father.'

'Won't the university be closed?'

'The students will have gone home for certain, but I think I heard Mr Meades say he likes to work there rather than at home.'

'Why's that?'

'I've no idea. I think he has two days at home every week during term-time.'

'There'll be nobody there to disturb him. I don't know if the students are always knocking on his door. His father said he was tutor to two or three extremely gifted people. I remember he told me that at Cambridge a tutor looks after your difficulties in life and a supervisor after your work. I don't think he'd be much good at telling you how to get it right if you lost your money or fell in love.'

'He married Adelaide.'

'My guess is that she married him. She was a social studies student, I think. His father laughed about cradle snatching.'

'Did she study maths?'

'I've no idea. I don't think so. She knows her way around whatever she did. If she decided to marry Henry she'd dazzle him if she set her stall out to do so. He'd be clay in her hands.'

'Not like Mr Meades?'

'Oh, I don't know. He's still got a roving eye, old as he is.'

Harriet had not arrived by the time she prepared the pâté and French bread for lunch. With a flourish Mrs Smith produced pots of Greek yoghurt.

'This is my favourite,' she said. 'I could live on it.'

'I wonder where the word comes from,' he muttered. She pointed to a dictionary on the kitchen shelves. His mother did not keep one with her cookery books, only a biscuit tin in shape of a small Oxford. He told her this as he reached upwards.

'You'd be surprised how often I use it,' she answered. 'Mr Meades said I should have it here, to hand. He bought another Chambers, more up to date.'

'Turkish,' he said.

She showed no interest.

It was past five before they had satisfied themselves that they had finished.

She wrote out his cheque as he was washing his hands. 'Many thanks,' she said. 'If there's some hiccup, could I call on your services again?' He agreed. 'Well, Miss Harriet's changed her mind or had it changed for her. I'd bet her mother's interfered.'

'You don't like Adelaide much, do you?'

'Adelaide is a daft name. So's Melissa, for that matter. I don't know what their parents were thinking of.'

'Melissa means 'a bee' in Greek. As does Deborah in Hebrew. Adelaide's "noble and kind".'

'What's Beatrice mean, then?'

'One who makes you happy.'

She threw her arms round him with enormous vigour, kissed him wetly on one cheek, then laughingly disengaged herself. 'And what's your name mean?' she asked.

'Timothy. Honoured of God.'

That seemed to sober her. She stood away from him, a table between them. 'Were your . . . are your parents religious?' she wondered.

'Not at all. I doubt if they know what it means.' He changed his mind as soon as he'd spoken. There was no doubt that Charles Hughes would have consulted books for the meaning of his son's name. It wouldn't matter to his father what the derivation was; only the knowledge of it was important.

'I've enjoyed your company,' Beatrice said.

'Thank you. Time's really flown.'

'Didn't you miss your friend?'

'He's a lively spark, but I think, I'm not quite sure, that I prefer female company to male.'

'Do you like Harriet?'

'She made a good impression on me. She spoke up for herself very well.'

'And she'll be very beautiful in a year or two.' He'd never thought of the girl in that way. Mrs Smith continued, 'That's what attracts men in the first place, physical beauty. I've noticed it times without number in dramatic societies. Even with clever men, mature men. They'd follow a pretty girl round with their eyes. Later they'll perhaps come to see that some-body less attractive physically might be miles better at acting, or be really stunning as a personality, but I'm talking of first impressions.'

She had just opened the door on to the outside corridor when the telephone rang, harshly, from close by. 'Hold on,' she said, dashing four yards to the phone. 'Ah, yes. Yes. Yes. I see. Yes. He's just about to leave. Yes. Would you like to speak to him?' In a different voice, 'It's Harriet. She'd like a word with you.' She waved the phone in her left hand, the flag of victory.

'Hello.'

'Hello. This is Tim. We've just finished. Mrs Smith and I.'

'I just wanted to apologise. I couldn't manage to come over. In the end.'

'Oh, that's all right.'

'It might have hindered you. My being there, I mean.'

'I don't think so. You'd have cheered us up.'

'Did you need it?'

'We worked pretty efficiently,' he said, 'but I always need encouragement.'

Conscious of the presence of Beatrice Smith, he found himself if not tongue-tied at least confined to banalities. Harriet seemed equally inhibited. She asked about Julian and in the end said she'd ring him next day in the afternoon, at two fifteen. He agreed. Her mother and father would be away from home.

'Does she still love you?' Mrs Smith asked comically.

'Desperately.'

'I'm glad to hear it. Does her mother know?'

She bent forward, then stood up on her toes to kiss his cheek. 'Be good,' she warned.

He went out from the far door thoroughly pleased with himself.

When next day Harriet phoned him she seemed breathless, half-frightened even, but wasted no time putting a question to him. 'May I come and see you tomorrow? At your house?'

'Sure. What time's best?'

'Afternoon. About this time. Two o'clock.'

'Yes. My mother will be at home.'

'That doesn't matter. Does she approve of me?'

'Everybody does,' he said unctuously.

'That's what you think.'

They had exchanged a few brief sentences before she broke off guiltily as if she expected her mother to burst in enquiring for what good reason she wasted time and money in this way. She had given him no notion why she wanted to visit him. When he told his mother she expressed her pleasure, but said she thought Harriet was growing fond of Julian.

'He's forbidden. By the parents.'

'Yes. So you told me. I understand how they feel, but I don't think it's very sensible on their part.'

'No?'

'I'll make a cake for the pair of you. Cutting and eating will give you something to do.' Melissa took a few steps about the room. 'Do you like her?'

'Harriet? Yes. What little I've had to do with her.'

'Young people usually make their minds up at once, without dallying. I know I did at your age.'

'But how long did it last?'

'Oh, I thought I was in love for ever, but it soon faded, for one reason or another. It hurt sometimes. The breaks. I thought I'd never get over it.'

'But you did?'

'Yes, and quite quickly. So much so that you now often find old folks of my age not taking young people's love for each other at all seriously. Quite wrongly in my view.'

Harriet arrived exactly on time and, to his surprise, chauffeured by her mother, who got out of her car, 'to give our place the once-over in broad daylight,' Melissa guessed. As soon as Melissa opened the door she dodged back into her BMW , but not quickly enough for Melissa, who asked, 'Is that your mum?' and dashed out to the front gate. Mrs Meades wound the window down and the two women were immediately immersed in rapid, high-pitched, vibrant conversation.

Tim, already in the hall, led his visitor into the small drawing room according to his mother's instructions.

Harriet looked round the book-lined room saying how pretty it was. 'Are these your father's law books?' she asked.

'No. They'll be down at his office. These are mostly my mother's. She did English at the university and has the habit of book collecting. Does your father have a lot of books?'

'A fair number. I don't know how much he uses them. And he'll have some at the univ, I guess.'

'Mathematicians seem different from the rest of us,' Tim said. 'I mean, they don't appear to understand the difficulties most of us find in the subject.'

'Daddy doesn't, for sure. I'd sooner ask Mummy for help if I'm stuck with my homework. He just says, "Yes, hm." And gives you the answer. In his head. And when I ask him to show me his working, to write it down, you know he'll miss steps out, because they seem so obvious to him. He claims that he's no better than most people at arithmetic, but that's because he doesn't do any more straight arithmetic than the rest. I don't believe him. He's worked some problem out before I've had the time to think about what I've been told.'

'What exactly is his line?'

'I don't know. He never talks to me about it.'

'Does he to your mother?'

'He might, but she's never mentioned it to me. He's quiet, and I think his work is a bit out of the way. One of the maths teachers at school told me she read one of my father's theorems in some mathematical periodical and she couldn't make head or tail of it. And they say she's pretty bright.'

Harriet seemed quite at home talking about her father. She sat clear-eyed in her chair, hands on the arms, head back as if she wanted not so much to convey information as to dazzle or puzzle her listener. He had no doubts now that she was pretty. Her pale skin was smooth, delicate, but thrilling as if full of hidden energy. She wore no make-up. Her voice spoke low, not in pitch but rather in volume, but had an electric edge (he could not exactly describe it, or wanted to) that made him agog for every next word. The nails were long though manicured, and shining. He noticed all this, but could not be sure why he did so, and why he approved so highly. Harriet sat comfortably in her chair.

A knock on the door introduced Melissa. 'Would you like tea or coffee?' she asked. Tim deferred to Harriet.

'Tea, please,' she said. Tim murmured agreement.

'Would you like it immediately, or would you prefer to go up to the billiard room for a game?'

Harriet dropped her eyes.

'We'll have it now, please,' Tim answered. 'Do you need any help with it?'

'No, thanks.' Melissa left, twinkling.

'She'll be bringing draughts in next,' he said.

'Or chess.'

'Or Scrabble.'

'Monopoly.'

'Snakes and Ladders.'

They laughed together at their mild impertinences.

'Yes,' he concluded. 'My mother doesn't think I'm capable of entertaining you without the help of board games.'

'Are you?'

'Oh, yes. For myself, I'd be satisfied just to sit here and look at you.' He offered this with some trepidation, but she smiled.

'Not exactly diverting for me,' she said. 'In fact, if you stared too hard I'd begin to wonder if I'd got a smudge on my face or a pimple. Or my slip was showing.' As she wore jeans that did not seem too likely. She moved the chat nearer conventionality to ask how Julian was faring.

'I've not seen him since the end of term. He'll be confined at home unless somebody gives him lifts. I've rung him twice, but there was nobody in. I left a message on their answering machine, but I've heard nothing from him.'

'Wasn't he supposed to be helping you with Grandpa's library?'

'Yes, but he wasn't capable after the accident.'

'He couldn't do it?'

'No. He had a sling and could get about marvellously well, but he couldn't carry anything.'

'Grandfather wouldn't have had him, in any case.' She'd speak the truth.

'So I understand.'

He said that he thought the Bishop family were going away over Christmas, but he didn't know where.

She said Julian would find something to do even with his fractures. 'He's very self-confident, don't you think?' she asked.

'We all try to score over one another with our so-called witty remarks at school. Aren't the sixth formers the same at your place?'

'Probably. I'm only a humble fifth former so I don't move in such exalted company.'

'You're too modest.' Anyone would leap at the chance of spending time with this beautiful young woman.

She sat, smiling pleasantly. 'Do you often use this room?' she asked.

'Do I? Personally? Not really. It's my mother's favourite, so that it's something of a compliment that she wanted us in here.'

'It's lovely.' A huge bunch of chrysanthemums stood in a Japanese vase by the fireplace. 'And aren't those dried flowers bright. They are real, aren't they? Not artificial?'

'No. Real. My mother hangs them up to dry and then sets them out in little pots and vessels.'

'She's artistic, is she?'

'Yes. She doesn't make a song and dance about it, but if it's a case of choosing a wall-paper or a picture, she has a very good eye.'

'You get on well with her?' Harriet asked.

'Oh, yes. There are sometimes snags. But I can't complain.'

'I don't know whether I should say this, but your father seemed, well, rather formidable.'

'Yes. He knows a great deal, especially about the law, and he'll make it clear to you when you're wrong.'

'You're more like your mother than your father, are you?'

'I have the virtues of both and the faults of neither.'

'Oh, witty,' Harriet said.

They were giggling over this when Melissa returned with a trolley. 'Tea up,' she called. 'It's straight Indian. Will that do?'

'Thank you.' Harriet dropped her eyes. She looked saintly, Tim thought.

'Two cakes. One a cream sponge, the other a fruit cake.'

'I'm fond of both,' Harriet said.

'Then you must try both. But you'll have to be quick. Tim here eats like a horse.'

'Neigh,' Tim whinnied. 'Neigh, lass.'

The three laughed, Melissa most childishly of all.

'Will that do?' she asked. Then to Harriet, 'You can always send Tim out to the kitchen if you get hungry.'

'Thank you,' Harriet said. 'I don't think that will be likely. My mother's picking me up at four-thirty.'

'So she told me,' Melissa said, slightly grim. 'And I'll not waste any more of your time.'

Harriet poured the tea and Tim cut the first slices from the sponge. It seemed friendly, domesticated, but to him slightly mannered. 'How are you spending the Christmas holiday?' he asked.

'They've set us some holiday tasks and I like to get them over early. Then I help my mother. Housework, shopping, that sort of thing. Thank-you letters.'

'No school friends round to see you?'

'No, not really. They phone if they want anything. One or two of us meet in town now and again. But I can always fill my time in. I read. And I go for a walk every afternoon, unless the weather's foul. It's all a bit boring, but it's different from school. There they cram every minute for you.'

'And you don't like that?' he asked.

'It's what they're there for. No, it's quite good, but I get a bit tired, exasperated with them.'

'If you had the time and money and opportunity to do exactly as you liked, what would you do?'

'I've never thought about it. It won't ever happen to me.'

'You might marry a millionaire.'

'I might not. And if I did I'd be spending all my time keeping him comfortable.' She laughed, embarrassed. 'Otherwise I'd be looking at the telly.'

'Do you do much of that?'

'No. The television's not highly regarded at our place.'

'Does your dad work away at his maths at night?'

'No. Not as far as I know. He looks through technical journals, or things people send him, and books. He always rereads Dickens's *Christmas Carol* in December. I think some teacher introduced it to him at school, or made him read it for himself, and he saw it done as a play, and then he started giving himself this Christmas treat. It's not very sensible.'

'Why do you say that?'

'If he gets so much enjoyment out of one book, you'd think he'd try some others.'

'But he doesn't?' Both had stood, for no reason, together by the window.

'Not as far as I know.'

'Perhaps it's a kind of certainty he gets. If his style in maths is so way out, then quite likely he wants now and then to do something ordinary, to prove to himself that he's a human being.'

'Oh, he's not like that. He reads his newspaper carefully every day and talks to us about the news when we have the evening meal. And he's been known to go down to the City Ground now and again for a football match.'

'Very good.'

'Oh, and he did say that the administrators had consulted him about the probability of something happening. He complained that he had to explain to them what probability meant, and he wasn't sure they'd any grasp of what he told them, because they asked him what he'd do. He seemed to look down on them rather.'

'I hope he didn't say so. Not to their faces.'

'No. He wouldn't. He's polite, almost always.'

'They must think highly of him?'

'Probably.' She giggled. 'Especially if they don't understand what he's up to. But he thinks they've worked themselves into positions of power, by ambition, he says, or crafty dealing, but without bothering to acquire all the necessary knowledge. They're like a motor-mechanic, he says, who wants to change a tyre, but owns neither a jack nor spanners.'

Now she spoke animatedly, moving her hands with delicate speed. Tim gave her an amusing account of his father's work. As he spoke he realised that he did no sort of justice to Charles Hughes's character, but was surprised at the sharpness of the sentences he chiselled for Harriet's benefit. She listened appreciatively.

She was describing how her mother had arranged for old Mr Meades, Harald, to come round for Christmas lunch, but said the whole negotiation had been difficult and that the old man was likely to call it all off at the last minute. Only one thing was certain: they were to be taken out by him on the day after Boxing Day.

'Mrs Smith won't be here, then?' he asked.

'No. It put my mother into a quandary. Should she invite Mrs Smith? She wouldn't ask Grandpa herself. My father had to do it.' Harriet took his hand.

'He didn't mind?'

'I don't know. It's said they don't see eye to eye, but he's never said anything very serious against him in my hearing.' They locked fingers.

They had begun to discuss the importance of Grandfather Meades's library when Harriet's mother arrived. When Melissa and Adelaide knocked on the door, the young people were back in their chairs.

Harriet, the calmer, congratulated Mrs Hughes on her cake and this exchange proved so successful that Mrs Meades was tempted, after some show of reluctance, to try a slice for herself. She ate daintily. 'You must give me the recipe,' she gushed. 'Unless it's an old family secret.'

'Out of an ancient Be-Ro book that my mother used.'

The mothers chattered with a vigour that seemed almost insane to Tim. They did not wish to stop their rapid exchange in case the young people intervened and thoughtlessly spoilt the occasion. He watched Harriet. She stood now, unembarrassed, her features composed into a pleasant expression, like some expert approving an effort from a gifted pupil. She nodded solemnly.

The manic chatter rose to its climax with a simple question from Adelaide Meades. 'On Thursday evening Henry and I are attending a lecture and dinner at the university, and so we wondered if Timothy would like to come round and spend the evening with Harriet. She'll feed you,' she said in a different voice. 'She's quite a cook.'

Harriet had blushed. Tim thought this had not been discussed beforehand between mother and daughter.

Melissa stood like a ballerina, all eagerness.

'If it's no trouble,' Tim said, 'I'd be delighted.' The stilted phrase doused some of the excitement.

'Are you a big eater?' Adelaide asked him.

'He'll eat you out of house and home,' Melissa answered for him.

'I can do my share,' he said.

Eventually Adelaide led her daughter to the door. Just before they pushed out into the front garden. Harriet spoke to Melissa: 'Thank you very much for having me.' She then turned to Tim, raised her gloved right hand and moved her fingers once or twice, like a small child learning to signal goodbye. He was suddenly gladdened by the movement, which seemed to dismiss the adults with their inane chatter and to mark Tim out as one who must be specifically favoured; the grown-ups could know, see, interpret as they liked but the young people by a small movement of fingers had been set apart. He made her a mock salute. She understood its import, he guessed.

When the door was shut, his mother turned to him, almost shouting. 'You seem to be in with them there,' she said. 'She asked me if you would go round one evening.'

'And you said?' Sarcastically delivered.

'That she must ask you.' Melissa moved him out of her way as she hurried to collect cups and plates and cake. He followed. 'She thinks that Harriet ought to have some time in the company of the opposite sex, but she's not sure, her words, of the girl's maturity. She's a bad chooser. She picks idiots like young Bishop who does his best to kill her.'

'If he's to be believed it wasn't his fault.'

'Very kind of you, but you won't convince her. He should not, he had no right . . . You know what I mean. He went swanking on the motorway.'

'Do you think she's reasonable? Mrs Meades, I mean?'

'I guess so. A bit excitable. I'm on her side in the Julian Bishop affair. If he's supposed to be at a dance with Harriet, he shouldn't be flying up and down in his jalopy.' Melissa, tray now emptied in the kitchen, walked and worked as she instructed him, 'But you're in her good books.'

'Why? She hardly knows me.'

'Harriet may have said something in your favour.'

'But her judgement is warped, isn't it?'

'Do you like her?'

'Yes, I do. She's quiet, but good company. Sensible. And quite entertaining.'

'What do you talk about?'

'School, parents, how to spend the holidays.'

'Does she get on well with her mother and father?'

'I think so. They're different.'

'Different in what way?'

'Her mother sounds a practical sort. Her father spends some time on way-out maths that nobody understands. And for the rest makes a comment on some news item.'

'What's wrong with that?'

'I think, I guess she'd like her father to confide in her now and then.'

'About what?'

'Her mother blew her top over the car accident, but her father didn't get excited. He just fell into line when her mother said she wasn't to see Julian again. She thinks, or led me to think, that he wouldn't have forbidden her, left to his own devices.'

'And so she was cross with her mother?'

'Not particularly. She understood how she felt.'

'Did she say that?'

'Not really. She was a bit shaken by the violent way her mother reacted, but I felt she conceded her mother's right to be so angry. She wouldn't have reacted that way herself.'

'Was she upset about Julian? Not being allowed to see him any more?'

'She's never said so. But, and again I'm guessing, I don't think she thought twice about driving down the motorway. He suggested it. It was a little adventure. She didn't see anything out of the way. They'd been, the family that is, on the motorway times enough.'

'And she doesn't think they're unreasonable to forbid her to see Julian?'

'No.'

'She couldn't have been too keen on him?'

'Or if she was, she's not saying anything.'

'A sly puss?'

'I don't get that impression. When she talks she seems balanced, open with me.'

'She's a really nice child,' Melissa said.

X

Just before Christmas, Tim met Mrs Smith in town. Winter
sunshine glared, but the daytime temperature rose barely above
freezing. Last-minute shoppers savagely clogged the street. Tim
had one errand, to collect a CD of the *Christmas Oratorio* for his
father, which he had ordered on the recommendation of *The
Times*'s music critics. He wasn't sure whether his father would
approve of his choice, but it was either that or socks and tie where
he was likely to be even further away from Charles's wishes. At
least he'd heard the old man say that he'd enjoyed a performance
of the work he and Melissa had attended earlier in the month.

Clumber Street was crowded; pedestrians, shoulder to
shoulder, made their slow erratic ways in either direction. Tim
found himself momentarily blocked outside a shop which sold
Victoriana. He spent the time staring at what looked like a highly
ornate wooden music stand. A firm hand touched him on the
back. Beatrice Smith.

'Which way are you going?' she asked.

He answered with a quick poke of his right index finger. She
indicated with her face that she too thought of going that way and
took him by the hand. They moved sluggishly forward.

'Isn't it crowded?' she asked. 'I don't think I've ever seen it so
bad.' When they reached the end of the street, and a slight
thinning was discernible, he indicated the direction in which he
intended to go.

'I've been in there,' she said, meaning Scott's the music shop,
'and that was pretty packed.'

'I've ordered my CDs,' he said. 'So if they've done their job, I
only need to pick them up.'

'You'll be lucky.'

She seemed particularly pleased with herself, a tall woman,
admirably if soberly dressed. Sometimes she waved with such
vigour that she seemed likely to clout some passer-by.

'You're going away for Christmas, aren't you?' he asked.

'How did you know that?'

'Harriet told me.'

'Little Miss Prim and Proper?'

'I see she's not in favour with you.'

'I wouldn't say that. I quite like her on the whole and Harald's besotted. He's taking them out for dinner soon after Christmas. That's unheard of.'

'And you?'

'I'm visiting a distant relative in Torquay. Her husband died a few months back. She's lonely and thinks the company of a widow of long standing will brighten her Christmas.'

'Will it?'

'I've always found her a lively sort. She's older than I am. I'm surprised she's making such heavy weather of her husband's death.' She jerked him to one side, rather violently, a warning that he was holding up the rush of shoppers. When she finally wished him the compliments of the season, she planted a kiss on his cheek as she pulled him to her. He watched her straight back and the bobbing brown velvet hat as she marched away. He wondered as he collected his discs if she treated old Mr Meades with such vehemence. He discovered he'd by no means mastered the length and spin of her bowling.

Tim borrowed his mother's car to drive himself to Harriet Meades's house. Melissa had issued a last-minute warning: 'Whatever else you do, don't take her out in the car.'

'I wasn't thinking of it.'

'Not now, but you might get a rush of blood to the head.'

When he arrived Harriet's parents were in the hall, ready to leave. They were in evening dress and were about to eat a formal dinner at the university. Adelaide appeared lively, delighted at the opportunities the occasion offered, but Henry looked heavy-lidded, half asleep.

'You'll look after her, won't you?' Adelaide gushed. 'She's our one and only.' She cackled with laughter, shooed her husband through the front door. After she'd gone, the air was heavy with her perfume.

'She loves it,' Harriet said, 'and hopes she's sitting next to somebody who's both interesting and influential.' The girl took

97

his hand and gently kissed him on the side of his face. They stood together listening for the departure of her parents' car. He turned to face her and clasping, pulled her into him. Her mouth eagerly sought his. They drew apart, breathlessly, and she took his scarf to hang in the cloakroom.

'Come and sit down,' she ordered, again taking him by the hand.

The room they entered was brilliantly lit by an elaborate chandelier of bright bulbs and two decorative wall-lights above the fireplace. She pointed him to an armchair and went across to a drinks cupboard. A silver tray with glasses waited.

'Would you like a sherry?' she asked. 'Dry, medium or sweet?'

'No, thank you.'

'Something else, then?'

'I'll have an orange juice, if you have it. Something of the sort. It's a condition laid down and inviolable that if I borrow my mother's car I don't take alcohol.'

She seemed to be searching inside the cupboard and came up with a tall glass, which she placed with some panache on the tray. She poured and brought the drink across.

'I haven't put ice in,' she apologised.

'Doesn't matter.'

'Do you think it's right that parents should lay down rules for their children?'

'Yes. Within reason. After all, it's her car and she doesn't want it wrecking.'

'You're a very reasonable being,' she said. He noticed that she was not drinking at all.

'I do my best.'

Harriet began to speak about the dinner her parents were attending. It was a function of the Walworth Society, a group of senior scientists named after one of its founders, a former professor of physics. A considerable proportion of the real notables of the university would be there, the vice-chancellor, two pro-vice-chancellors and the registrar, a formidable figure, all in relaxed mood so near to Christmas, all talking freely of their schemes, confiding their most cunning ambitions to Adelaide, at least according to Harriet. The younger and wilder lecturers were all away with their families on the ski slopes and so the really powerful could enjoy themselves, knowing that in the last few days they'd met and made firm the foundations of their own pet schemes.

'I didn't know that universities were such places of in-fighting,' Tim said.

'That's just my mother's idea. She may be wrong. She thinks Daddy wouldn't have got this personal chair without some prompting from her.'

'Is your school like that?' he asked.

'I don't know. And at the univ. there are Senate and Court, whatever they are, to be kept an eye on, as well as all sorts of outside bodies now. My mother chunters on about them. Daddy's been taken up by all sorts of foreign universities. They are interested in his research. He has no end of invitations to go abroad. He isn't keen but my mother makes him go. And that's what made him so much in favour with the authorities. His name's often mentioned in mathematical journals, and it gets the univ. here a good name.'

'And has this always been so?'

'With Daddy, do you mean? No. He worked for years and nobody took much notice. His stuff was tricky. But then some trendy American economists took up one of his theorems and one thing led to another. He'd always been a conscientious teacher, Mum says. He'd mark their papers and get his exam marking done before anyone else, but now there are all these big noises, men at all the mathematical conferences and congresses, touching their caps to him and mentioning him in their journals, and then it gets into the magazines. My dad laughs and says it's just as likely to go out of fashion as quickly as it came in.'

'How do you know all this?'

'My mum. She talks of nothing else. Especially just before an occasion like this Walworth dinner.'

'And are you interested?'

'I'm interested that people, some people, think Daddy's some sort of mathematical genius.'

'Does your mother?'

'I just don't know. She wants him to be somebody in a position of power at the university, but I don't think she's any notion what he's doing.'

'Does he not explain?'

'I think he tries, from what she says, and from what I've seen,

99

but I think, I'm sure in fact, you have to be a mathematician to grasp it.'

Harriet spoke with the quiet confidence of an adult. She asked if his parents discussed his father's work. Tim enjoyed answering, showed off describing one of his father's cases, which he and a clever barrister had won against the odds and their expectations. He remembered Beatrice Smith's nickname for the girl, 'Miss Prim and Proper', as she sat opposite, eyes bright, taking it all in, chasing him with questions. This was not how he had imagined they'd talk together. They were the products of their upbringing.

'In a minute or two I shall have to go and finish off our meal,' Harriet said, standing so rapidly she startled him. She walked across, plumped down on the wide arm of his chair, put an arm across his shoulder. She leaned down across him, her breast pressing into his head. The position was by no means comfortable, but he was surprised by her boldness. She was faintly perfumed. He pressed his face against her. Awkwardly she pressed her mouth to his. He bent his head back, painfully. She stroked his face when she withdrew her lips. No Miss Prim and Proper about this. He pulled her to him so that she fell, pinning him to the chair. They kissed, breathlessly sweet. Suddenly she pushed herself upwards to stand. 'You sit there,' she ordered. 'Or find something to read.'

'I'll just sit and recover,' he said.

'Good. It won't be long.'

She slipped from the room. He stood, pulling down hard at his jacket and then, over at a mirror, straightening his hair. He picked up two books which were lying on the table top: *Travels with a Donkey* by R. L. Stevenson and *Variety of Men*, an old hardback, by C. P. Snow. He looked at the list, nine people, and hesitated between Einstein, Robert Frost and Stalin. Plunkett, their English master, had given a talk to the sixth-form society on Frost and had spoken ambivalently of him, a good poet but a flawed man. This had led to an interesting discussion in which he and Julian Bishop had pressed Plunkett whether a man of poor character could write poems worth reading. The teacher had no difficulty and made, in Tim's view, his point with masterly ease. Julian had remained unimpressed, grumbling all the way home that Plunkett was obtuse, couldn't see the obvious.

Now Tim chose Einstein, turned up the page, in honour of this mathematician's house. Would this book belong to Professor Meades? Before he started the essay Tim turned back to the unmarked flyleaf and then to the author's preface, and read that, slowly and carefully. Snow made out he was not attempting much, had written the book for fun, but the boy wondered if one wrote about great men whom one has luckily come across for 'fun'. That word would have to be modified; he allowed his chin to drop low as he considered this. The smell of Harriet's powder touched his nostrils.

Harriet, out in the kitchen, seemed busy to judge from the occasional clashes. Tim had not progressed far with Einstein's life, but Snow had impressed him. The writer worshipped the genius but tried to keep a clear head, make objections to his own views. Einstein appeared as everyone would want to be. He did it his way. Oh, to be in that world class. 'The truth was, no university in the nineties could have contained or satisfied him . . . But the university did not offer him the lowliest post there after he'd graduated.' What would Einstein have thought, felt? He'd no money. He taught sporadically, then took a job as an examiner at the Swiss Federal Patent Office, got married and then, at the age of twenty-six, published his ideas to upend the world of physics. Tim paused. That was the beauty; Einstein did something that no one else had managed. He reorganised our view of the universe. Most who scraped through the university's final tests were seen by their teachers as idle, crept along with the rest of their careers if they were foolish enough to continue with the subject and ended up, at best, as decent, law-abiding citizens, schoolteachers, research workers in industrial labs, businessmen, good fathers of families, loving husbands, useful nobodies, yet troubled from time to time with the same thwarted ambition, laziness, half-baked victories. That was worrying, Tim concluded. This mediocre man was everybody. The Einstein saga raised the heart only because the young patent examiner happened to be the new Copernicus, the one among billions.

'Soup's on the table,' Harriet's voice called from outside.

He tiptoed out to the kitchen, which was empty, though permeated with a delicious odour of cooking, and out through another open door into the dining room. There candles flickered over a polished table with lace and silver.

'The far end,' she ordered.

He sat down. The table put a great distance between them. Why were they not close?

'Make a start,' she said. 'Don't let it get cold.'

He started. The soup was deliciously thick, with lentils, and hot.

'All right?' she asked.

'Lovely.'

They ate in silence. Tim felt he should say something, either complimentary or interesting, but enjoyed his soup so much that he didn't waste time or words. He finished well before she did, but when she laid down her spoon she asked, 'Would you like some more? There's plenty.'

'Yes, please.' His voice betrayed his eagerness.

Harriet returned with a saucepan to fill his plate. 'Not very elegant,' she apologised, 'I should have taken your plate out.'

'You've not spilt a drop,' he said.

'Too good to waste.' They laughed. 'Go on,' she urged. 'Get on with it. I'll tell you now what the next course is. My mother asked your mother what you'd like best. And what do you think the answer was?'

'Steak and chips.'

'No. She said pizza. Isn't that right?'

'Oh, yes.'

'Your mother said, "Fill him up with stodge." And so . . .'

She was outside some little time and then called to him to bring his soup plate to the kitchen. She handed him his pizza, well sauced, vegetables colourful, enormous in size. 'Your mother said you could eat any amount. And it's a shop affair, out of a packet. That's safer. The rest is mine, or my mother's.'

They carried their plates in in a shy procession. He was delighted to place his on the table without the slightest accident.

'"Let good digestion wait on appetite,"' she quoted.

'*Macbeth*. Banquet scene,' he replied, pleased with himself.

They ate with pleasure. He described an enormous pizza the family had been served in Italy. He'd done marvels with that, because his mother was a small eater, and his father rather disliked the dish and downed it only to convince himself that complete holidays in Tuscany meant consumption of Italian food.

'That seems a sort of lawyer's decision,' she adjudicated.

'Typical. Thought out. He'll always make sure he isn't missing anything.'

'My father likes his meals.'

'Even those he eats abroad?'

'Yes. He says that his view of food is like the drunkard's judgement on beer. It's all good, but some is better than others.'

They chattered easily to one another, even though the table's length divided them. He helped clear the plates, and she brought on meringues, fruit salad, cream and ice cream. Tim did well again, but he noticed she barely covered half the base of her dish. At the end, he turned down a second helping of pudding, claiming the pizza had done for him He then bossily decided that they should wash up together before they had coffee. She refused his offer, saying the washing-up machine would cope. He opened the machine; it was empty.

'There,' he almost shouted. 'Let's not leave work for your mother.'

Harriet yielded. She washed the dishes with a pretty efficiency, donning an apron. He flashed round with a red tea towel. Once the chore was over, she made coffee, instant at his request, and they returned to their original places in the drawing room. Tim felt, not without embarrassment, that he was smiling all the time. He felt at ease, pleased with himself, with Harriet, with the wide world.

After a time she suggested that they sit on the settee together. They kissed and she leaned into him. 'What time are you due home?' she asked.

'Doesn't matter. They know where I am.'

'I have my orders to throw you out just before ten.'

A bout of kissing occupied them. They drew back breathless. He refused more coffee. She stretched across his lap, face upwards, then moved up so they could kiss more easily. Her tongue reached into his mouth. Again they fell apart.

'Hard work?' he ventured.

She smiled, stroked his face, which was smooth.

Tentatively he placed his right hand on her left breast. She made no demur. Her eyes were closed, but her mouth smiled. Her hand slipped under his and she unbuttoned her blouse. 'Put it inside,' she said.

He blushed, amazed at her boldness. Her face seemed serene as ever. He obeyed her order. She wore no brassiere, and his hand fingered the small, warm, rounded softness. Now he cupped it, then fingered the nipple which stood proud.

'That's nice,' she said. 'Be gentle.'

They kissed again with fervid awkwardness. Because of the position of his hand it seemed like paradise. They sprawled uncomfortably, but out of themselves.

'I love you,' he said, whispering, 'I love you.'

'Do you?' she asked.

'Yes.' He shut her mouth with another kiss.

Her skirt had ridden up her thighs. Her face, straining towards his, grew angelic.

Finally it was she who drew herself upright. She straightened her skirt and buttoned her blouse. She stood. He lay half back, head on a gold-tasselled cushion.

'I'm thirsty,' she said, in a voice that lacked passion. 'Would you like a drink? Lemon? Orange?'

'Yes, please.' He sat up.

'With ice?'

She was off towards the door without waiting for his answer. Tim rearranged himself decorously upright on the settee. He stroked its rich velvet covering. The room had become different, highly coloured, magnificent. He focused on a picture opposite; it seemed to be an elegant gateway in Venice, in some palazzo, all gold, deep browns, audacious orange. He breathed deeply, a man satisfied but uncertain of the cause of his satiety.

Harriet returned with a tray, tall glasses of lemonade.

He was glad she'd chosen that, there seemed more varieties, and had given him ice. He'd opted for neither, but she'd read his mind. He fancied that if she'd filled the vessels from the cold tap he'd have been equally pleased.

She carefully placed his drink on a small table near the settee and moved away to sit perkily on the armchair she had originally occupied. She raised her glass. 'Your health,' she toasted him.

'And yours.'

She was the Harriet of a month or two back, smart, not easily knowable, her blouse buttoned, skirt straight, tights silken, shoes glittering. She had combed her hair. He noticed with refined pleasure how neatly she now sat.

'I love you,' he said. She raised her glass again. 'I mean it.'

'You're a nice boy.'

He doubted that, but bowed his head to her, and then pointed to the picture he'd been studying in her absence. 'Where's that?' he asked.

Harriet paused as if she had trouble in identifying the location. 'Venice,' she said, in the end.

'I could guess that.'

Her eyebrows rose. His intervention was misplaced. She still struggled, it appeared, to answer his original question. 'It's some palazzo not far from the hotel where we were staying two years ago. I forget the name, and the famous man who once lived there. Some young student was making quick watercolours of it. He sold one cheaply to my father. It was thirty-five pounds, I think, and though that sounds a lot in local currency because you get so many lire to the pound, it's really a good buy. We had it framed back home.'

'It's very good.'

'I like it,' she answered.

They talked about Professor Meades's taste. He sometimes had a rush of blood to the head, she claimed, went to an exhibition and bought three or four pictures. Her mother was not always pleased.

'Does she get on to him?'

'Yes. If she doesn't approve. I expect all wives do.'

'Will you complain to me when we're married?'

'When.'

Her word, lightly spoken, fell heavily. This was Harriet the person of reason, who could look on things as they were, weigh them up and make a balanced judgement. The girl who had overwhelmed him with mouth and tongue as she rolled on him, who bared her breasts to his touch, had gone, been changed back. She smiled at him as to a baby, exaggerating to make sure that the expression was understood.

The twenty minutes left before ten o'clock passed slowly. When he stood, on her instruction, at ten minutes to the hour to put on his outdoor clothes, they fell into each other's arms and stood kissing, swaying in the middle of the room. At one minute to ten, as if she had been watching the clock all through their bout of hugging, she broke away, said it was time to button his coat.

In the hall he managed this and said, 'Would you like to go with me to the cinema this week? Will you have time?'

'Yes, please. I'd love to. There's a bit of a snag. We're out to dinner one night, but I'm not sure when. I'll find out and give you a ring, and we'll fix it up.'

'And perhaps you'll look at the local paper and find out if there's anything worth seeing?'

'Yes, sir. But don't suggest that we go by car. My mother will have a fit.'

'As you say.'

They kissed again and she opened the door. He bent for a last touch of lips on lips, and then he was walking down the drive, sharply. A quick breeze rattled the twigs of trees and bushes. The lights of town, straight garlands or irregular patterns of lamps, pitted the dark distance. He glanced at his watch. Five minutes past ten. He carefully closed the front gate and headed towards his mother's car.

XI

Harriet telephoned the next day. She had consulted her mother and the young people arranged to visit a cinema slightly out of the town centre but on a bus route. The Tuesday after Christmas was the chosen day; the film *Angela's Ashes*. On the Tuesday she rang again. Tim feared she was about to cry off; everyone seemed to be suffering from 'flu or bronchitis these days, but she had another suggestion. On Friday evening her grandfather had invited them to dinner, just the two of them, at his house in the Park. The meal would be served at six sharp so that they would have plenty of time to eat and to talk, and yet she would be home by ten o'clock, her mother's inevitable hour.

'It surprised me, when he rang,' Harriet said. 'He insisted on speaking to me. He'd been talking to my mother and I guess she had mentioned your name. I thought he'd been ill or depressed or away, from what Daddy said, though he did take us out on Boxing Day.'

'What does your father think?'

'Nobody has consulted him.'

'He seems, your grandfather, I mean, rather fond of you.'

'Is that surprising?'

Harriet enjoyed the film rather more than he did. He would have preferred some ancient James Bond glossy rubbish. Even *Titanic*. One went to the cinema to be entertained. Harriet had cried from time to time, and had taken her hand from his to forage for a small, lace-edged handkerchief to dab her eyes. Tim preferred a handkerchief to the screw of tissue most girls used. He enjoyed both her soft-heartedness and his feeling of superiority.

He accompanied her to the bus, boarded it with her to her evident pleasure.

'My mother will be glad you've seen me all the way home,' she confided. Harriet looked at her watch. 'We're in good time. We'll get a cup of coffee out of them.'

Sometimes she spoke like this, as if her parents were childishly unreasonable. He could not make out why this was so, but attributed it to her wish to appear, to him at least, independent of her mother. Some of his form-mates had confided to him that they were already engaged on torrid love affairs. Though they rarely provided corroborative detail, they spoke with confidence, even treating him as if he too were already experienced in sexual encounters. He had been surprised that Harriet had made access to her naked breasts so easy and wondered if she had learnt this from some other boy, possibly from Julian Bishop, who had boasted of his amatory conquests. They walked through the darkened streets, pausing to kiss, though never for long. They arrived at her home well before the appointed deadline.

Mrs Meades must have been waiting and bustled into the hall. 'Come in,' she called. 'Would you like a cup of coffee? The kettle has just boiled.'

Adelaide led them to the kitchen, which blazed with light. Harpsichord music clanged and was turned off. She parked Tim on a high stool. Harriet immediately disappeared. Fiddling with crockery, Adelaide questioned him about the film. When she had heard his opinion she asked, 'Would it be suitable to take my husband to see?'

'I'd think so. Yes, though Harriet thought more of it than I did.'

She placed coffee and a plate of chocolate biscuits on the table beside him. 'I hear Grandpa Meades has invited the pair of you to dinner on Friday.'

'Yes.'

'And you're going?'

'Do you advise me against it?' he asked impudently.

'Of course I don't. In fact, he enquired of me what he should feed you on. So he must be taking it very seriously. That's good, I suppose, in that he'd not shown a great deal of interest in Harriet before the end of last year.'

'Perhaps he doesn't like small children.'

'He's at the age, surely, when the majority of grandparents see most of them.'

'He's unusual, you think?'

'Oh, he's that all right. He gets his own way, like most rich people. He's very well-to-do, you know. And he's not so mobile as he was. He visits London, I know, and has a couple of holidays abroad. But he doesn't live a very social life. He reads and plays the piano and turns out for the odd concert.'

'Mrs Smith looks after him.'

'Ah, the enigmatic Mrs Smith.' Adelaide exhibited dislike in her emphasis.

Harriet reappeared.

'How are you thinking of getting to Grandpa Meades's?' Adelaide asked Tim.

'Bus. Shanks's.'

'I'll run you down and back,' Adelaide said. 'I'll ask him what time he's thinking of throwing you out.'

'Telling him,' Harriet said *sotto voce*.

'Same thing,' her mother answered, unabashed. The two women grinned at each other, excluding Tim.

On Friday evening at exactly three minutes to six, Adelaide delivered the two young people outside Harald Meades's door. She did not wait, but drove off immediately.

Mr Meades appeared, in carpet-slippers, light-grey suit, with a red, jaunty waistcoat. His collar seemed preternaturally stiff round a green-and-gold silk tie.

'Is it cold out there?' he asked, leading them along the outside corridor. 'I've been frozen all day.'

They rid themselves of scarves and outer garments in the cloakroom. He led them upstairs. Warmth pleasurably enveloped them.

'Come and look at your library,' he invited Tim. They followed the old man, who made remarkably quick progress up the curving staircase.

'Sherry?' he enquired as they entered the room. He poured schooners of dry wine for them all. 'I decided on a picture. After much misgiving. I don't know whether it's suitable. Trixie thinks I'm just a dirty old man and perhaps that's so.'

He led them along and they lined up in front of the new acquisition.

Two lovers embraced naked on a sheet or bedcover, beautifully if formally drawn, the edges magically twisting into scrolls. The man had his thin, muscular back to the painter and his left leg

109

disappeared downwards into the sheet. The woman's left arm clasped him by the neck, her long fingers dividing one to three along his shoulder. Her brown hair spread out in dark waves behind her as if the artist had lifted and arranged it to mimic a streaming banner-like pattern in the wind. The effect was unrealistic; no breeze could have stretched and left those long, heavy billows. The man clasped her to him, his strong left arm imprisoning her right, while her free fingers fondled his neck, his cheeks. He sat, it seemed; she lay, convincingly unreal, yet solid, strong but magical. His head was thrown back to kiss her ear; her face dropped to her collarbone, loving herself until he forced her to love him again. In the two opposing corners outside the sheet the background, floor or bed, writhed in pale gold.

Meades gave them a short time to judge the picture. Tim looked and nodded but Harriet took two confident steps to her left to view it from another angle.

'What do you think, then?' he asked.

'He's a marvellous draughtsman,' Tim answered.

'They seem strained,' Harriet added. 'Look at his head.'

'Passion.' Meades stroked his mouth, smirked. 'This is not nearly so disturbed, tortured, tense as some of his earlier pictures. I couldn't make my mind up and then I decided on this painter. Do you know who it is?'

They admitted their ignorance with monosyllables.

'Egon Schiele. This picture's nineteen seventeen, I think. He died the next year.'

'Was he very old?' Harriet asked.

'No. Under thirty. Eighteen ninety to nineteen eighteen. Austrian. Do you like it?'

'Yes,' Tim said. 'He combines realism and imagination.'

'Exactly.'

'Isn't it, well, slightly light, in colour, I mean, for its place?' Harriet hesitated her way through the sentence.

'Good point. I thought that myself and imagined I'd choose something full of dark blues or perhaps staring whites. But then I saw this in a book and I hovered, hovered between this and another Schiele called *The Family*. I decided on this. I've never seen either, though I've often been to Vienna.'

'Is it a big picture? Originally?' Tim asked.

'Yes.' Meades took from his pocket a small notebook, as if he had prepared for this and other questions. 'Thirty-nine and three eighths by sixty-six and seven-eighths inches, a hundred by a hundred and seventy centimetres.'

'Oil?' Tim asked.

'It is. There's a man in London who does this sort of reproduction. From photographs and he employs trained assistants. Costs a great deal of money, I can tell you. But this is said to give a marvellous impression of the real thing.'

'Could it be mistaken for the original?' Harriet asked.

'No. I doubt it. I don't think so. But it suited my purpose here.' He looked his young guests up and down as if to put them to some stringent test. 'Do you know why I chose it?' He raised a finger, compelling them to hear. 'I'll tell you.' Another pause. 'All you see of the woman's face. You're looking down on her. You see the foreshortened forehead, the eyebrows, the nose and that's about it. And yet you know, I knew, she was beautiful.'

The door opened, and Mrs Smith came in and stood for a moment listening to the last part of his discourse with some amusement. Meades lifted his head to her.

'Dinner is served,' she said.

'Trixie doesn't approve of this picture,' he remarked.

She did not reply, but politely bowed her head, turned and left the room. They followed her downstairs. In the dining room Mrs Smith immediately served soup, hot and delicious from a pot on a heated trolley.

'I can taste the lemon in this,' Meades said.

'Good. If you'd have said nothing I'd have put more in next time,' Mrs Smith answered, attacking her own soup. 'It's leek and potato.'

'I can recommend Mrs Smith's home-made wholemeal with it,' Meades enthused.

'We're both trying it,' Harriet replied. 'It's excellent.'

At the end of the course Tim stood to help Mrs Smith clear the dishes. Meades beamed at him and continued to talk to his granddaughter. When Tim brought in the vegetables the two were chattering about playing the violin. On his next return it was about continental tramcars.

They settled to their roast pork, carved by Mrs Smith, and apple sauce, made from their own Bramley crop, Meades boasted. They drank a fruity white wine. The old man did not eat heartily, but continually complimented Mrs Smith on her cooking, desperately as if she would clear the table unless she was sufficiently praised. Tim received a second helping to the admiring smiles of the rest. He had finished this while Mr Meades was delicately still feeding himself with his small, neatly arranged forkfuls. They had to wait almost five minutes for him to complete the course. When he finally laid down his knife and fork he said, 'I feel a better man for that,' like a grace.

Tim again helped pack the trolley and wheel it out to the kitchen. Mrs Smith gave instructions as to the disposal of uneaten comestibles, the swilling of gravy-blemished plates under the hot tap, explaining each time why it was worth while to complete the task. She spoke cheerfully, patted his bottom in encouragement, seemed completely at her ease.

'When I cook,' he confessed, 'my main difficulty is getting the different things ready all at the same time.'

'Yes,' she admitted. 'But practice gives you confidence. You'd be surprised how far out you can be and yet come up with a successful result.'

She made no attempt to deal with the third course until the second was tidied away. 'It'll give him time to talk to Harriet,' she said. 'And that will be to the advantage of everybody. He's been very off colour these last few months.'

'What's wrong? Anything serious?'

'Old age. Depression. He can visualise himself cooped up in one room of this house all day and every day, and he hates the thought. I hoped when he'd finished tinkering with the library that that might have set him right, but no such luck. We'll have to wait for the spring. That's next.'

'We're past the shortest day,' Tim said.

'I haven't noticed any difference yet. But now he's taken up with Henry and his family it might improve the situation. Listen to the pair of them going at it in there. With me, he'll sit all day and never open his mouth unless he has to.'

They listened. Vaguely they could hear the rise and fall of light voices. They could make nothing of the content of the conversation. Beatrice Smith had now taken the lid from a steaming saucepan and had hooked out with a long carving fork a basin, which she placed on the work surface. She left this for a moment before attacking the knots in the string holding the cloth cover in place. She puffed and blew on her fingers, muttering. 'By God, this is hot,' she complained. Then, after another foray, 'Got you.' She undid the string, which she dangled from her fingers held high in front of her face.

'What is it?' Tim asked.

'Christmas pudding. Do you like it? I was surprised when Harald ordered that.'

'Did you make it yourself?'

'Yes.' She had turned the dark, shining shape out on to a plate. 'You can buy them in the shops and I'm sure they taste just as good as anything I make.' She took down the custard jug from the top of the cooker. 'Just take that in, will you, and come back for the cream or he'll think we're never getting round to afters.' She laughed. 'He's told me many times not to call it that.'

When Tim placed the custard on the table, Meades and Harriet stopped talking to watch him.

'I thought it was never coming,' the grandfather said. 'What on earth were you up to?'

'We had to deal with the remains of the last course.'

'Why?' Meades snapped.

'Mrs Smith has a system,' Tim said solemnly. 'She looks ahead.'

'No brandy burning,' Mrs Smith told them on entrance. 'Custard and cream. Both or neither.'

They ate; Meades's portion looked minute but he flooded it with custard. He seemed intent on enquiring about Beatrice Smith's system.

She answered patiently, 'I learnt it from my father. He said that one should clear up whatever you were doing, because then you knew how you stood.'

'There you are,' Harriet said to Tim. 'We are influenced by our parents. To some extent.'

'Some more than others.'

'Did you make a mathematician of your son?' Tim asked Meades.

'No. I don't think so. He found the way himself. Once I learnt where his strengths lay, I encouraged him of course.' Meades took a large white handkerchief from a pocket and blew his nose. 'And', he portentously addressed Harriet, 'your father has achieved exactly what I wanted for myself and never managed.'

'What's that?' Harriet asked.

'A beautiful daughter,' Tim laughed. The others joined, Meades only dutifully.

'I was always bookish,' the grandfather said, 'but what I would have liked to be was an expert in some out-of-the-way subject.'

'Such as?' Harriet, sharply.

'Oh, Old Irish or American Indian languages. Some half-forgotten tongue, let's say, of which I was a master. I've heard it said that some Irish people used to smile when they heard Dr Robin Flower speak Irish, because of his English accent, but after half an hour they realised that he'd forgotten more of the language than they had ever known.'

'How does Professor Meades fit into this?'

'Ah, yes.' Meades leaned back from his still unfinished small portion of pudding, as if Tim had reached the heart of the discussion. 'Yes. Henry has found, or invented for himself, some obscure branch of mathematics, which is difficult and not well understood even by fellow practitioners. And he is the expert.'

'Why is that so good?' Harriet asked.

'Because he demonstrates his mathematical intelligence. And the odd thing is that now and again some piece of mathematics proves itself useful in the world. Some physicist or economist takes it up and uses it to extend the boundaries of his own speciality.'

Meades topped his flowered plate with his spoon, and helped himself to another small mouthful of Christmas pudding and custard.

'Was Daddy good at maths as a small boy?' Harriet asked.

'Yes. Very quick. Very much so. He'd have some problem over and done with while I was still thinking about it. He worked hard at it, but I guess he enjoyed it.'

'Were you pleased?' Harriet asked.

'Yes. I was glad he did well at school. I expected it. He was an all-rounder, did outstandingly well at all his lessons, but I must confess that I was surprised when it became clear that mathematics was the subject where he really excelled. I'm an old fuddy-duddy and I suspect that if you read history or English literature or geography, you'll know more about life than if you spent your student days in a lab or wrestling with mathematical brain-teasers.'

'Is that right?' Mrs Smith asked.

'I don't know these days. Computers, information technology, seem to be in the lead now. They do a lot of your work for you. I read that in a test in America between a computer and medical consultants, the computer made a more accurate diagnosis of illnesses in real patients than the medical experts. I don't know. The machines can only give out what some human being has put in.' He paused. 'And a great deal of money is made on computer programs and so forth. I don't really understand it, though I have a computer in the library, but money is what counts these days. People go for the price, not the quality. We are judged by our bank accounts.'

'Hasn't that always been so?' Tim asked.

'To some extent. But people paid lip-service to the achievements of artists and musicians and philosophers even if they were poor.'

He ate the rest of his pudding slowly and in silence, as if saddened by his conclusion. Mrs Smith offered more wine, but only she and Meades partook. Tim helped her clear the table.

'Where are you having your coffee?' she asked Meades.

'Where do you suggest?'

'The drawing room,' Beatrice said, without hesitation. 'Take Harriet and your wine in there, and we'll be with you shortly.'

Outside in the kitchen the percolator bubbled away. Mrs Smith emptied the wine bottle into her glass and drained it. She prepared the coffee tray; Tim packed the dishwasher and wiped down soiled surfaces.

Before they departed for the drawing room Mrs Smith walked across, twisting a small piece of mistletoe which she held over his head. 'Compliments of the season,' she said. She kissed him on the mouth. He tasted the wine on her breath. She forced her tongue into his mouth, and arms round him pressed her body into his. She was bigger than he imagined; her breasts seemed heavy, her belly seductive; her legs against his stood strong as pillars. She broke away.

'Yum, yum,' she said. She barely smiled. 'You carry the coffee. I'll open the doors.' They made the trip across the corridor without mishap. She indicated to Tim where he was to place his tray. Harriet and her grandfather looked red-faced, pleased with themselves. 'I think you have all you need. You

115

know where the whisky is,' Mrs Smith said. 'I've one or two things to do.' She made them an ironical bow.

'Such as what?' Harriet asked when she'd gone.

'She always keeps irons in the fire. Letter writing. Lists. She makes a great thing of the laundry.'

'Needlessly?' Tim asked.

'I wouldn't say so. She's very efficient. I think she has a part in a play at the Sherwood Rooms. Don't ask me what it is. She'll give me the details in due course and if I feel like it I shall turn out to see it. The company's quite good. And she's quite a talent.'

'Do you go out much at night?' Harriet.

'No. That's why I'm so pleased to see you two and hear you talk. Beatrice, Bea, Trixie's all right, but I think she looks down on me. I'm a useless old man, a drain on society, only tolerated because I've plenty of money.'

'No,' Harriet said.

'Does she say as much?'

'No. But I can tell.'

'That's one thing I have difficulty with,' Tim said thoughtfully, 'making out just what people are thinking. Especially when they say nothing.'

They played with their coffee cups and chocolate mints.

Harriet drew herself up to speak. 'They tell me', she said, 'that you've not been very well.' She sounded grown-up.

'They,' her grandfather mused, 'they?' He also rearranged his position, disposing for the moment of his cup and saucer. 'When you get to my age, the seventies, you can't expect to be, or to feel, fit.'

'Why's that?' Harriet asked.

'The machine is wearing out. And you don't, therefore, take the exercise you did. And at this time of the year, you feel down in the mouth. And one of the remedies we take – eating between meals – only makes us worse. Now I'll use the proper pronoun. I ought to be perfectly content. I have a convenient and beautiful house, always warm. I have my books, and my computer and my garden. Mrs Smith is always about to attend to my bodily comforts. I can travel if I wish, and I do sometimes, or stay at home. There are cultural events galore, both here and in London, and I'm strong enough to take advantage of some of these. And yet, yet . . .'

116

'Haven't you quite a lot of friends in Beechnall?'

'No. I've been too preoccupied with my own concerns. Acquaintances, yes. I have plenty of them. But there,' he held up a finger, 'hardly a month passes without news of the death of one or another of these. And the thought strikes me that they have just as much right to be alive, to occupy a place on the earth, as I have. And some of them, more. Some have made a real mark, "left the vivid air signed with their honour".'

'Who's that?' Tim asked.

'Who wrote that? Stephen Spender. I suppose nobody reads him these days. Perhaps that exaggerates the importance of the people I knew. They were not "the truly great". But there.'

'Tell us about one of them,' Harriet begged.

Meades began at once. 'My old classics master. He died at the beginning of this month. Eighty-four. He was only twelve years older than I was. A marvellous teacher. He had very strict standards. But real judgement. He didn't make a fuss over little errors. But he could drop on you like a ton of bricks. He left the school at the same time that I did. He became headmaster of two schools, and then he went to some kind of academic post at Cambridge, and finally head of a college there. I think of the influence he had on me, and I was no sort of scholar in Latin and Greek. And yet. I still think, now, at my age, if I'm in a quandary, "What would old Rowley say?" Rowland Raikes, that was his name. His influence on people must have been enormous.'

'And did he think of himself as a successful man?' Tim asked.

'Ah. It's interesting that you ask that. An old school friend of mine went to see old Rowley just a few years ago. He'd retired to a very nice house up in the Lake District. He'd no real connection with the place except for holidays spent there. He seemed, my friend said, to be physically pretty well and he'd kept all his marbles. But he was downcast. His life was over and he'd pretty well wasted it. When my friend suggested that it was not everybody who became Master of a Cambridge college, he said he had been elected to fill a three- or four-year gap until the man they really wanted could come back from America to do the job. And Dr Raikes said, "That's what I've been doing all my life. Plugging gaps. Efficiently, yes, but . . ."'

'What should he have done?' Tim asked.

'There's no saying. He was old, and at a loose end, and tired,

117

and I guess, if he was anything like me, that whatever course his life had taken, it would have seemed misguided. He perhaps thought he should have stuck to his sixth-form teaching of Latin and Greek. He wrote a very good little book on Homer while he was still teaching me. And it's said he was doing a book on Sophocles, which he never finished. He would have had less free time as a schoolmaster than as a head, but he knew then what he wanted to make clear to his pupils about Homer. Once he left the classroom, he was too busy organising this, that or the other, and accepted invitations to sit on committees and the like, all of which he did extremely well, I'm sure, but there was no book, apart from the Raikes Report on the Teaching of Classics, which he could look to to keep his ideas alive when he was dead. It's sad.'

They sat in silence. Harriet looked beautiful in this light, pale but healthily alert, interested and interesting.

Meades took a sip of his wine, twirled the glass by its stem, painfully cleared his throat and began again. 'And Raikes was a gifted man, who had accomplished a great deal.'

'Was he right? To feel as he did?' Harriet asked. Tim silently approved of her question.

'I don't think he had a great deal of choice. Very few of us can override our feelings, master them, especially when one is old. When I tie up my shoelaces, it's a major undertaking. I bend and I can't get my breath. It's as though I've carried some heavy weight for a long distance uphill. My heart's banging and I'm trying to set myself right with gulps of air through my mouth. To tie my shoes, something you do in no time without ever thinking of it. But it shows me the state of my heart and lungs, and I wonder how long I have left when such a small undertaking half kills me. If I walk out on a cold morning, I'm not exhilarated like you, I'm struggling.'

'Can't your doctor do anything for you?'

'Doctors. Oh, they provide me with tablets and examine me, but they don't understand. To me, ageing is a natural process, which we must all expect, which we must learn to put up with. They help with their medicines. All the doctors nowadays were trained in the era of instant cures. First the sulpha drugs and then penicillin. All they need to do is to diagnose properly and then reach for the correct bottle, and in a day or two you'll be right as rain. No bedside manner is needed. You swallowed the cure and you were better. They hadn't mastered everything, but that, they thought, was only a matter of time. Now, ironically, they're beginning to learn differently. Bacteria grow to be immune to these wonder drugs, and dirty hospitals, no longer hand-scrubbed by young nurses, with the sister or matron breathing down their necks, encourage these super-bugs to thrive.'

'And won't scientists discover something else?' Tim asked.

'Possible. *Homo sapiens* is very versatile. But just now we're in a period of doubt. And I, old and feeble and depressed, will have to try to put up with it all.'

'Surely you have some pleasure in life?' Harriet objected.

'Yes. Moaning and groaning to you young people.' They laughed, slightly self-consciously, all three. 'Listening to music, reading something marvellous, walking out on a bright day. Much the same pleasures as younger people of my temperament. Of course, physical pleasures are out, be they mountain climbing or sexual intercourse.'

'Didn't Sophocles say that he was glad to be rid of his sexual drives, that he felt like someone released from the clutches of a cruel master?' Tim posed his question with a serious face.

'Well, yes. Old people are not immune from the concomitants of sexual desire. Attraction to the opposite sex is still there. Even, I believe, love, that complex and wonderful amalgam. But we know we're ugly and misshapen, that nobody in their right mind could be sexually drawn to us.'

'I don't know,' said Tim. 'The papers are full of photographs of beautiful young women married to aged and frail men who look old enough to be their fathers if not their grandfathers.'

'But don't you find these wrinklies', Meades laughed and coughed over the word before he returned to complete his sentence, 'are very rich men or men of power, presidents or prime ministers?'

'Don't young people have such matters in their minds when they make their choice of husbands?'

'I'm sure they do. But they don't have the obstacle of ugliness and weakness to cope with as well. They choose people who are physically attractive. Very often people not unlike themselves in looks. And if they're rich, or outstanding in some way, yes, that's all to the good.'

119

Tim glanced over at Harriet and wondered in what ways he resembled her. She seemed to sit, to preside over this conversation like a judge. Her beauty gave her the right to evaluate her grandfather's words. Tim dismissed this view. She looked up and smiled suddenly at him as if to encourage him.

'You must be tired of my complaints,' Mr Meades ventured.

'By no means,' Harriet answered, a schoolmistress to a diffident pupil. 'Did you get on well with your parents?'

'Yes and no.' He divided his answer, his face revealing something of his surprise at her question. 'They were both eccentric and rather old when I was born in the late twenties. My mother was forty and my father a little older. I must have come as a surprise, and not altogether welcome at that. My father, though his health was uncertain, was a great worker. He'd often not be home till eight or nine. So I saw little of him except on Sundays, and then he'd be tucked away in his study. I saw him for meals and occasionally, very occasionally, we'd go out after lunch for a walk. My mother tried her best for me. She read books to me and answered questions, and put me to piano lessons, but I don't think she'd much talent for dealing with small boys and they sent me off to boarding school when I was eight. In a way it suited me, I suppose. I could fight my corner and made some good friends, and was never accosted by paederastic schoolmasters, even if such existed at the place. I was lucky, in that at both prep and public school I was well taught, and that was by no means always the case.'

'What about parental love?' Harriet asked.

'What about it?' Tim judged the grandfather's answer rude.

'Didn't you miss it?'

'No. There was very little overt show of affection in our home. And so, never having enjoyed it, if that's the word, I never missed it. There was plenty to occupy me with lessons and games and clubs. And I suppose that determined the sort of life I was to lead, as a schoolmaster and a bookseller, and prepared me for it.'

'But you married Grandma?'

'Yes. Amazingly. While I was still at Oxford.'

'Did your parents approve?'

'They gave me the impression that they considered marriage rather an insignificant part of life. I may be wrong, of course. My father collared me one day, or rather ran into me, and said he hoped I wasn't spending too much time with the girl, that's what he called her, and warned me that if I made a poor shot at my degree I could expect no more financial help from him.'

'And he meant it?' Harriet asked, quietly breathless.

'I'm sure he did. Fortunately I did well in my final exams and he came up with money from time to time. If, for instance, we had to put down a deposit, or moved from one job to another. Nothing very lavish, but it helped us through. I was lucky in that the Army didn't want me. Your grandmother had also started to teach by this time and we made our way.'

'You were happy?' Harriet did not want her grandfather's story to end.

'Yes. We both liked our jobs. We got on together rather well, especially considering our ignorance and upbringing. My wife, Joan, was brought up strictly nonconformist, a Baptist. She was baptised by total immersion. I think she felt rather embarrassed by it, later on.'

'Did you go to her church?' Tim.

'No. We didn't live in Beechnall and my first school was an Anglican foundation. We attended the parish church and services in the school chapel.' He breathed deeply. 'I don't suppose it meant much, really. Any attraction was aesthetic. Your grandmother was a very good pianist, much better than I ever was. She had a performer's diploma. One of the first pieces of house furniture we bought for ourselves was an upright piano. We used to play duets. It improved my playing a great deal. And Henry was born a year or so later.'

'Mrs Smith didn't look after you then?' Harriet asked, then answered her own query. 'She's not old enough.'

'No. Though her mother worked for me. And an aunt. She used to come up sometimes in the school holidays. Your mother was fond of her.'

'When did my grandmother die?'

'Later. When your father was at Cambridge. Just after he'd taken Part III. We had his result a few days before she died. She was so delighted. And Beatrice was working for us then. She'd married very young, at seventeen or eighteen. She looked after your grandmother marvellously well in her last illness. She had cancer, but we didn't expect her to die. A heart attack killed her.'

The young people were silenced. Meades delivered this

information in the quietest of voices, but with a serious face, unmarked by grief. He sighed, took another sip at his wine; he was as abstemious with that as with his food. He sighed again, rather like a ham actor.

'But that's all history.' He tapped his knee as if to drum further words into being. 'She'd only be seventy-seven now and they tell me that's no sort of an age, especially for a woman. We'd been married twenty-seven years. I often wonder what sort of husband I made. I was busy and that meant we spent very little time together. Holidays in France. Concerts and theatres. Otherwise I was just like my father. Except I knew I wasn't acting fairly. He didn't. It was his wife's duty to be there at his beck and call at any time of the day or night. And he was far from generous. I saw to it that your grandmother was never short of money. Not that she needed it; she had means of her own. And she was a woman who could occupy herself. She made friends; they visited each other, went on outings and to classes and recitals. She learnt Spanish. She practised the piano. She and two other women formed a piano trio and gave recitals. One year, Trixie's theatre group put on a musical and she played for rehearsals and performances. It was only in her last year that she was really ill and even then she went out, when the hospital was half murdering her with chemotherapy.'

'An interesting life,' Tim ventured.

'An interesting woman. And that's where I didn't do either her or myself justice. I was so busy as a schoolmaster, then as a bookseller and entrepreneur, that I didn't realise what pleasure we could have had, had I made the effort to know her better and join in her activities.'

'But had you the time?' Harriet asked, excusing him. 'You had a living to earn.'

'No, my dear. By the time my father died he left me a rich man. Both his brothers had died unmarried and bequeathed their businesses to him. He sold off one of his elder brother's shops, just the premises, and rented out another three. And that meant I had no need to work.'

'Why did you?' Harriet again, fresh-voiced.

'Ah. It had been drilled into me that one had to pursue some useful occupation. In my case teaching, then buying and selling books or property. And if I'd spent my time idling at home, or cruising round the world, or following some scholarly pursuit – I suppose I was capable of that – it would have gone against my upbringing. I should have been pleasing myself and not doing my duty. That's wrong, of course it is, but that's the way I reacted.'

'And you regret it now?' Tim asked boldly.

'Yes, I suppose I do. I could have spent my time better. On Sunday evenings Joan and I used to play duets together. In this house. We lived here then. That seems odd. I've altered the place. Before, Joan saw to the decoration and the pictures. This room, it's been repainted of course, but in the same colours that she chose, and these pictures, they're ones she bought.'

'It's a beautiful room,' Harriet said.

'It is. She had taste. But I took it all for granted. She was just over fifty when she died. There were so many things she could have done. She was a headmistress, but she had so much time for the home. I could kick myself when I think about it now. I knew then I wasn't playing fairly by her, taking advantage of her energy.' He made an exclamation of distaste and slapped the thighs of his trousers.

'Did she complain?' Harriet asked.

'Hardly at all. She sometimes was annoyed. She lived a full life. She retired at the age of forty-six to enable herself to do all the things she wanted. And then, after a few years, she began to be ill. It seems such a waste.'

'But you weren't to blame for her illness,' Harriet protested.

'I wonder,' Meades answered. 'I wonder.' He sighed again. 'One never knows. I think she would have worked a few years longer in her school. I don't know. I never pressed her to retire. Henry was away at school or Cambridge. But she retired. I'd made by that time enough money to keep us, well, modestly. I don't know why she gave up. She was successful, very much so, but she suddenly announced that she was retiring.'

'Did she often make these unexpected decisions?' Harriet asked.

'Not really.'

'And you could think of no good reason for this?'

'No.' Meades drew in a heavy breath. 'No. It's twenty-one years ago since she died. I've often wondered whether she had a suspicion that she'd only another four or five years to live, and decided to live them at home and in her own way. But that's mere superstition. She never said anything of that kind, then or later. She just filled her life for the first years with music, and visits, and friends, and I'm glad now she did, though it meant I was often enough left to fend for myself.'

'Did her trio ever perform publicly?' Tim asked.

'Yes. Three times to my knowledge. For charity. They mostly performed at home. They practised in this house, because we had the largest, most convenient room.'

Meades rose, almost jumped from his chair, and stood as if trying to infuse himself with hospitality. 'You've had enough of my reminiscences,' he said. 'Let's play a game.'

Tim wondered what remarkable pastime the old man was about to suggest. His usual position, legs wide, arms swinging arhythmically searching for a meaningful gesture barred nothing. Russian roulette? Strip poker?

'Such as what?' Harriet bringing them to earth.

'Monopoly. Scrabble. Some card game. Why, what did you think? I spy with my little eye . . .'

'There's just about time for that,' she answered. 'It's twenty to ten. It won't be long before my mother's here to pick us up.'

'So she will. Adelaide's a good timekeeper. Can I offer you a last drink? One for the road?' He had relaxed now, was jovial, with hands in trouser pockets. They refused. 'Then perhaps you will excuse me. I fancy a malt whisky. I can't get you to indulge with me? Then I shall only be a minute or two.' He closed the door behind him.

Tim immediately moved across and kissed Harriet. Her mouth sought his; she pressed eagerly into him. The outside bell interrupted their pleasure.

'That's my mother,' Harriet said.

'It's not ten to yet.'

'She'd sooner be early than late.' Harriet picked up her small handbag, snatched a tiny handkerchief, wet it with the end of her tongue and tidied Tim's lips. 'Sit down now,' she ordered and examined her own face in a small round hand mirror with a silver back. She made minor adjustments to the flawless beauty. Tim watched, entranced.

Meades came in, red-faced, his glass of whisky in his hand. 'My apologies. I couldn't find the bottle.'

'Did you hear the doorbell?' Tim asked.

'I did. But Trixie will have gone down.'

They heard women's voices chatter on the corridor outside. After a brief rap on the door, Mrs Smith ushered Adelaide into the room. Both were grinning broadly, as if sharing a joke.

'Come in, come in,' Meades shouted. He still stood. 'Our favourite ladies.'

'I'm not too early, I hope,' Adelaide said. 'There seems a lot of late traffic about, but I was more than lucky with traffic lights.'

'The Gods wanted you here in good time to make our evening,' Meades said. Behind his back Mrs Smith pulled a tart face.

'Have they been good?' Adelaide.

'Yes. They've excelled themselves. They not only ate well, but I expect that with Trixie's cooking, they sat and listened to my everlasting list of complaints about life and death and old age. Moreover, they asked questions that showed they were listening and were interested.'

'And that's not usual?' Adelaide again.

'Not in the experience of old men without influence. Or at least this one. I might as well be talking to myself.'

'You often do,' Mrs Smith gritted.

Meades drew in a breath and waited. Tim expected him to explode into crude abuse, but the moment passed. 'I expect that's right,' he said. 'But it's been great for me. I feel stronger for it, more cheerful.'

'Good,' Adelaide answered. 'I'm glad of that, because you have been invited together with our family to see the New Year in at Timothy's home. I spoke to his mother on the phone tonight and she invited us all, and you and Mrs Smith, to celebrate at her house. You didn't know that, did you, young man?' To Tim, who had taken Harriet's hand. 'Your father, who, according to your mum,' the nouns displayed their status, 'doesn't drink, will drive us back home, so you can tope to your heart's content.'

'Do you think', Meades spoke with formality to Mrs Smith, 'that we shall be able to manage that?'

'Yes.' Mrs Smith turned to Adelaide. 'Please thank Mrs Hughes for us both.'

Coats were fetched. Talk seemed to have died. At the door the young people remembered to thank the host for his hospitality. He received their sentences as if his mind was elsewhere.

Adelaide dropped Tim off first. He and Harriet kissed awkwardly on the back seat, but they had made their gesture.

'Give me a ring, won't you? Before the thirty-first,' she said.

'With pleasure.'

Both grimaced.

XII

The party on New Year's Eve proved acceptable. They had a
buffet supper at nine of which all, on their own confession, ate
too much so delectable were the dishes. For the house of a
teetotaller, wine, in good supply, kept them garrulous and
happy. Harald Meades had been, with two friends, to visit the
church at Little Gidding and he described the outing in slow,
portentous tones. It had been a dark day, but he had felt, he said,
much moved. One of his fellow travellers, so he called them, a
clergyman, the retired Dean of a Cambridge college, had some
connection with the community there. Meades described the
skies, Nicholas Ferrar's tomb, their car journey, which had
seemed wild in the extreme with the most ancient member of
the trio at the wheel with his foot never lifted from the
accelerator. The place seemed to speak of heaven, Meades
grinned, and the car ride suggested they'd soon have first-hand
experience. The old man spoke at his best; civilised humour
flavoured his description of the trees, the clouds, the rose beds
where one or two flowers still bloomed. Once he stopped to
quote Eliot:

> You are here to kneel
> Where prayer has been valid,

and there was suddenly about this wine-heavy room a silence. It
was as if Meades had become a priest of some esoteric but simple
cult, Tim thought, though the voice remained almost jovially
secular. The boy, on a small settee, sat close to Harriet, who
whispered to him, 'I think I'm drunk.' He held her hand and
Meades walked across, though not a tall man, to tower over them.

Professor Henry Meades sat next to Melissa Hughes and, when
she was not hospitably leaping up, they talked rapidly together,
in low voices, heads close. Only once did Tim catch any of their

127

conversation, 'a man I knew who had lived much of his life in China', then the voice dropped, continued but inaudibly. The expression on their faces conveyed interest, serious concentration rather than pleasure. Perhaps, Tim's wine-flushed imagination suggested, Henry was attempting to coach Melissa, guide her through some mathematical theorem, both knowing he would fail but determined to impress the other. Over at the far side of the room, in two armchairs placed together, Adelaide furiously talked to her father-in-law, smiling, irrepressibly determined to stimulate her companion who sat, red-faced, like a Buddha now, after his poetry. Both would break off to hurl a question elsewhere in the room, Meades to ask Harriet the year of Eliot's birth, the answer to which Tim supplied and was rewarded by a kiss on the ear, or Adelaide to enquire about the heating of the room, or to comment on the bronze beauty of the chandeliers.

Most surprising of all, Mrs Smith had paired with Charles Hughes and they occupied the largest settee, with friendly propriety. Beatrice Smith had dressed the most soberly of the women, but with the most instant and striking effect. She wore a Celtic cross at the neck of her dark-green dress. Her tights, of a delicate shade of green, were smooth above highly polished, silver-buckled shoes. Her hair had been swept up into a bun, leaving her neck exposed in its whiteness. Though she was ten years older than Adelaide, and twelve than Melissa, she looked younger than both. They smiled, gestured with their features, flashed eyes; her face was smooth, lightly made up, pleasantly expressive of her enjoyment, but adult, not setting out to impress or dazzle, merely to show her unmistakable gratification at being one of the party, and at the same time assessing her emotion exactly, exaggerating nothing. Her hands, long-fingered and white, lay in her lap, calm, at ease.

By her side, with perhaps a yard between them, sat Charles Hughes, stiffly leaning slightly towards her, either plying her with questions or haranguing her, emphasising his discourse with small accompanying hand movements. He was extending himself to entertain her, but seriously. Tim could not hear what his father said, but guessed he was explaining some point of law, or describing an incident in a court. The delivery would be dry, but his father knew how to make his points both clearly and thus catch interest. Once Mrs Smith threw up her hands as if he had surprised her, shocked her even. Her mouth rounded, but her green eyes were ironical.

'What's he telling you?' Adelaide shouted across the room.

'The iniquity of relatives,' Hughes answered for her.

'What a topic for a family party,' Adelaide commented.

'Where better?' Mrs Smith riposted, earning a laugh from Adelaide and a guffaw from Meades.

'It's getting on for midnight,' Melissa warned. 'I've put the champagne ready. Tim will help me carry it out. I'll give you a call in a minute, and then you can get your coats on. It's cold outside. I shan't stay out there long, that I can tell you. We've just one firework, a huge super-, hyper-rocket.'

'Already on the launch pad,' her husband said, and Mrs Smith nodded satisfaction.

They filed into the hall for outdoor clothes with some reluctance, but once outside in the chill they chatted about the weather. Hughes pointed out the single rocket, which was certainly very substantial. The Council House clock began to chime, the sound large, distantly detailed in the frosty air. On the first stroke of midnight, as lesser bells clanged from a church tower, Melissa raised a finger to Tim, who twisted, after a short struggle, the cork from the wine. He'd already removed the silver paper and the wire work. He upended the bottle towards the first glass.

'Not a drop spilled,' he boasted, directing the foaming stream towards the second glass. When all eight were topped up, including his father's to Tim's surprise, Charles Hughes called out. 'A very happy New Year' in a stentorian voice. 'And century, and millennium.'

They shouted back and drank.

'Moët et Chandon,' the professor whispered to himself.

Fireworks now scarred the sky with streaks and bunches and globes of light.

'Now,' said Charles solemnly, 'we must make our single contribution to the *new* century, and I invite Beatrice to send this monster skywards.' Mrs Smith, some yards away, stepped staidly across to where the rocket stood poised, slightly out of vertical, in its tower of bricks. Tim and his father had built this supporting edifice earlier in the afternoon.

Charles pulled a cigarette lighter from his pocket, snapped it on, and then in the still air lit a long taper. 'Madam,' he said, and handed the taper over to Mrs Smith. He bent forward to point with his finger. 'Please, your attention, please. Light the blue touchpaper and retire.'

Mrs Smith swiftly, efficiently, lit the fuse, doused and handed back the taper, and the two stepped away together.

The fuse burnt dully, slowly. Harriet dug Tim in the ribs with delight that nothing had happened. All stared intently at the faint glow at the base of the rocket. Silence hung close, while round the rest of the neighbourhood minor explosions lit, bit and echoed.

'No,' said Charles, not altogether confidently, 'give it time.'

Suddenly the rocket exploded into a ferocious violence of sparks as it whooshed upwards, trajectory as planned. The size of the burst, the speed of the ascent were stultifying. There was nothing of the majestic and stately rise of the projectiles from Cape Kennedy, with the preliminary clouds of obscuring smoke, the flash of fire and the godlike slow power as the machine rose. Here it was all hurry, scurry, bustle, sizzle, but so wild, unexpected, loud that Harriet stepped back, and her arm through Tim's dragged him with her. They recovered from their stagger to stare upwards with the rest.

Now the rocket was high, lost in darkness until a deafening bang shook them and a circle of generous light burst like a flower. Another crack and a further blossom, green and beetroot red, then another, splitting this time into two teardrops of gold, and a repetition and, after a significant pause a detonation, terrifyingly loud, heralded a kind of curtain, a net of lights, which then dropped to earth, each part extinguishing its own beauty as it fell.

'Um,' Meades said, 'a spectacle. Impressive.' The others murmured appreciation.

'Yes,' Charles answered, taking Mrs Smith's arm as if they had been jointly responsible for the planning and manufacture, 'I think we can claim satisfaction there.' He did not bow.

'Indoors,' Melissa ordered. 'It's too cold to be loitering out here.'

As they bundled up the wide steps into the hall, Adelaide said to Tim, 'I'm glad that's over. I hate fireworks. I always have.'

'Never mind,' Tim said. 'It pleased the little ones.'

Adelaide laughed and removed her coat with deft speed, handing it over to the boy to be hung. 'Don't let them hear you,' she warned.

The party broke up almost at once and Charles Hughes's Daimler waited on the drive. They discussed his route briefly: first the Meades family, then the grandfather and Mrs Smith. When they had left, Tim and his mother made an effort to clear away the débris of the feast.

'How do you think it went?' she asked.

'Very good. It really was. And everybody seemed happy.' He juggled with plates. 'No, nobody is complaining.'

As they passed on the way to and from the kitchen he said, 'What about Dad, then?'

'Oh?' His mother stopped.

'He seemed to be hitting it off with Mrs Smith. I've never seen him quite so jovial. And talkative.'

'Do you know what she said to him? Or so he reported to me? "Isn't young Timothy really handsome?"'

'*In vino veritas*.' He laughed.

Later, as they packed the dishwasher, he enquired, 'What was the prof like? You seemed to be able to get him to talk.'

'He was quite interesting. Not at all like his father, who's a bit of a show-off, in my opinion. He prepared all that stuff about "Little Gidding", including his snippet of quotation.'

'About prayer? Is he a religious man, then?'

'Not according to Henry. I asked him. A literary type. Wishing he was anything but what he was, but changing his mind with every book he read. A dilettante, he said. Henry, the son, was shy, but a good talker.'

'What did he tell you about, then? Algebra?'

'He didn't waste his time on that. He told me he intends to go out walking, rambling on Sundays with some club. He wants me to get Charles to join them.'

'Does Adelaide go?'

'Yes. Twice so far this season. He's not started yet.'

'How much do they do? Miles?'

'No. About six to eight. Every so often they lay on a heavy day, twelve, fifteen. But that's on Saturday, not Sunday. He says it's all very casual. Nobody's forcing anybody to do anything.'

'Will Dad go?'

'He's getting worried about middle-aged spread, so it's possible.'

They heard Charles Hughes's car in the drive. He hadn't loitered about his delivery home of his guests.

'He's had his skates on,' Tim said. 'It must have been that glass of champagne.'

Melissa laughed out loud. 'He didn't have any. Rapidly changed his glass for one of apple juice. Sleight of hand. If you didn't notice, it's not likely the others did.'

Charles Hughes made his usual, quietly impressive entry.

'Coffee?' his wife asked. He declined. 'All safely delivered?' A solemn nod. 'Were they all happy?'

'Yes. Or drunk.'

'And at your expense,' his wife commented.

'I think it went very well,' Hughes said. 'Everybody seemed to find something or somebody interesting.'

'Did they say so?'

'Adelaide did most of the talking for them, but the others seemed to agree.'

'What did the prof say?' Tim asked.

'He admitted he did not want to come out, but he found the evening both restful and stimulating. And,' he turned to his wife, 'you'd fed us to perfection. The exact words.'

'*Ipsissima verba*,' Tim said.

'And what about the other two?'

'Mr Meades was rather quiet. Mrs Smith said she'd not had such a pleasant visit for years. Nobody was pressing her.' Hughes yawned, but did not bother to cover his mouth. 'I'm tired,' he said. 'And all Tim and I did was shift a few chairs and build a launching pad.' He sighed. 'You must be worn out.'

'Let's to bed, then,' his wife answered.

Two days later Tim met Harriet in town. The arrangement had been made by phone. They sat together in a coffee bar, jungle-thick with plants, and with Tudor-style windows, starchy cloths on the tables. Coffee was served at a counter in wide cups, with demerara sugar. The place stood supremely neat but almost empty.

'My mother wouldn't be pleased if she knew I was here,'

Harriet began. Sometimes she seemed to enjoy putting a blight on the occasion. 'She thinks I'm working away at my Latin set books.'

'Have you much to do?'

'Not really. We're doing the *Georgics*, Book Four, and I've been carefully over the part we've read, and prepared the next hundred lines so that I'm ready when we start again.'

'You enjoy it?'

'Yes, I do. Mrs Partington is very good at explaining it and quite amusing. She can be that because she has no trouble with discipline.'

They sipped their coffee. He explained that the cups were broad, more like soup-bowls, so that the drink would cool more quickly and customers would either have to leave the shop, or order a second.

'Some people I know', Harriet objected, 'make one cup last an hour or more. They come in here out of the weather or to rest their legs.'

'But the proprietors depend on most people acting decently,' he said. 'And I guess it works out.' Harriet laughed at his optimism.

They talked without difficulty and he, the decent boy, fetched second cups.

'Did your parents enjoy the New Year's Eve party?' he asked.

'Yes. They were determined to. They'd been invited to several others. My mum says that Dad's quite a celebrity these days so that everybody wants to know him.'

'And does that please her?'

'Yes. I suppose so. She's no idea what it is exactly that has made him so highly regarded.'

'Does that matter? I mean, that she doesn't understand his mathematics?'

'It doesn't seem to. They're not much like each other. My mother's volatile and he's quiet; they live in worlds of their own. They must always have been like that.'

'Do they love each other?' he asked.

'Do your parents? Or anybody's? They must have, I suppose, at one time, but they never show any signs of it. They get on well enough, or seem to, these days. She has a job she likes and he, she says, is lucky. He invented, or whatever, this sort of maths he

133

does. It isn't like maths at all, people have told my mother. But he started on it as part of his Ph.D. Many of his teachers thought he was cracked, but his professor at Cambridge, he's dead now, a man called Wood, supported him and used his influence to get him a job up here. Apparently he's very good at teaching the ordinary stuff, you know, that the students do for their degrees. Nobody ever set questions on his sort of whatever it is, though there were always a few mathematicians who were convinced he was on to a good line and reported favourably on the books he wrote so that they were published. And gradually he became known, through these specialist journals, and in the last few years some high flyers in America have used his techniques.'

'To do what?'

'God knows.' Harriet giggled. 'I think somebody used some theory of his in economics and some way-out physicist has been proving things about the universe with a line Dad has been following.'

'That must be very satisfactory for him. To find that he's been right all these years and other people wrong to ignore him.'

'Do you know, I don't think that occurs to him?'

'It would to me.'

'And me. But he was so interested in these theorems he conjured up as a young man that that was enough. He wanted to know where he was going, mathematically. And it's opened up developments. He'd done all his best creative work before he was thirty, he says, and he's been dotting "i"s and crossing "t"s ever since, and it's given him a great deal to do. Sometimes he says that even now – he's nearly forty-nine, though to hear him talk you'd guess he was ninety – something completely new crops up.'

'And your mother's not jealous?'

'I don't think so, but then I don't exactly understand my mother. She seemed pleased when they made him a professor. And when he goes back to Cambridge to lecture, or to America, she threatens to go with him, and boasts like blazes about all the mail he gets and all these lectures he's invited to give and the references to him in books.'

'So she's happy?'

'My mother's never happy. Excited sometimes.'

'Elated?' he suggested.

134

'Yes, that's about it, but never happy. She fears the worst. Even if everything is turning out perfectly, she harbours some doubt at the back of her mind that something will spoil it.'

'Why is that?'

'I don't know. Both her parents died when she was young. Perhaps that was it.'

'But she always seems so lively?'

'I know. Everybody says what good company she is. And so she is, full of ideas.'

'She's not like that at home?'

'Yes, she is. But recently I've begun to have my doubts. I wonder if she isn't acting a part.'

'Aren't we all?' Tim asked.

'No, I don't think I am. Or not very often. I mean, if I were acting, I'd be talking about something other than my parents. I guess not many people of our age do that.'

'I don't know. It's a popular subject. I met your grandfather one night when I was wandering round town and he told me that his parents were mad.'

'I wonder if they were.'

'I doubt it. Eccentric, like him, but not lunatics.'

They talked together. He was only partly interested in what she told him, but he knew he would prefer her company to that of any other person. They walked hand in hand to the bus stop.

'Back to your Virgil,' he said. 'What will you do with it?'

'I'll go over the part we've studied. That's what Mrs P. will test us on when we get back.'

'Have you got "mocks"?' he asked.

'You can bet we have.'

'They're good for your soul.'

She waved from her seat; he saluted as the bus drew out, and the day grew darker.

XIII

Tim saw nothing of Harriet during the week or so she dedicated herself to the school exams. One afternoon he arrived at his front gate and saw that Harriet's father preceded him up the drive. Professor Meades, hearing the gate click behind him, turned round, muttered a greeting and waited by the front door. 'I've called to see your mother,' he announced.

'I don't know if she's in.'

'She said she'd be at home. Unless I've got the wrong day.' He opened his coat and pulled out a diary. 'No, right day, right time.'

Tim let the visitor in, relieved him of his coat. 'Has Harriet finished her exams?' he asked.

The professor appeared quietly startled by the question. 'I assume so. By now. It appears she's done particularly well from what we hear.'

'You'll be pleased.'

'Yes. Yes. I think so.' Henry Meades gave the impression of an absent-minded academic, concentrating to produce an impossible answer to an insoluble question.

'She's clever,' Tim said.

'Yes. So her teachers say.'

'Don't you think so?' Tim asked, annoyed by the man's lack of generosity.

'As far as I can tell.'

At this moment Henry Meades was rescued by the arrival of Tim's mother, who swooped on them, reprimanding her son for not letting her know at once that her guest had arrived. She disappeared with the professor into the drawing room, while Tim made for the kitchen, the kettle, tea bags and biscuits. Within five minutes she had joined him to provide Henry with coffee.

'What's milord want?' Tim asked.

'Don't you like him?' she replied. 'Milord, indeed.'

'I hardly know him.'

'Well, you'll get the chance, because I've invited him to stay for dinner and we're going up there when I can find out when your father's free. His wife's in Leicester.'

Melissa seemed pleased, humming to herself as she filled the mugs. 'Mugs for friends,' she commented. She whirled out, still singing, though he could not recognise the music.

He came down from his room, his homework, to find his father newly arrived and rather put out by the presence of a visitor. This was, Tim guessed, designated as one of Charles Hughes's 'free' evenings, and he did not want it spoilt by the unexpected. The meal seemed to raise his spirits and at the end he sat at the head of the table, dabbing at his lips with a napkin and beaming. No wine had been served, 'Henry's driving,' Charles had said; they drank water or a particularly delicious home-made concoction of oranges and lemons. Tim guessed that his mother had knocked that off without fuss or preparation as she'd made the meal for three stretch lavishly for four. A woman of parts, his mother.

During the meal Charles explained how people managed to get an injunction in the middle of the night. This was amusingly delivered, especially when he described the reactions of one tetchy judge dragged from his bed in the small hours. Melissa gave a curiously restrained account of a meeting that morning, which had been protracted and boring, towards the end of which they had tried to discuss a pithy phrase for an advertisement for a new cheese spread, which itself had not yet been given a name.

'Will it be popular?' Charles asked.

'If we get it right, it will. But the end of a long meeting is neither the time nor the place for inspiration.'

'Have you tasted it?'

'No.' This was part time work she'd recently taken on.

'Then how can you think up a pithy phrase or anything else?'

'You'd be surprised.'

'Don't you connect it in some way with a marvellous event that seems to have no connection? That's not altogether clear. I mean, can't you suggest that the success of a good-looking young couple's honeymoon is due in some miraculous way to your cheese spread?' Henry Meades spoke slowly, but without force. What he said surprised them all, as they did not expect him to comment.

137

'You're a cynic,' Melissa teased.

'No. Just simple-minded.'

The date for the meal with the professor's family had been fixed already before Tim had come down to dinner. His mother announced it at once, as of importance, the Friday of the next week.

'Harriet will be very disappointed if you can't come,' her father said.

'He'll be there,' Melissa promised.

' "Though hell should bar the way",' Charles.

'It so happens', Tim said, 'that I am free that evening.'

'We are relieved.' His mother spoke sarcastically.

At nine thirty Professor Meades left. His daughter, out until then at the home of a friend with whom she was working on some complicated historical project would have to be picked up at nine forty-five. Adelaide, it appeared, was away for the night. She and a friend had arranged to see *A Doll's House* in Leicester where the friend lived.

'I enjoyed Meades's company,' Charles Hughes said.

'He doesn't say a great deal.'

'No, but what he does say is worth hearing. I thought, I think it every time I talk to him, that he'll be so entrapped with his mathematics that he barely realises what is going on around him. It's not so. He's shy and he doesn't want to ram his ideas down my throat, but he's not inhuman. Less so than his father.'

'Do you understand what he does at his work?'

'He teaches.' Charles laughed. He teased his wife only when he was delighted 'You mean his research. No, I've no idea. He never raises the subject with a layman like me. Though his name came up when I was talking to a client, a young man on the arts side at the university. I mentioned Henry to him. He said he didn't know him personally, only by reputation. But it was rumoured amongst the ignorant, that's what he called himself, that Henry was an original, but in more than the unravelling of the usual out-of-the-way topics, in more than an unusual route. He also claimed that he taught degree mathematics in a very clear manner. Rather quick, he said; you had to hang on, but with real clarity and an eye to the difficulties his students would find. That's not always the case, but with an outstanding and thoroughly independent mathematician pretty well unique. Yes,

I know, Tim. You're either unique or you're not, but you grasp what I mean.'

'Is Harriet a mathematician?' Melissa asked Tim.

'Not as far as I know. She's clever, but not especially at maths.'

'There was something I liked about Henry,' Melissa said.

'What was that?' her husband asked. 'His blue eyes?''

'No, his modesty. You could see that Adelaide had ordered him round, and he'd fallen into line and come obediently to fix the invitation. While she was away. And he was not to phone.'

'She wears the trousers?' Tim asked.

'You know her better than I do,' his mother said.

Adelaide rang within the next few days to ask if the Hugheses would mind if she invited Harald Meades to dinner on the night that was planned as exclusively theirs.

'No, not at all,' Melissa agreed.

'It might mean that we'll have to ask Beatrice Smith as well.'

'My husband will be pleased about that.'

'Melissa.' The tone of protest died as she continued, 'There's a good reason why we should invite him. You'll perhaps remember that the house behind his was burgled some little time back. The police made some progress and just a few days ago another two men were arrested. Well, two nights ago somebody or, more likely bodies, fired rifles at the house, smashing several windows. The police think that these may have been members of the same gang as the lot held in custody.'

'Goodness.'

'There's been quite an outbreak of the use of firearms in this city in the last few months. Again the newspapers suggest it might be gang warfare.'

'Did it do much damage?'

'Several big picture windows smashed, upstairs and down. Glass everywhere. Nobody was hurt.'

'Were there people in the house?'

'The man and his wife. They were in bed.'

'Did Mr Meades hear anything of this?'

'Yes. It woke him. The rifle shots. I got all this from Trixie Smith.'

'She was at home?'

'She was. Heard it all from the other side of the house. They both got up, but saw nothing. But what has upset Mr Meades is

139

that when the police came round it appeared that the shots were fired from his garden.'

'Why was that?'

'It puzzled me, but they could easily get to the back of the house and then they're not likely to be observed. The gardens are big and Mr Meades's has a bank by the end wall between the two properties with bushes in front. That made it straightforward to fire, and if they then slipped over the wall into the next garden there's open access to the street by means of a small alleyway at the side of the house. They couldn't open fire from the garden next door because of trees and bushes; there's quite a spinney. Then presumably they slipped out into the road and were driven off.'

'And Mr Meades?'

'He's been depressed this winter, according to Mrs Smith, but he seemed to be snapping out of it. He enjoyed the meal out with Henry's family and their trip up here. He sat in his library, as he used to, but he felt about this crime as he did about the last, that he was somehow involved in it. Trixie tried to argue him out of this frame of mind, but he was quite unreasonable. She asked him how he could have prevented it, but it made no difference. He'd arranged the perfect shooting gallery for any crooks who wanted to blow his neighbour's windows to smithereens. I don't know.'

'Is there anything we can do?'

'Well, yes, there is. Trixie suggested that I went to see him and I thought that if you could come with me we might talk him somewhere near sense between us.'

'When?' The length of the syllable denoted Melissa's lack of enthusiasm.

'Tomorrow afternoon. I suggest two o'clock. I've the afternoon free and I'll call round to collect you.'

Meades's house stood silent matching the grey coldness of the day.

'He's got it on him,' Mrs Smith complained. 'He won't listen to music. Tells me to turn that damn row off. He must feel ill.'

'What's the doctor say?'

'He's given him some tablets, but I don't think Harald takes them regularly. I keep warning him that he can't expect to get better if he won't do as he's told, but he just tells me to mind my

140

own business. I think he must be in pain. Anyhow, you'll see for yourself in a minute.'

She led the visitors to a small, comfortable room. Mr Meades, in an armchair, had stretched his legs on to a padded footrest. He opened his eyes to find out who had interrupted him, but closed them rudely as if he deemed their presence beneath his notice.

'Sit down,' Mrs Smith invited the two. 'Tea or coffee?'

They made their choice, but Meades still had not spoken. 'I'll bring you tea,' Mrs Smith told him, but he said nothing in return.

The whole visit failed. They drank their coffee in silence. He answered one or two of their questions. He was in pain, arms, joints, shoulders, back. He was short of breath. He could not talk to his doctor; the man was a fool, who thought there was little wrong with him. His chin sagged to his chest and it was some minutes before he opened his eyes. He ignored questions and advice or offers of help.

'Look at me,' he said in the end, his voice barely rising above a whisper. 'Every day now I feel I'm hanging on to life by a fragile thread.'

'In that case you ought to be in hospital,' Adelaide said. 'If your own doctor's useless then go and get a full check-up in the private sector.'

Meades looked up at her helplessly, eyes bloodshot. 'No,' he said and his voice sounded strong.

They left soon after, both having kissed him. He showed no recognition of the favour.

'You see what he's like,' Mrs Smith said, once they were outside the room. She had stood without a word against a far wall. 'There's no helping him.'

'I'll see what Henry says,' Adelaide answered. 'We'll come back in a few days. Keep in touch with us, will you?'

A day or two later Henry Meades rang Melissa. 'I'm worried about my father,' he said, almost immediately. 'Adelaide told me how he was. It was good of you to go round with her. As far as I can make out there wasn't much difference between your reception and mine. He hardly said a word, kept his eyes closed and was much more likely to groan than give me a reasonable answer.'

'Adelaide thought he ought to see some specialist privately.'

'I mentioned this to him, but he wouldn't hear of it. The only animation he showed was when he shouted me down about this.'

'Why would that be?' Melissa asked.

'He's really depressed and very afraid. He thinks that he has something seriously wrong with him, something the doctors can't cure, and he doesn't want to know about it.'

'But you'd think that he'd want to see if something could be done.'

'If he were in his right mind, yes, but his pain and his depression won't allow it. He's no longer reasonable. Adelaide, who's not the sort to hang about, rang his doctor, who said he couldn't really go calling in on the off chance. He must have an invitation. She then rang my father to tell him what she'd done. He told her to keep her nose out of it, that he knew whether or not he needed medical help.'

'I see.'

'I understand that you and Adelaide planned to visit him again in the next few days, so I thought it was my duty to let you know exactly how things stood. Adelaide is not always forthcoming. She's enthusiastic and when she starts something she doesn't like obstacles to be put into her path if she can help it. That's good in many ways, but I thought I ought to warn you before you are dragged into something you'd rather be out of.'

Henry Meades made the same point again, twice. She must please herself how she acted. Speaking for himself, he was only too grateful for the support she was giving his wife, but he wanted her to know exactly how things stood.

When Melissa reported this phone call to her husband, Charles stroked his chin, and smiled. 'Would you say he was genuinely concerned?' he asked.

'Why should he ring otherwise?'

'Because it may be', Charles spoke slowly, 'that it is an excuse to get or keep in touch with you.'

'What does that mean?' She knew quite well.

'That he's attracted to you and looks round for any opportunity to speak with or meet you, or catch your interest.'

'Do you think that's likely?'

'I don't know. I'm like him. I want you to be aware of all the possibilities. He seems not quite on this planet in some ways, though I must admit that the impression he made on me was generally favourable. I liked him. He made no effort to impress. But he doesn't seem ordinary. Perhaps on account of his mathematical training, or the genetic endowment that determined his future in the first place. I don't know.' Charles shook his head. 'What are you going to do about it all?'

'Carry on as before. I'm hardly involved. I feel a bit sorry for the old man. He appears to have been deserted, abandoned somewhere along the line. Possibly it's his own fault. I think Adelaide was pleased that I was there. She's scared, perhaps.'

'She thinks you'll defend her?'

'She thinks Mr Meades will be, by age and upbringing, much more polite to her if I, a comparative stranger, am there.'

'Yes. Would you be flattered to have an admirer?'

'I never gave it much thought,' Melissa answered drily. She was deeply shaken by her husband's suspicion, which seemed a judgement on her gibes about his entanglement with Trixie.

Three days later Adelaide rang early and asked if Melissa would go with her to visit the invalid. Arrangements were to be as before, unless there was some snag at the old man's end. She'd ring Mrs Smith. How did he seem? Much as last week, as far as she could make out.

They chatted cheerfully in the car, but the weather struck cold as they got out at Mr Meades's gate. The sky stretched uniformly grey, the leafless trees dark and oddly misshapen, the wind penetrating.

Mrs Smith was long enough answering the bell. She apologised at once. 'I'm sorry, I was upstairs straightening his room.'

'He's down, then.'

'Yes, we have a visitor. He rang up yesterday and appeared an hour later. He's an old friend, though I've never heard him mentioned before. But he's here, according to Harald, for three or four days.'

'He was pleased that this friend came?' Adelaide asked.

'Nothing'll please him these days. But this man, Paul, rang out of the blue; he was in these parts and rang on the off chance that it would be convenient for him to call, and before he'd been in the house for an hour, it was sealed, signed and delivered that he was going to stay a few days.'

'Is he with him now?' Adelaide.

'Yes. Waiting for you. "A little feminine company will do us both good," Paul had pronounced. So be ready.'

'I can see that you don't like him.'

'I don't. "Do this, do that." That's his line. "I'm giving the orders. Bow down and worship."'

'Perhaps', Melissa suggested, 'that's what Mr Meades is in need of, and a few short, sharp commands will do him good, make him snap out of his depression.'

'It's not him he's ordering about,' Mrs Smith snapped, 'it's me. Paul Gooch, that's him. Saint Paul Gooch, I call him.'

'What does he do?'

'I've no idea. If Harald had been well, he'd have clued me up on what he did and where he came from. Not that we had all that number of visitors, but when we had somebody he'd tell me about them, what they'd prefer to see or do. But all this came in such a ruddy blush.' She giggled; the spoonerism revived her. 'Come along now, you female company.' She led them cheerfully down a corridor.

'And you've no idea what Mr Gooch does for a living?' Adelaide again, not willing to be found unprepared.

'No. He'll be retired, I expect. He came in a Roller, so presumably he's not short.'

Mrs Smith shouted and knocked.

They waited, to silence within and without, until the door was suddenly pulled open by a tall man in a dark suit. He held out his right hand. 'Oh, Mrs Meades and Mrs Hughes.' He laughed at the knowledge, waving them forward with a sweep of his arm. 'And which is which?'

'Adelaide Meades.'

He shook her hand, bending forward. 'Ah, yes. Harald's daughter-in-law.'

'Melissa Hughes.'

Gooch turned from one to the other and, smiling, took Melissa's hand. He seemed enormous. Neither his height nor his smart suit diminished the size of his paunch. His voice sounded velvety deep, but made no great noise. He expected people to listen to him. 'I'm delighted to meet you both. See, we've put out chairs in preparation.' He paid no attention to either Meades or Mrs Smith.

Melissa and Adelaide did not sit as he indicated, but walked across to Meades to enquire how he was. He thanked them, said he was slightly better, held out a limp hand. Expressing pleasure

144

at the improvement, though Melissa saw few clear signs of this, they backed away and into their chairs.

'Good,' Gooch pronounced. 'Good.' He moved ponderously over to his seat, opposite Harald Meades, and reaching into his pocket drew out a handkerchief, still stiff and square from the ironing board, shook it open and blew his nose. All this was done without noise. 'Good,' he pronounced again, returning the hand-kerchief to a pocket which he straightened. He reminded Melissa of pictures of Henry James, though on a grander scale. She had no idea how tall James was. People never divulged this in their memoirs or biographies. The information would appear in their passports, and was likely to be accurate, unlike conjectures about unhappy childhoods, broken marriages or trouble with censors or publishers.

'Drink?' A voice from the back of the room. 'What can I get you to drink?' All chose tea, Earl Grey, except Meades who asked weakly for a glass of warm water.

'I hope we're not intruding,' Adelaide began. 'We had no idea Harald had a visitor.'

'You'll do him more good than ever I shall.' Gooch leaned forward. 'I'm afraid Harald has allowed himself to sink too deeply into his own concerns and, though that might be excellent for young people or men of genius, it's bad policy for those who are beginning to get on in life.'

'Is that so?' Adelaide's voice was not without menace.

'We cannot allow it too often. We have too few distractions. We rarely go out. We cower in the same place, day after day, thinking the same sombre thoughts, feeling the same pain.'

'I'm sure', Melissa answered, at a loss, 'that Mr Meades has plenty to entertain himself with indoors.'

'Entertain,' Gooch said, 'ah, entertain. People of our sort, Harald and I, need something other than entertainment.'

'He has his library,' Adelaide interrupted.

'Yes. But a book needs considerable effort on the part of the reader. It's not like television. One switches on and whether you pay attention or not it continues to put out its message. The book is dumb until a reader bids it speak.' Adelaide turned her face away from the archaism. 'Harald's low spirits have prevented him from reading. You young people do not quite know the energy, the mental energy, required.'

These exchanges were made without any attempt to draw

145

Meades himself into the conversation. He sat still, fingers clasped, as if he did not understand the language, but the expression on his face was pleasant, complacent, as if they flattered him.

'You must be stimulating him,' Adelaide said.

'We went out for a short stroll this morning, though the weather was not altogether attractive. We walked about the streets, and I asked my usual hundred and one questions. There is much of interest to a stranger in these avenues and crescents.' He drew in an enormous breath. 'I wonder if there is a printed history of this estate.'

The women expressed ignorance. Melissa thought they might find a line or two in *Highways and Byways*. 'F. L. Griggs did the illustrations,' she said.

'No, I don't know him. I shall utilise my stay here to find out about him. I expect you know of him, don't you, Harald?'

Meades looked up as if he hadn't quite followed the question.

'F. L. Griggs, the artist?' Gooch said.

'F. L. Griggs.' Meades looked heavenward, repeating the name, but gave no answer.

Mrs Smith entered with the tea. She made something of a ceremony of pouring, issuing cups and plates, explaining the varieties of biscuit. Meades seemed slightly more animated as he drank. He chose a chocolate digestive biscuit at which he stared before returning it to the plate.

Gooch was in full flow before Mrs Smith had finished her duties. He explained to Adelaide, and Meades incidentally perhaps, how one could draw comfort and encouragement from some fortuitous happening. 'I recall', the voice still low but impressive, 'sitting in my house last spring. I was in what Wordsworth called "in vacant or in pensive mood" and glancing up from my newspaper – it is one of life's pleasures for the elderly man to take to his armchair and open his newspaper, isn't that so, Harald? – I saw that the window was chock-a-block with flowers from a shrub, magnolia stellata, in the garden with a pink spire-cherry behind it. The window seemed packed with blossom and by a happy coincidence the wireless, the radio, was playing Handel, an andante from the *Water Music*, a favourite of mine over many years, and I suddenly felt elevated, content beyond measure.'

' "O Lord, how rich the times are now",' Meades intoned suddenly.

Adelaide gasped. 'What's that?' she asked. 'It's a quotation, isn't it?'

' "The rainbow and the cuckoo-bird". It's by W. H. Davies, the Super-Tramp.'

'And he saw and heard the two together?'

Meades nodded, gratified, and sank back into torpor.

'Exactly, exactly,' Gooch said, beaming. He went on to an anecdote about a holiday in France, when his wife had lost a ring and found it sparkling outside the hotel at a moment when the sun emerged from clouds.

The visitors stayed for another half-hour, taken up by Paul Gooch's monologues. Even Adelaide seemed loth to interrupt, though the frequent glances towards her father-in-law suggested to Melissa that her friend would have liked to have included him in the exchanges. When they rose to leave, Gooch having pressed a bell to summon Mrs Smith, Harald Meades brightened, half smiled, said in a normal voice that he had enjoyed their company and hoped they would call again soon. He stood to shake their hands, and seemed in the few moments he was on his feet to be his fit and everyday self. Mrs Smith came in and Gooch shook hands, thanked them, said they had not only done Harald good but also had cheered him. 'Visiting the sick is not one of my gifts,' he whispered, head turned away from his host.

Outside in the corridor Beatrice Smith asked them bluntly, without preliminaries, how they had got on with Paul Gooch.

'Too fond of the sound of his own voice,' Adelaide pronounced. 'I don't think I'd fancy him at my bedside if I was ill.'

Mrs Smith chuckled in appreciation. 'He wouldn't be allowed anywhere near my bedroom.'

Two days later Mrs Smith rang to see if Tim and Harriet could pay a visit at the weekend. She had, she said, rung Adelaide first, who had willingly freed her daughter.

'Didn't she ask Harriet first?' Melissa enquired.

'Of course she did. This is the twenty-first century now.' She coughed. 'I expect you'll ask Tim, won't you?'

They arranged the visit; the young people would meet at two o'clock or thereabouts on Saturday outside the Council House. A second arrangement was then broached: a visit by the mothers on Tuesday, the day before Paul Gooch returned home.

'Mr Gooch said you two did him a power of good,' Mrs Smith encouraged.

'Is there a Mrs Gooch?' Melissa asked, out of order.

'There used to be. I'm not sure about the present.' Melissa heard a deep indrawing of breath. 'You know what he's famous for, don't you?'

'No. I have to depend on you for information.'

'He won the Victoria Cross. As a mere boy, Harald says. Sixty years ago. That's why Harald admires him so much. You must let me tell you about it, when we've both got an hour or two to spare.'

'Does he boast about it?'

'I've never heard him as much as mention it.'

'That's to his credit.'

'Yes. And he's done Harald good.'

Tim said little about his call on Meades. He and Harriet had stayed an hour, had been regaled with tea and chocolate cake, and had then walked round the Lace Market before he had delivered her back home in the dark soon after five. Adelaide seemed particularly pleased to see him and insisted he stayed the evening, after he had informed his mother.

The boy said they had chatted to Mr Meades who had seemed comparatively normal. Gooch had talked a great deal and Harriet had surprised them all with a brief disquisition on metaphor which had particularly pleased the old men.

'Was it clever?' Melissa asked.

'They'd been doing it at school with their English teacher. She, Harriet, is full of ideas. She was very good about dead metaphors. Mr Gooch was quite excited as if he'd never heard of them before.'

'Had he?'

'I expect so. He seemed well educated. But she was leading off about "examine", which is something to do with "examen" the tongue of a weighing-balance in Latin. She'd taken it from Fowler, she said, *Modern English Usage*. I didn't exactly follow it, but Fowler and Harriet both made out it was dead now in modern English.'

Melissa found herself pleased with this.

148

The two mothers paid their visit. Mrs Smith announced as she let them in that Meades was better, much better, and that he and Gooch were going on a holiday to South Africa in a fortnight's time.

'Why South Africa?' Adelaide asked.

'To visit another friend.'

This time Mrs Smith led them up to the library where the two were walking round. They lined up in front of the Egon Schiele to greet their guests.

'You're going to Cape Town,' Adelaide said after the preliminaries, 'to visit a friend?'

At this both men laughed uproariously, but made no attempt to explain the joke. Mrs Smith left to bring up the Earl Grey.

'You're looking better,' Melissa told Meades. 'By a long chalk.'

'You've recovered the old twinkle in your eye.' Adelaide turned towards Gooch. 'I don't know what you've been telling him.'

Gooch set off on a long modest explanatory ramble. They all made pleasant sounds of agreement. Gooch threw back his head as though he approached some climax. The three listeners braced themselves. The orator made them wait, occupying the pause with urgent hand movements. 'You'll be delighted, and proud, to learn that your children played a not unimportant part in the recovery. I date the marked improvement to their visit on Saturday last.'

'Did they talk to you?' Adelaide asked Meades.

'Oh, yes. In a really interesting way. About the English language. They spoke as I would never have dared when I was their age.'

'Did they talk sense?'

'Yes. And they seemed to know a great deal. You get the impression that nowadays children learn very little in schools, that all they can do is to play about with computers and retain nothing of the information they have conjured on to their screens. And the public examinations make little demands on their knowledge and intelligence, even "A" Levels.'

'I doubt whether that's true,' Adelaide grumbled.

'It's certainly not so with your children. They were really learned.'

149

'I'm pleased to hear it,' Adelaide muttered.

Gooch waved his fingers, cleared his throat to attract attention. 'But the best thing of all was that they were in love.'

'And how did that cure Grandpapa?' Adelaide enquired.

'When you reach Harald's age, and my even greater length of days, you take great pleasure at observing young people in love. It reminds us, me particularly, of the time when we were their age, and had fallen for some young lady.'

Harald Meades nodded to himself as if his friend had made some notable discovery, or expressed it in memorable language. His right hand caressed the knee of his trousers.

Gooch began again. 'Their concentration on each other was extraordinary. It was as if they could not take in enough of the beloved other. We might not have been there. Oh, they were polite, but when they were left free, they devoured each other with their eyes and, if I may say so, with their exhibition of approbation of each other. It was remarkable, gripping, ineffable. I thought at first it was I, and I only, who noticed it, but then I happened to glance at Harald. He was as caught up, as rapt as I was. We talked about it afterwards.'

'We did,' Meades said. 'And it wasn't done by large gestures. These were two young people, to all intents and purposes sitting still and yet, yet, exuding love. I should be pressed to say exactly what it was about them.'

'And still the wonder grew,' Gooch continued, 'that from so little we could deduce so much. When I see young people in shop doorways, or at bus stops, clinging on to each other, kissing with never a thought for what the rest of the world thinks of their behaviour, I feel nothing but embarrassment. But with Harriet and Timothy I could not help recognising that love is uppermost, making lust subservient.'

Melissa thought this over; she made little sense of it. It was Gooch's imagination at work.

Adelaide was now chipping in. 'Will it last?' she asked.

'That we can't say. No one knows.' Gooch made his expression of ignorance sound like wisdom. 'And if they should stay together, the nature of their love will change.'

'For the worse?' Adelaide snapped.

'Most people would answer that in the affirmative, but I am unsure. Human nature is so complex. The love of middle-aged people, with very little show of outward affection, may be an expression of an emotion that is deeply valuable, that has passed, is passing through experiences that are difficult. Something of the purity of young love has disappeared, its "wild surmise". But, it is of value.'

'It may not be love at all,' Adelaide argued. 'People have just got used to living together. They can't be bothered to risk the economic consequences of a split.'

'A good many people do,' Melissa said. 'A good proportion of marriages fail.'

'We're not arguing about marriage,' said Adelaide. 'It's love, love, love.'

'Yes, yes, yes,' Gooch mocked. 'But to see these young people in the first throes, no, that's not right, ecstasies of a new attachment, without any opportunity to demonstrate these publicly, and yet emphasising their affection in every glance, head or hand movement is to old men like us a miracle, not only their showing of these signs, but that we, to whom nothing like it will ever happen again, are granted the grace to recognise and interpret them.'

They talked on, or at least Gooch did. Once or twice Adelaide contradicted him and small arguments developed, which he appeared to take in his polemical stride. Mr Meades occasionally added his comments and this indicated to the women that he had begun to rearrange his life. His most fluent interventions were about the Egon Schiele *Lovers*, which he said Gooch did not find exactly suitable to be placed in the position of honour in a library.

'It's not pornography,' Gooch said, 'and certainly it's a painting of talent.'

'But . . .' Adelaide sarcastically.

'But there is a certain depiction of strain, of discomfort which makes the whole not what I should choose. In a library one needs peace, lack of movement, stasis even, stoppage, so that when one lifts one's head from a book, whatever the subject matter or the effect, one can be stilled, no, not exactly comforted, nor even disenchanted, but rested for the moment.'

'What sort of picture would you have?' Melissa asked.

'A landscape. A meadow, hills not mountains, a quiet sea, clouds.'

'I agree with Harald,' Adelaide said. 'And his ambivalences.'

151

When they prepared to leave, they kissed both men, pressed cheeks. Meades stood, almost jauntily, until Mrs Smith appeared to lead the visitors out.

'Have a great time in South Africa,' Adelaide said.

'I think we shall,' Meades answered.

'I am certain,' Gooch boomed. Then Meades looked suddenly small, shrunken, not fitting his clothes, afraid of not being up to the moment, pitiful. He straightened to wave, became himself again.

Downstairs Mrs Smith thanked them for calling. 'I suppose his nibs was leading off? Old Man Gooch?'

'He doesn't impress you, then?' Adelaide, stirring it.

'He doesn't. He never stops talking.'

'He's talked Mr Meades into a holiday in South Africa,' Melissa said.

'Yes, he has, though I'm not sure it's what he needs. He should keep warm here with his books and wait for the spring.'

This time Beatrice Smith kissed both women. As they drove home, Melissa tried to sort out her thoughts, but with difficulty. There was no doubt in her mind that Paul Gooch had an effect on Meades, had dragged him from his self-regarding depression. She voiced this view to Adelaide who was at the wheel.

'You're probably right,' Adelaide answered. 'But I'm not sure, either. If he's helping Harald, that's all to the good, but I'm by no means sure of the method. There's too much of the school bully about him.'

'Do you think he talks sense?'

'My view is that he talks to impress. When he was describing Harriet and Tim, I wondered how near any sort of truth he was. He was telling us what he thought we wanted to know, what we'd like to hear, to make us believe that our children were out of the ordinary.'

'And that's not so?'

'I shouldn't think so. We both think highly of our children, but they're no Romeos and Juliets. I'm glad Harriet has found a young man who's nice, whom I approve of. It will bring her out, help her grow up, but without any of the worst side effects. Or, at least, that's what I hope. But when he blethers on about these signs of love passing between them, I think that I've never noticed. If they were holding hands or exchanging kisses, I could understand that, but all this about throes and ecstasies makes me think he's trying to impress us with his language or his sensibility.'

'You don't believe what he's telling us?'

'Not in the first place. Now he's expressed it in words, God knows what he believes himself.'

'And Meades?'

'My father-in-law is a selfish man, and now the opportunities in his life are becoming more and more limited, he's angry and then depressed. I don't blame him; I'd feel much the same in his place. Probably I shall if ever I reach his age. And it's done him good to have a personality, a somebody, a VC, at his beck and call all day, loading him with advice and ideas and encouragement as well as reproach and criticism. He feels the better for it. Paul Gooch is a man of parts, as you can hear; I'm beginning to talk like him.'

Adelaide made a neat transfer into the next traffic lane. She expressed no anger at some fool driver in front of her who had suddenly, and without warning, pulled up, leaving Adelaide either to stop as quickly or safely find the way round him in the next lane. Fortunately there was little traffic. Adelaide did not comment, or even turn towards her passenger silently seeking a word of congratulation on her quickness of response.

'Perfect,' Melissa said, by way of praise. Adelaide breathed deeply.

When they arrived at Melissa's house, Adelaide refused to come in, saying she must get back to the office for half an hour, before hurrying home to feed her husband and Harriet.

'Can't they prepare a meal?' Melissa asked.

'They can both cook, but I have to spend so long helping them to make their minds up and then helping them to lay their hands on the ingredients that I might just as well do the whole thing myself.'

She grinned, not displeased with her lot, waved and drove off.

Both received a postcard from South Africa, where Harald Meades claimed to be flourishing. The weather was far too hot and bright, 'I've taken to wearing sun-glasses constantly,' but the company, the food, the scenery were all admirable. 'I feel all the better for crossing the equator.' Professor Henry Meades had gone to the United States to lecture and also sent his modicum of

153

cards, while Melissa heard two scientists on Radio Three make very favourable reference to his research. She rang Adelaide who seemed less than impressed.

'I'm glad,' she had said. 'I can't pretend to understand what he's up to.'

'Has he ever tried to explain to you?'

'Yes, but we get nowhere. My mind seems to close. I don't expect to grasp anything and so I don't.'

'Does he mind?'

'Not too much. I think he'd like me to follow what it is he's doing, but so many mathematicians have failed to understand him that he's hardly surprised that I'm not getting anywhere.'

'Did it bother him that his colleagues weren't convinced?'

'He probably was in the first place. But he's rather like Harald. He thinks that nobody owes him anything, and if he's going anywhere he's going under his own steam. I believe some people have helped him from time to time. His professor at Cambridge supported him against some big noise there, somebody who was noted for his publications but who made no bones about saying that Henry's work was mumbo-jumbo, not mathematics at all.'

'Has this man changed his mind?'

'I don't know. I think he's dead. Now, of course, when people are coming round to use his theorems, and finding out that they work in some way, it's a lot easier even at his own university here. Before that there were some who wrote him off as some kind of nutter. Now he's genius class. Henry doesn't help himself. If people don't want to believe him, then it's their fault, not his. They are capable of reading what he's written. It all gets published these days, which wasn't always so, and if they won't or can't read it, it's their lookout not his. They get these inspections at universities now and the inspectors always praise his teaching, and I think some of his colleagues find it odd that he can make that sort of mathematics so clear to his pupils, but can't make his own stuff more approachable. But they're probably non-mathematicians. I don't know. He's sitting pretty and I guess he likes that. He's worked for it; I'll give him that.'

'Did he never get discouraged?'

'I guess he did. But he didn't make a big thing of it. He had a job which he quite liked, and he was really immersed in his own work. He'd be discouraged if he made a breakthrough and nobody could see it. But he never complained much. Not to me.'

'But didn't it make him miserable about the house?'

'Henry's hardly a bundle of fun even if all's going well. But by the time we'd been married a few years and Harriet was born he began to get inklings of success.'

'And that changed him?'

'I'm not sure. Yes. It must have. Though he's not one to make a song and dance about anything. He did apply for a chair here, the headship of department, but he got nowhere. Now he's become so well-known he's the pride and glory of the place, or at least that's the story. Not from him. And I'd bet that when he comes back from this conference in Pittsburgh he'll have received two offers of chairs.'

'Would you go?'

'Go where?' Adelaide wasn't paying attention.

'To live in America?'

'I wouldn't mind. I could try it until I grew tired of it. It wouldn't do to think of it just now until Harriet's finished her school studies.'

'And your job?'

'There's nothing inherently irresistible about that. I try to make it as interesting as I can for myself, and I quite like a little income of my own, but I shouldn't grieve beyond bearing if I had to give it up. I've already had a spell out there, but I was young then and could put up with practically anything.' She sighed. 'I must get away. There's always something to do. You know Harriet and Timothy are going out on a ramble on Saturday.'

'He's not said anything to me.'

'Oh, dear. It must be getting serious.'

XIV

Mrs Meades picked up Tim on Sunday at twelve. She had issued orders that they'd eat what little lunch they needed at the Crown in Newholme from where the expedition would start at one o'clock sharp, to give them three hours' walking before it was too dark. Tim was surprised that Professor Meades was also in the car, dressed for the country and with thick walking boots.

'You don't mind our coming?' Adelaide asked Tim once they set off. 'Henry and I have said time enough lately that we ought to get some exercise every weekend. And so we decided that today was ideal for starting. I went with this group on a couple before Christmas with Harriet and we quite enjoyed it. We divide into two parties, one that works hard at it and the other which rambles. You can take your choice. Both lots will aim to be back at the same time.'

'Which do you usually choose?' he asked.

'Oh, Mummy's amongst the fast movers,' Harriet said. 'That's where we are. Yomping.'

They entered the pub where a dozen or so middle-aged people were already seated at the small round tables under dim lights. A few ate chips and pies in baskets while the others mainly concentrated on half-pints.

'Are you hungry?' Adelaide asked Tim.

'No, not really, thanks. We've not long had breakfast.'

'Like us,' Harriet said.

'You surprise me,' Adelaide interrupted. 'I had it firmly fixed in my mind that your father would have got you up early and on the way to church.'

'My father? No, it's his one self-indulgence. In bed until ten a.m. on Sunday.'

'And then what?'

'A long bath, a look through the *Observer* and then about twelve, twelve thirty we have brunch.'

'You've not eaten, then?' Adelaide asked.

'Oh yes, I have. I'm up at nine and did some reading and eating all morning until you arrived.'

'And what does your father do? In the afternoon?'

'He washes up, after lunch, and then he'll read the paper again if he's not busy.'

'Doesn't he garden?'

'No. No, we hire a man to do it.'

'And if he is busy?'

'If he is he'll have brought some work home and he'll put an hour or two in at that. Otherwise it will be a book or perhaps even the papers again.'

'Not the telly?'

'No. He and the TV set don't mix well.'

'And after dinner?'

'He washes up again. And I sometimes help him. Then he reads and looks at the BBC news, and occasionally he'll tune in to some programme, if it's historical or educational. And he likes to talk about it when it's finished. I don't think my mother's very interested, so it's up to me.'

The professor returned with four glasses, two sparkling glasses with slices of lemon for the ladies, two dull halves of what turned out to be bitter shandy for the men.

'I admire your father,' said Adelaide. 'He seems to have his life so well organised.'

Tim raised his glass. Harriet looked puzzled. Adelaide seemed determined to air her views on the character of Charles Hughes whether the rest wanted it or not. She did not seem put out that the others did not show any interest. The atmosphere in the pub was subdued; a shout of recognition sometimes greeted a newcomer, but excitement was notably lacking. Suddenly and out of character Professor Meades rose, made for the bar and returned with four packets of crisps, which he distributed.

'We'll share ours,' Harriet said to Tim. 'One now, one later.' He opened his packet, tearing it really open as they moved to sit shoulder to shoulder.

Adelaide looked disdainfully at her packet. 'Put mine in your bag,' she ordered her husband, 'if you please.' He stared at his own open packet as if he could make something new of it. Harriet had told Tim that some mathematician had said of her father:

157

'You can't put a daisy in front of your pa's face but he'd make something of it.' He ate slowly as if to pass the time, and in his bemusement offered the packet to the man in the next seat who rewarded him with an account of his West Highland Walk, undertaken last September in foul weather. Henry did not answer at all, but looked interested, and passed over his packet. The man crackled the bag and continued.

At five to one a loud voice bawled, 'Outside for PT. "B" party with Jonah today, "A" group with me and Edgar. We start dead on the hour.'

The pub emptied smartly. Outside the sky loured brown rather than grey. Tim and Harriet held hands.

'Do you reckon we s'll have a drop?' the West Highland man asked Tim.

'I doubt it. Not according to the weather forecast. But you never know.'

'You don't that.'

At exactly one o'clock the 'A' party set off. They marched for perhaps a mile along the road. As there was no pavement, they faced the quite frequent traffic. The group kept closely together and turned right into a field where they climbed a slope. Heavy clay, with puddles, made progress difficult, but the 'A' party pressed on fast. Tim felt breathless.

'How will your father like this?' Tim asked Harriet.

'Oh, he'll be all right. He used to be a good cross-country runner. He had a half-blue at Cambridge. He goes out running now once or twice a week.'

They reached the crest of the rise and turned right. Here water stood about in long pools in cart ruts. Harriet in some way seemed elated. Two red spots glowed on her cheeks. The leader halted them and pointed out a wood perhaps a mile away as their first halt. 'It's not much help stopping here today,' he said, 'but if you do this again on a fine day there's quite a view. There's Cooke Hall that way, and Lark Hills, and further round a glimpse of Beechnall, and the old abbey at Shirebrook.' All they could see was mist and, now it was raining again, a fine, fast drizzle. 'Forward,' he shouted. 'Try not to get too far behind. I don't want anyone lost.' The road now sloped gently downwards.

They reached the wood, and were ordered to walk along the edge. 'This side,' the leader said. 'It'll be drier.' They moved off at a sharp pace. Adelaide dropped back to join the young people.

'Where's Daddy?' Harriet asked.

'He's deserted me. He's up at the front there.'

She could see Henry, steaming along but without strain. He did not appear to be talking to anyone, merely thrusting forward, keeping the party up to speed. Harriet and Tim held hands, swung arms together. Adelaide talked, mainly to or at Tim, and seemed quite at home, never breathless, never falling behind. At the end of this path by the wood they found they were right by the edge of the north–south motor road cutting. They had heard traffic, but Tim was surprised how close the road was to this out-of-the-way place.

'Far too many people out driving by the sound of it,' Adelaide commented.

They walked along the side of the wood for perhaps half a mile when the path and the M1 seemed to veer violently away one from the other. Now the path entered the wood and narrowed. Adelaide dropped behind the youngsters, who could just about walk side by side in the semi-darkness. Now they could begin to go gently downhill and quickened their pace. People spoke more, Tim noticed; perhaps it was because they had to raise their voices to talk to those in front or behind. When the road flattened it also widened and after a while they could make out through the trees on their right a silver gleam, the narrow end of a lake. They were sheltered here from the rain.

'What's that?' Harriet asked her mother.

'A reservoir. Cresswell Reservoir. It's not a natural feature. I believe it was dug out to feed the canal, though that's gone now. I'm not sure when that would be. Eighteenth century, or early nineteenth. I guess there'd be a small natural lake there, and they'd started with that and extended it.'

'Is it used now?'

'No. It's a feature. I believe you can get a licence to fish there. It's well stocked, I'm told. And I did hear that many years ago the Marsden family up at Lark Hall used to have water parties in the summer.'

They now emerged from the woods to press on uphill along a B road. Again they took to the fields by way of a five-barred gate. The drizzle had stopped, but the clayey ground clogged their soles. After twenty minutes' long pull they halted.

'A good view from here,' the leader announced, 'on a fine day. You can see the motor road, the reservoir, Lark Hills House and Bellswood Colliery.' The countryside, draped heavily in mist, revealed few beauties. Every fence, hedge, bush, tree dripped. 'Are we all here? We're in good time. There's just over a mile and a half of this stuff, and then about the same on a road. That'll give you half a chance to get the clay off your boots. We shan't stop again. It's all very straightforward. Right.' He turned towards Henry Meades as if asking permission to move. Henry turned and the trek began again.

Adelaide had moved away from the young people and had joined two tall women. They could hear her voice from time to time. Harriet and Tim walked gloved hand in hand.

'Nobody in his right mind would come out on an afternoon like this,' Tim said. Another heavier shower beat into their faces. Hoods were pulled up, but the pace did not slacken. For elderly and middle-aged people these walkers showed admirable stamina.

'It's exercise,' Harriet replied. 'And it keeps people warm. And when they get home and into a hot bath they'll feel delighted with themselves. Achievement is the be-all and end-all.'

'No matter the uselessness of the achievement. Nor its side effect: colds, coughs, sneezes, running noses, pneumonia?'

'If you're properly prepared you shouldn't suffer from any of those. And some of us like the company we're in.' She glanced at her companion.

'I love you,' Tim answered. They snatched a kiss.

Soon they had reached the road where the first group increased pace. The going, slightly downhill, seemed easy. Talking petered out as if the walkers concentrated on a fast, triumphing finish. The leader waited for them at the entrance to the pub car park, greeting them with a short sentence or a wave, a salute of congratulation.

'We're in good time, but it'll be dark early today with all this cloud cover.' He gave a special welcome to Tim and Harriet and as she moved towards the car where Henry already had the doors open, the man signalled towards Tim and bent for confidential conversation. 'Who's the gent over there?' He motioned towards Henry.

'His name is Meades.'

'I've not met him before.'

'His wife's been walking with the club once or twice last season.'

Tim pointed out Adelaide, who at the moment came in through the gate, now in the company of a bespectacled couple who laughed as the husband shook water from his tweed hat. The leader greeted them with a large, cheerful bow, laughingly acknowledged.

'What's he do?'

'He's a professor of mathematics at the university.'

'Is he, by God? He can't half move.' He looked towards the Meadeses' car. 'I remember the wife. A lively little woman. She had no difficulty keeping up with us. But him. My word he can push you. He's not your dad, is he?'

'No. Though I'm with him.'

'If he drives as fast as he walks you'll soon be home.'

'His wife will be at the wheel.'

'Like that, is it?'

'Her car. Bigger than his.'

The leader, still making sure all were home, said he hoped to see Tim again. Back at the car Tim joined the others who were cleaning clay from their boots; they had implements with them, bradawls, small screwdrivers, skewers and sharp pointed knives. When their task was over, they placed their boots on the thick sheets of newspaper in the boot of the car.

'Look at my hands,' said Harriet.

'Tap in the corner of the yard. We'll have a quick swill,' her father answered.

'You go. I'll leave mine to dry on. As good as a beauty treatment.'

Henry was already on his way, allowing his wife no time to finish her sentence.

Back at the Meades home, they washed again and sat in the warm kitchen, mugs of tea or coffee in front of them. Adelaide chattered and questioned, but her husband said not a word, though the expression on his face was one of satisfaction. When Adelaide and Tim had finished their second cups, the hostess issued her orders. 'Leave the kitchen to me now, will you? Otherwise there'll be no dinner to eat.'

'Can't I give you a hand?' Tim asked politely.

'Thank you, no. You go and get yourself into Harriet's good

graces somewhere.' Then to her husband, 'You'll find the newspapers on the table of the breakfast room.'

Thus dismissed, Harriet led Tim straight upstairs to her bedroom, a large room with two armchairs, as well as wardrobes, a dressing table and bed rather dwarfed by the size of the other furniture. The room was, to his surprise rather untidy with scattered books, articles of clothing and underwear. The desk under the large sash window was almost clear, the two piles of books on it neatly stacked.

'Is that where you work?' he asked.

'Yes. Sit down.' She pointed to one of the chairs. He obeyed the signal. She crouched on the arm, bent to kiss him enthusiastically. He ran a hand up her leg. She allowed this for a brief time, then removed his fingers.

'Nothing too intimate,' she said. 'Adelaide is likely to fly upstairs without a sound, and burst in on us. And then the fur would fly.' There was about her tone of voice something of her mother, swift in censure. She struggled up and her knee caught him hard in the testicles.

He shouted in pain. 'God,' he said. 'That hurt.'

'I'm sorry.' She laid her hand on his genitals, then straightened herself. 'I'd better get out of the way before I do you some real harm.'

He pulled her on top of him; they kissed violently.

'Does it still hurt?' she asked.

'Bearable.'

After another frantic bout of kissing, she moved to occupy the other armchair, pertly. She talked about the sex lessons they received in school.

'Are they any good?' he asked.

'Yes. As far as information goes. They issue us with a book that has explicit pictures in it. Erections and all. And we're told to show this to our parents.'

'Don't they know about it?'

'Adelaide read it avidly. Perhaps it made up for what she's not getting. No. The reason we have to show it to the parents is that some of them might otherwise object. You'd be amazed. The PE mistress knocked her knee on a piece of apparatus and said, "Damn and blast the thing." Next morning one of the girls in our class said her father had written a letter to the headmistress,

162

complaining that such behaviour was not up to the standard he expected the school to set.'

'She must have told her father.'

'Of course she did. To cause mischief. She knew how her father would react.'

'Doesn't her father swear?'

'Like a trooper, she says. Don't you get issued with these pamphlets?'

'Yes. But nobody would think of showing them to their parents.'

'You mean you wouldn't?'

'No. My mother would glance at it and say it was sensible. My father would nod and probably say nothing, or mention the courts as a source of recondite knowledge.'

'That's a good word.'

'Abstruse, obscure. Latin – put away, hide, store out of sight. *Abstrudo-ere, abstrusi, abstrusum.*'

'That same girl whose father complained, said in class that people of our age never thought about their parents having sex. And Miss Bradley, the biology mistress, blushed very red. She stuttered something about sex being a private matter. I guess she thought we were going to ask her if she had it.'

'Has she?'

'I've no idea. She's no beauty, but you never know. The ugliest people find somebody frustrated or hideous enough themselves to want them.'

Tim jumped from his chair and pulled Harriet from hers. Lips locked, their fingers explored each other's bodies. Suddenly in the middle of a deep kiss, she pushed him away, hissed, 'Sit down.' He staggered back and across to his chair. She was already seated.

The door flew open and Adelaide marched in. 'Hello,' the mother said cheerfully. 'You two all right?' She looked from one to the other. 'Would you like a drink?' They declined her offer. 'Or a jam pasty?' She was carrying a tray with two confections on it. She held it out first to Tim. 'You have the bigger one. That's yours.' Thanking her the boy did as he was told. Adelaide swiftly proffered the tray to her daughter who said, 'I like these, though they are fattening.'

'Is there anything we can do for you?' Tim asked.

'No, not really. We shall eat in half an hour's time. These will just temporarily blunt your appetite.'

'Where's Daddy?'

'In his study, I expect. I haven't seen anything of him since I gave him our boots to clean. He'd make a good job of them and enjoy it. Then he'd be off to pursue his thoughts. I tell you what you can do,' she turned to Tim. 'Come down and lay the table. When you've finished eating.'

She bounced over to the window where she stood staring out. 'Nobody's doing anything untoward out there.'

'You couldn't see them if they were,' Harriet answered.

'No. That's shut the night out. I hate these short days.'

'Why doesn't your rambling group start out early at this time of year, ten or eleven in the morning? It would give them another couple of hours,' Tim wanted to know.

'They do if they have some big walk in mind. Otherwise two or three hours at a sharp pace suffice. That's what the "A" party wants. The others, the wimps, idlers and elderly, can toddle along when or as they like. And if they set off at the same time people can change their minds which lot they go with.'

'Who draws the programme up?'

'A little committee of men. Dictators.'

'Are they efficient?'

'Yes, I think we can say so, can't we, Harriet?' Adelaide rushed for the door. 'Eat up, you two, and then down you come to sort the spoons and forks out.'

She quietly closed the door. Harriet frowned, slapped her thighs and whispered, 'I told you she'd come up.'

'I never heard a sound.'

'No, I'm used to her. I can pick out her every movement. I have to, for my own peace of mind.'

'She'd have been cross if she found us snogging here?'

'If she'd found our clothes buttoned up and undisturbed, she'd have been very sarcastic. Otherwise, neither of us would have dined down there tonight. And there'd have been a smart message to your mother. She's like the ramblers' committee. She knows how to organise things.'

'You don't seem to get on very well with her?'

'She likes her own way And she finds it satisfying. I'm beginning to know her tricks of the trade. And Daddy doesn't much care what she's up to. She can have a free hand as long as she doesn't trespass on the two or three areas which he considers his.'

'Why is she like this, do you think?'

'We all like to be on top of everything.' Harriet brushed a crumb from his mouth. 'She's quite good at it and doesn't ever like to relinquish her superior place. She's a bossyboots.'

Harriet kissed him hard on the mouth, pressing herself into him. 'Enough,' she said in the end. 'Waiters, below.' She took his hand, swung his arm, vigorously as if to erase the embarrassment of their conversation. As they walked together down the stairs Tim admired her the more. Compared with himself she seemed grown-up, adult enough to know exactly what she wanted, and why she could or could not have it. He would not have thought of criticising either his mother or father to Harriet. They did not, his father especially, see eye to eye with him often enough, but Tim did not find the fault exclusively theirs, blaming their old-fashioned ideas or upbringing. Perhaps Harriet was more deeply wounded by her mother than he by his father, and so was more ready to get her own back by any means. Or was it, he wondered, that girls felt more strongly about these domestic upsets. He did not know. On the corridor below she kissed him again just as her father emerged from one of the doors. He beamed absent-mindedly at their antics and said he hoped her mother was well on with dinner.

'We're just going to set the table,' Harriet answered.

'Are you? Well done. Large plates. I'm hungry.' He cleared his throat. 'How are you, young man?'

'Well, thank you.' Tim was surprised at the question.

'Did you enjoy the walk?'

'Yes. Very much, though the weather wasn't ideal.'

'Never mind. I've dried and cleaned your boots with the rest. That's my chore. It occupies me completely. Yet without too much difficulty. One can't make too many errors.'

He nodded brightly to his daughter and walked towards the stairs.

'He's only just come down, turned straight round and gone back,' Harriet said. 'He must have forgotten what he wanted.'

The two entered the kitchen, where Adelaide whooped a greeting.

'Dining room?' Harriet asked.

'Where else?'

'We're only four.'

'I see.' Adelaide now outlined the menu, named the colour and place of the cloth, the table napkins. The wine, a German Riesling, was already in the fridge. Tim cheerfully followed Harriet round, and carried after her the cutlery and linen that she handed to him. They laid the cloth, set out mats, knives and forks once the curtains were drawn and the lights ablaze. He straightened the cutlery, brought out on instruction from the kitchen a huge cruet, its silver at a high gloss and the glass sparkling.

'Put it near Henry's place,' Harriet said, pointing at the far end of the large dining table, 'and then perhaps he'll manage a sprinkle or two of salt before Mummy stops him.'

'Why would she do that?'

'It's supposed to be bad for him. He has high blood pressure.'

'He doesn't act as if he has.'

'You can't distinguish any signs of it, even in yourself, or so I'm told, but unless you do something about it you might quite possibly have a stroke or a heart attack. And one of the things you can do is deny yourself salt.'

'You don't want to kill him off, do you?'

'Of course I don't. I'm not sure I believe it. Not with the moderate amounts he takes. It's just another of Adelaide's little ploys to make his life uncomfortable.'

They hugged again without haste before returning to the kitchen where Adelaide ordered Tim to uncork the wine. When he finished this, Adelaide said they had five minutes while she made the gravy. 'You just hold hands for a moment, and then I'll give you a call to carry things in.'

The meal was unexceptional, chicken breasts with four vegetables, but delicious. All except the cook ate with relish. Adelaide spoilt the mood by claiming that slaving over the stove had taken away all her appetite. The two men had second helpings. The pudding was a huge apple crumble with custard and cream. Again Henry and Tim did it double justice. The boy noticed that Adelaide did not drink wine, saying she must drive him back home.

'Oh, I can easily walk it.'

'You've done enough walking for one day.'

In such moments she seemed utterly charming, as if she concentrated the whole of her efforts to please him. After dinner, they played Scrabble, if not very seriously. Adelaide talked the whole time. Amongst other snippets she gave the news that Mrs Smith had rung to announce that Mr Meades was already in England, but would not be back in Beechnall until the weekend, as he was spending a few days in London.

'How did he seem?' Henry asked, rather impersonally.

'Grumbling, Trixie said, but she interpreted that as a sign of good health.'

'Who's he staying with?'

'I've no idea. If she did tell me I've forgotten. Is it important?'

'No. I thought I might ring him.' He watched her raise her eyebrows. 'Word of welcome.'

'You'll have to ring Trixie first.'

'I might do that.'

At a quarter to ten, Harriet was despatched to make final chocolate or coffee. At ten fifteen, Adelaide ordered Tim to get his overcoat on. She gave him five minutes to say goodbye to Harriet; it was not unduly difficult for them when each lover understood exactly how the other stood in respect of her clock.

As she drove him home Adelaide not only praised him, but confided that Henry also approved of him.

'He's fond of Harriet, you know. He doesn't show much affection, but she's pretty and does well academically, and doesn't get into trouble, with drugs, idiot boys and wild raves. One reads such things even in the broadsheets these days. And that's what Henry wants. A trouble-free, good-looking girl, who doesn't interrupt whatever he's doing at the time. He's selfish in a nice sort of way. He doesn't demand a great deal. If I gave him the same meal every day he wouldn't mind. We work on a rota and I keep to it religiously. We did tonight. I might go out of my way if we have a dinner party. I'll chance my arm then, take the whole day over it, use the books. But,' she gurgled over her steering wheel, 'I think it's nothing like as good as what I cook ordinarily. Still, I quite enjoy these high days and holidays. It stretches me. The rest I do for convenience's sake. After all, I work very nearly full time and I have to look after myself.'

'Does he notice?'

'Oh, yes. Most dons are interested in eating. During term he stays for dinner every Tuesday evening. He has some late meeting and then the meal and a bit of social conversation, and comes home by taxi.'

'So he can drink?'

'Yes. But don't think he comes staggering and singing up the drive. It's a quiet, unembarrassing enjoyment. It's possible his voice is slightly slurred, but he's not going to do anything that'll cause scandal. He's too interested in his own progress.'

Adelaide spoke with her usual candour, at ease in her seat, the right gloved palm tapping the steering wheel. She seemed in no hurry. 'Harriet's a bit like her father, don't you think?' she asked.

'I would have said she was more like you.'

'In what way?'

'She seems to know her mind and isn't afraid to speak it.'

'Naïve, you mean?'

'That's the last thing I'd call either of you. No, she thinks things out, and often rather quickly, and is prepared then to tell you her conclusions. I'm quite different. I can't make my mind up. I see so many snags and objections that I'm uncertain.'

'You're like your father? A lawyer in the making?'

'I doubt it. My dad knows the law books thoroughly, but I'm not sure of anything.'

'You're fond of Harriet, aren't you? You know that.'

'I could give a dozen reasons against taking my reasons for liking Harriet seriously. Do you notice that neither of us has used the word "love". "Fond", "liking", they're the things we said.'

'We're trying to exclude emotion from the discussion; we're keeping it reasonable.'

'And is that sensible?' Tim asked.

'I suppose so,' Adelaide answered. 'We're trying to read the truth and not cloud our vision with strong feelings.'

They argued on, strongly, but fumbling their way. In the end she said her family would miss her. She said she had enjoyed herself, that he was an interesting, clever boy. The flattery was so blatant that he squinted at her in the light of a street lamp to make out hypocrisy in the darkened face.

She leaned over him to unlock the door of her car and, straightening up, bent forward again to kiss him. He felt the smoothness of her arms and breasts for a moment, but then she drew away, her face serious. 'Goodbye,' she said, dismissing him.

'Goodbye.' He scrambled out. 'Thanks very much for the lift.'

She raised a hand, twinkled fingers and drove off. He fumbled for his keys.

'Who brought you home?' Melissa called from a bedroom.

'Mrs Meades.'

'Are they all well?' His mother emerged, fully dressed. She did not wait for an answer. 'Your father's downstairs. Get yourself a drink or something. You won't be hungry.' She disappeared. He wondered what she was doing at this time of the night. He never knew with his mother. She clearly wasn't washing her hair or manicuring her nails. Probably she had decided to sort out clothes ready for the onset of spring. He wondered if she'd decided on this chore so that she could observe the street and his arrival.

Downstairs his father looked up from a newspaper. 'How were they all?' he asked.

'Thriving.'

'Good. Did they mention old Mr Meades? Is he back yet?'

'He's back in England, but still in London.'

His father tapped his teeth with a fingernail. 'I wonder what he finds to do at his age in London?'

'You go pretty often, don't you?'

'Committees of the Law Society. Lucas's Chambers. That sort of thing. These are part of my work.'

'No socialising?'

'Not really. We're too busy. It's true I may stay overnight, but I've reached a time of life when comforts of home appeal more than excitement abroad.'

'Aren't these Law Society meetings interesting, then?'

'Yes. On the whole, they are.' Charles Hughes stroked his chin. 'There are some people there who are too fond of the sound of their own voices, and I often think that I and one or two others could do twice the business in half the time, but there we are.' Charles leaned back as if he was glad to have a companion to talk to, an equal. 'There's one man in particular I dislike. He nit-picks and critically assesses, or so he thinks, matters that other people have looked into really carefully, and he does it with such an air of superiority.'

'Is he popular with the rest?' Tim asked.

'Not really. He has a crony or two. But the other day he had been asked to introduce one of the topics and he made a hash of

169

it. He was slapdash and I rather suspect that some had carefully prepared so they could catch him out. One old chap, an emeritus professor of law, just set about him, pointed out mistake after mistake.'

'And did that embarrass old know-all.'

'He's not old. Younger than I am. He saw he'd made a fool of himself. He'll take good care that it won't happen again. It's done him no good with the profession. I could name several who are pleased he's made a fool of himself.'

Charles Hughes spoke to his son as to an equal, Tim thought. Whether it was a moral tale, to warn against overwhelming pride, or merely an interesting bit of gossip the boy could not decide.

'You'd better go on upstairs to get some beauty sleep in,' the father said. This re-established the status quo. Tim left without a further word. The old man seemed pleased with him. A good conclusion. Why did he not ask about the ramblers' club?

XV

A day or two later Tim, walking home from school, met Mrs
Smith. He'd been strolling along the road in no hurry since he
knew there'd be no one at home for another hour, had turned into
Clement Avenue where he lived when he saw Beatrice Smith
walking down the hill.

'What are you doing here?' she asked, robbing him of opening
words.

'This is where I live.'

'Is it? I didn't know that.'

'I thought perhaps you'd been to see my father. Or mother.'

'No. I've been visiting an old friend, Kate Cullen, who used to
perform with me at the People's Theatre.' She laughed at her
choice of 'perform'. 'She was a professional at one time and then
left the theatre to marry. She helped me a great deal. Now she's
ill in bed and I went to see her.'

'Is she better?'

'That I don't know. I don't know what's wrong with her. It
might be nervous trouble. Or old age. She spends much of her
time in bed.'

'Is she old?'

'Not really. Early sixties, I'd guess.'

'Would you like to come in for a cup of tea or coffee?' he asked
to his own surprise. She accepted this offer. He led her into the
kitchen and began his preparation.

'You rang the bell three times,' she said, 'and then unlocked
the door. Der, der, der.' She imitated the bell.

'A family code. To let the rest know that I'm bringing a visitor
in. I always do it. We all do, even, as today when there's nobody
at home.'

'Why is that?'

'It's an idea of my father's. He doesn't want to appear in his
gardening clothes if some important person comes to see him.

My mother thinks some notable once called and he appeared at the door without a tie. Mark you, that would be unusual because he mows the lawn, when he does, in a collar and tie.'

'But not often?'

'No. We have a gardener. Both my parents work.'

Mrs Smith chose Earl Grey and he served it in china cups. She refused his offer of chocolate biscuits but praised his tea.

'Kate Cullen's husband brewed something up,' she said. 'It tasted like mud. Now this is something like.'

She was complimentary and envious of Mrs Hughes's kitchen. 'This is what I'd choose for myself. It's quite large and light. My place is big enough in the Park, but it's so old-fashioned, and built in the basement so that we need the light on all day. It makes the place look dirty. Not that it is, the amount of time I and Bella spend cleaning it.'

'It'll be cosy in winter.'

'I suppose so, but it's gloomy, depressing. Mr Meades, Harald, won't have it changed. I've been on to him time after time. You wouldn't like it if the coalman delivered a ton or two of coal in your library. Not that we use coal. All gas and very up to date, the heating.'

'And what does he say?'

'He pulls a long face and says, "Trixie, if you want to convince me about this or any other point you'll have to draw your parallels from somewhere nearer reality."' She laughed. 'It might be that his wife had this kitchen kitted up and he keeps it in sentimental memory of her.'

'Is that likely?'

'No, I shouldn't think so. It's not important to him. The food I serve is up to standard, and where and how it's done doesn't cross his mind. He's never thought I might like somewhere more congenial to work in.'

Tim listened. She did not appear distressed, but recited her grievances like an amateur actress at an early rehearsal of some play without much conviction.

'Is he back yet?' he asked.

'No. He's still in London. He sent a card telling me he'd let me know in good time. But that was some days ago. I don't think my convenience crosses his mind.'

'Did his wife spoil him?'

'That's not my impression. She's been dead over twenty years now. I was comparatively young at the time. But from what I gather, what she said went. At that time he was occasionally teaching and watching over the bookshop.'

'Who ran that?'

'He had a manager. A Mr Caunt when I was first here.'

'Was Mrs Meades away from home very much?'

'Much as you'd expect. She had friends and a club, and attended a class or two. She liked cookery and showed me quite a few things, fancy dishes, you know.'

'Did you live in?'

'Not until a few months before she died, when she began to be really ill. I had a husband I was supposed to be looking after, at first. But I separated from him and bought my flat, or at least he did. It was fortunately one of his monied periods so I did all right. He died soon afterwards, quite unexpectedly.'

'Yes. And then you moved in later?'

'It seemed sensible. Harald pressed me and I felt sorry for his wife. She was in her fifties, a big woman, knew her mind. I think he depended on her to some extent. I don't know. I was growing disillusioned with all ideas of marriage. They were no lovebirds, but they could disagree without smashing every pot in the house. Unlike some.'

'Was Mr Meades much as he is now? In temperament, I mean. I know he was much younger.'

'Yes, I suppose so. He'd always got some scheme on hand. It was an interesting house to live in. At the end she was in and out of hospital, and when she was at home she stayed in bed. She had a bed made up downstairs in the room next to the dining room.'

Beatrice Smith suddenly clapped her hand to her wrist and squinted down at her small gold watch. 'Goodness,' she said. 'Look at the time. I must shoot off.'

'Can't you please yourself? While the cat's away?'

'If only I could.'

She was up and out of the house within two minutes, apologising for her speed of departure. 'Thanks for the tea,' she said, striding down the drive, waving.

His parents seemed interested that Mrs Smith had called in. Over dinner both questioned him. She had been visiting whom?

173

'Kate Cullen. She was a notable at the People's Theatre, or so she said. She had been a professional actress at one time.'

'And where does she live?' Melissa asked.

'Wemyss Drive, or thereabouts? You don't know her?'

'No. Do you, Charles?'

'The name seems familiar, somehow. But not really. I can't pin it down.'

'Did she say anything about Harald Meades?' Charles Hughes asked.

'He's still in London. Says he'll give her due warning of his return, but he hasn't done so yet.'

'She seemed a sensible woman to me,' Charles said. 'She'd have things under control.'

'She's lived in the house since just before Mrs Meades died. More than twenty years.'

'Hasn't she got a home of her own?' Melissa enquired.

'Yes,' her husband answered. 'She has quite a spacious flat.' He made his lawyer's wise face. 'I think I ought to give her a ring to find out how Meades is doing, and when he's coming back.'

'You do that,' his wife answered.

After the meal when Tim and his mother were clearing the table, Melissa said, half humorously, 'I think your father's rather taken with Mrs Smith.'

'And that enquiry was just an excuse to get in touch with her again?'

'Something like that.'

'Ah, but is she interested in him?'

'I haven't seen many or any signs of it, but we don't know. She didn't particularly question you about your father?'

'Not that I remember.'

'I know you think your father, and Mrs Smith, are well past such matters. Don't you?' Tim said nothing, but thought of staring at the shapely legs up the ladder in Meades's library. 'Your father cuts quite a figure in this city. Amongst lawyers, and with charitable and hospital work. And there are women who are greatly taken by demonstrations of male power. Did you know that?'

'No,' he answered. 'Are you?'

'When I see it,' Melissa, dismissively.

On Friday night at dinner Charles Hughes announced that

174

Meades was coming back to Beechnall by train and that he, Charles, was to meet him at the station. Tim glanced across at his mother, but her face showed nothing. 'He's not at all well and I thought that was the least I could do. I shall meet Mrs Smith at the station. I did offer to drive round to the house first, but she wouldn't have it, so I shall park and then meet her there in the foyer, and the pair of us will go down to the platform and between us get him and his luggage up the stairs.'

'Aren't Henry and Adelaide available?' Melissa asked.

'No, they're going to York to meet some relative of Adelaide's. This has been arranged for some time and Meades's announcement of his arrival came as usual at the last minute. So you won't be seeing anything of your bien-aimée this weekend.'

'That's all you know,' Melissa said. 'If the weather's decent they, Henry, Addy, Harriet and Tim, will all be out on a ramble starting at ten thirty sharp.'

'Beatrice said nothing of that.' Charles seemed in no way put out.

At lunch on Saturday he gave his family an account of Meades's arrival. The old man not only looked ill, but was in a foul mood. The train had been crowded, the first-class carriages as bad as the second. It had arrived three minutes early, but this won the rail services no compliments from its disgruntled traveller. When they got him, with difficulty, to his house, he flatly refused to go to bed.

'I was up in good time this morning. I'm not ill. Otherwise they would have sent me home by ambulance.' He'd chosen an armchair in the library, where Mrs Smith had wrapped a tartan blanket over him.

She, showing Charles out, said once Harald had been left alone for an hour, he'd begin to understand how tired he was and would allow her to put him into his bed. 'Once he's put on a public performance, he'll be more amenable. I know the sort of meals he likes and I'll see to that. If he's no better by Monday I'll ask the doctor to call. He lives just up the road.'

'He looks quite ill,' Charles Hughes warned. 'Is he?'

'He's not been well for some time now. But he varies from day to day. He can put on an act, if he sees any advantage in it.' She frowned. 'In these last few months, he's aged visibly even to me and I see him every day. It's not facially, but in his body. He's beginning to lose weight, though that might be an advantage; he's very short of breath sometimes; he has high blood pressure; he's very slow in his movements and he can't seem to make his mind up. I think these are all ailments of old age. I try to persuade him to eat sensibly and take a bit of exercise, and suggest things that might catch his interest. I can't always make out what is happening.'

At this moment the handbell which Mrs Smith had placed on the table by Harald's chair was violently rung from the library.

'Go on, go on,' Mrs Smith complained. 'Ring away.' She was in no hurry to rush upstairs. 'It'll do him good to wait.'

'May he not be ill?' Charles asked.

'If he is, he'll have to learn that I can't leave everything I'm doing to be at his beck and call. Once he realises he's back at home he'll settle and act more reasonably.'

'You're a hard woman,' Charles said flirtatiously.

'Oh, I don't know. I've been with him long enough.' She thrust her hand through the crook of his arm. 'It's the only way to treat you men.'

Charles drew away from her, earning him the sort of disapproving look a baby might have earned from its frustrated mother. He wished her good morning. She grinned at his stiffened back.

On the next day, Sunday, the Meades family picked Tim up for an outing with the ramblers' club. The weather was sharp, the ground hard and the sky cloudless. This time they met at a farm building where they parked in a field.

'No drinks this time,' Henry Meades told Tim. 'Serious stuff today.'

The atmosphere in the car had been strained. Adelaide snapped at her family. Harriet did not show any pleasure at his arrival, nor attempt conversation, but sat scowling in her corner of the back seat as far away from him as possible.

Only the professor seemed comfortable. 'Coldish,' he said. 'But it'll be fairly warm as we walk and the sun gets higher. Have you brought a thick anorak?'

'No. Medium.'

'Sensible.'

They sat with their legs out of the car doors pulling on their boots.

'You're quiet,' Adelaide told Harriet. 'You've barely exchanged a word with Tim.'

'No,' her daughter said, with finality.

'The day is yet young,' the professor said cheerfully.

They moved over to the field gate for final instructions. The same leader as on their last outing greeted them.

'Morning, professor,' he called loudly to Henry. Several looked up, suspecting perhaps that the use of the title was ironic. The leader began his description of the route. He described it as straightforward, but said that he and Ted Gentle had mobile phones, and he bet several others had. He asked for a show of hands. At least a quarter had. 'There shouldn't be any need for 'em,' he said. 'The way is dry and pretty reasonable, but you never know. I hope you've all brought drinks with you. There are no pubs or shops. It was all on the handout. It's speed and stamina we're after today. Any questions? How long? Back here between three to four hours. It's not the marathon. Don't get lost or abandoned. Mobile phone wallahs, hands up again.' He glanced at his watch. 'I guess all who are coming are here, so we'll make a start.' He set off, looking back as if the party could barely be trusted to reach the road without disaster. After that he straightened his cloth cap and set a good pace.

Tim joined Harriet, who still had nothing to say to him. 'Are you all right?' he asked after five long, silent minutes.

'Yes. I don't much feel like talking. I've a headache.'

'I've not annoyed you, have I?'

'You will soon if you go on chattering like this.'

'Who has got out of bed on the wrong side this morning?'

She did not deign to reply, merely increased her pace. He easily kept up with her. He obeyed her ukase about silence. After they had completed half an hour and their faces had begun to redden, he asked her about a bird call.

'I don't know. I didn't hear it.'

'Would you like a drink?' he asked, indicating his pack.

'No thanks.'

He had asked two other questions, both miserably half answered, one about a distant village the other about a television programme. He did not mind for they were striding along now, up and down the hills. He opened his anorak at the neck; Harriet wore a pretty navy-blue waterproof hat with a brim, which hid her sour expression.

At the top of the rise their leader stood on the broad grass verge and signalled the rest to join him. 'Are we all here?' he called. 'Is anybody missing?' People made a show of looking about them.

'The Blacks aren't,' one woman answered. 'Colin and Enid Black.'

The leader stepped out into the road. The others looked along it with him.

'No sign,' he said. 'No.' He leapt with alacrity up to his place of vantage. 'I think it will be worth waiting, in case anything has happened. Does anybody know them? Are they experienced walkers?'

'A bit on the slow side,' somebody ventured.

'She's not been well,' a woman said. 'She had 'flu over the Christmas period.'

'It's ten past twelve,' the leader informed them. 'We've made very good time. We – I've just worked it out – must be about halfway round. So I suggest that we park here and eat our sarnies. We're out of the wind and if it rains hard we can shelter in that little coppice on the other side of the road. I know it's a bit early for eating, but we can wait for the Blacks to arrive. If they don't turn up soon, I'll be asking for a volunteer to go back with a phone.'

The group scattered to both sides of the road and pulled out their provisions. Tim joined the Meades family who'd found a sheltered hump under a hedge. Adelaide issued steaming coffee from an enormous flask taken from her husband's rucksack to all four. Tim pulled out the ham sandwiches with lettuce and tomato which he had packed up for himself. Harriet, he noticed, had perched herself to his left. He was within a yard or two of her parents, but she had distanced herself from them all, five yards beyond him.

'Are you all right out there?' her father called.

'Very comfortable.'

Adelaide passed a mug of coffee for the girl to Tim, but he had to stand and make a step or two to hand it over. She took it from him, with only a mutter of thanks. The walkers seemed quiet now, concentrating on food, relaxed, watching the sky, which brightened. Rags of blue promised better things.

'They're here,' a man shouted, pointing down the road. 'The Blacks.'

All watched the two dark figures climbing the hill with slow competence. As they arrived, the leader stepped out to greet them. 'All well?' he asked, friendly, without condescension.

The couple answered cheerfully. Mr Black said, quite loudly, in answer to the questioning eyes of the party, that he'd had a bad attack of the cramp. He stopped and rubbed his calf as if to make sure that they all understood the exact location of his pain. He looked odd, leaning on his stick, lifting a leg, massaging it in warning. Tim could not recall seeing the couple at the meeting place. They seemed healthy enough, properly prepared.

The leader was now answering a question.

'We've done a little less than halfway,' he said. 'The rest is a bit more hilly than the first half. Have you got a mobile? No? I see. Not here.' Tim could hear the leader's voice, but not Mr Black's. 'Yes. I wondered if it might be easier if you had a rest and then went back the way we've come.' Black muttered some sort of objection. 'It's entirely up to you, of course, and I'm not sure whether it would be sensible for you to go on your own.' Almost immediately a nondescript middle-aged man shouted, far too loud as if from nervousness, 'We'll go back with you, Colin. We've got a phone. And we'll get about as much exercise as by going on.'

Mrs Black spoke for the first time, thanking the man and making no bones about it.

'That's settled, then,' the leader said. 'A friend in need is a friend indeed.'

The Blacks settled by their companions-to-be, unpacking lunch with noisy aplomb.

People now began to stand, pack away wrapping paper. They clearly did not want a long break. The leader went across to the Blacks, spoke quietly with a serious face, but smiled as he left them.

'I'll give you five minutes,' he shouted out. 'Then it's away to the woods.'

' "*Nous n'irons plus aux bois*," ' Tim said to Harriet, ' "*les lauriers sont coupés*." '

She did not answer.

179

When the party stood to move off, and it was all done efficiently, with no time wasted in last-minute changes of mind, Adelaide accompanied Tim to the road. He looked about for Harriet but she was on her own near the tail of the group.

'Have you and Harriet quarrelled?' Adelaide asked.

'Not as far as I'm concerned.'

'She seems very off.'

'Yes, but I've no idea why. I thought it might be the time of the month.'

'Possible. Is she often like this?'

'No,' the boy answered. 'This is the first time. You know, I always thought how well-balanced she was. Things must upset her, but she seemed able to put up with them.'

'You're sure there's nothing wrong between you?'

'No. Not to my knowledge.'

'Look, Tim, I know I've no right to ask you this.' She lowered her voice to a tactful whisper. 'Are you and Harriet having sex?'

He paused before replying. He felt his cheeks burn in the cold air. 'No. We don't. I know you'll think I'd say that whatever the truth. We do not; we have not had sex.'

Again a break, as if she used the moment to weigh his answer. 'She's sixteen now,' Adelaide began. 'The legal age. We talk about it and she tells me that some of her friends, girls in her class, are no sooner sixteen than they're dashing off to some clinic to get on the pill. And they tell them all about condoms, to keep themselves clear of AIDS or sexual diseases. Did you know?'

'Did I know about these clinics?' he asked.

'No. About these girls going down to those places, bold as brass?'

'They see doctors there. Properly qualified experts, don't they?'

'I suppose you're going to say that's better than having casual sex and hoping for the best.'

'Yes. I'd say that.'

'The doctors don't pass the information on to the parents. They leave it to the girls themselves to tell their parents when and if they think fit. Or wait until their mother finds the packet of contraceptive pills lying about in a drawer.'

'Would you be angry if that happened to you?' Tim asked.

'I'd explode. And even if I knew that eighty per cent of girls of that age were on the pill, and it won't be anywhere near as high as that, I'd still be concerned, because I'd want my daughter amongst the twenty per cent.'

'But she is.'

Adelaide, without losing pace, put her hand on his arm. 'You're sure, Tim,' she said, her voice strong in supplication. 'You're telling me the truth?'

He felt the pressure on his inner forearm. She looked at him, but their speed did not slacken. She was asking him, not demanding, but he could not help deciding that she would rather have been ordering him or sinking her teeth into him, forcing him to subject himself to her will. 'She's a beautiful girl,' he said hesitantly. 'But she knows her mind. If she wants something she'll do her best to bring it about. I think she's a bit like you.'

'Yes.' Adelaide's voice was dull now. 'But what's got into her now? She seemed furious with the whole world at breakfast. She didn't want to come. I insisted.'

'Is it her school work?' he asked.

'It may be. She's never complained before. She's clever and she works hard. I thought perhaps her period was late and that worried her. You say not.' That sentence carried menace again, as if she suggested that the devious Harriet was deceiving him. They marched on unspeaking.

Tim broke the silence. 'Your husband seems to be enjoying himself.' He pointed ahead where the professor led the party, making speed.

'Oh, him. He wouldn't know how to enjoy himself.' She sniffed. 'See if you can find out what's worrying Harriet, will you?'

Adelaide stepped away, as if to catch up with her husband. Tim looking back saw, to his surprise, that Harriet was a mere four or five yards behind him. He slackened his stride, allowing her to draw level. They did fifty yards together without speaking.

Harriet was first. 'What had the witch to say for herself?' she asked nastily.

'She was', he spoke slowly, with emphasis, 'worried why you seemed so unfriendly or off colour this morning. As I am.'

'And what conclusion did you reach? You and the wise witch?'

'She didn't know. I didn't. I'd be pleased if you'd tell me.' He coughed. 'I might be able to help.'

'I doubt it.'

'Try me. In the absence of anything better.'

'Katie Riddell,' she said. 'You were out with her. Last week.'

'Oh, Katherine. Is that her name? Riddell?' He smiled. 'That would be Tuesday or Wednesday. I was walking down to Arnold to collect my mother's car for her. It was in for a service. And we met at the corner of the road and walked to the garage together. She did whatever it was she was doing, library, I think, and I arranged to take her back. It's a longish walk, and uphill. How did you know about this?'

'You were seen. And she was dressed up.'

'You should send your spies to a good optician.' His words belied his misery.

'You took her home in your car?'

'I don't deny it.'

'And stood in the street outside her house snogging her.'

'She kissed me, certainly.'

As far as he could recall, the incident took place in an empty road. The walls of the large garden were high, there were six or eight steps upwards from the street gate to the bottom level of Katherine's grounds. Moreover at this time of year the evening was dark and the pavement dimly lit by an old-fashioned street lamp. He had politely climbed out of his mother's car to retrieve Katherine's books from the back seat. He glanced at them; the top volume had 'Inorganic Chemistry' in its title. While he was still awkwardly holding the pile, she had thrown her arms round him and glued her lips to his. In his surprise he managed to hold on to the books. Clearly this was not to be a snatched goodbye kiss. Her tongue forced its way into his unready mouth. They rocked together, but the books hindered him. She more than made up for his awkwardness and in the end he stepped back breathless from her embrace. He held out the books. She took them, straightened the pile and smiled graciously. She bobbed and dashed a kiss on his mouth; she was taller than Harriet.

'Thanks for the lift,' she said.

'A pleasure.'

'I'll see you again,' she said, and walked smartly to the gate and steps. He stood watching her, still taken aback, caught off guard, by the development. Katherine did not look back either at the lower gate or the upper, though she took her time closing both. He sat in the car, wiping his lips on a none too clean handkerchief. He had enjoyed the encounter; of that he had no doubt.

'Had you met her before?' Harriet was now asking him.

'Yes. I'd seen her at joint sixth-form meetings.'

'Had you spoken to her?'

'A time or two. By way of politeness. And I'd danced with her at the last sixth-form social. A waltz.'

'And you fancied her?'

'She seemed nice enough.'

'But you didn't know her name?'

'I knew it was Katherine. And I'd seen her once or twice in the street, and we spoke. We never stopped for long; we were usually going in opposite directions. She lives quite close to me.'

'You'd never kissed her before?'

'No.' His denial fell leaden, defiant. He lied. He had kissed her cheek when they lowered the lights as they danced.

They paused awkwardly. He opened the cross-examination. 'Who were your informants?' he asked.

'Two girls in my class. One lives just opposite and the other had come to tea with her.'

'And they just happened to be looking out of the window? It was getting dark.'

'Presumably they heard the car.'

'They can't have very interesting lives,' he countered, 'if they have to look out of their window every time a car draws up.'

'Maybe so. But they recognised Katherine and they thought it was you with her. And another girl who was listening said she'd seen you two together walking down Arnold Main Street.'

'Kissing?'

'No, she didn't say that. Why was she going all that way to the library there? Ours is much closer.'

'I asked her that. The Arnold one has a bigger selection. Especially of scientific books.'

'And did she get what she was looking for?'

'I asked if the visit was satisfactory and she said "yes".'

Again silence.

'And no more kissing?'

'There hadn't been any. I told you that. She didn't kiss me until we got out of the car outside her house. She was thankful for the lift.'

'Why did you have to get out of the car?'

'To open the back door and lift her pile of books out. One of them had fallen on the floor. I straightened them.'

'And then she kissed you?'

'She did. She threw her arms round me.'

'Out of gratitude? For the lift?'

'I suppose so.'

'And', Harriet continued doggedly, 'you didn't step back or try to fend her off?'

'No. I was taken by surprise and a bit off balance holding the books.'

'Was it just one kiss? Short and polite?'

'No,' he spoke now with exasperation. 'She kept it up. For a minute or two.' Now he was beginning to be angry. She'd no right to ask these detailed questions.

'And what are you going to do about it?' she asked.

'I don't understand you.'

'You think you can go about with any girl you like at any time you like?'

'I haven't said that,' he answered, steadying his voice.

'You haven't said that, no. It's not what you say, it's what you do.'

'You're thoroughly unreasonable.'

'I'm not.'

They walked now, getting nowhere in silence. He knew if their roles had been reversed he would have been as jealous. Harriet seemed to be fumbling in her anorak pocket, found a bit of a tissue. She dabbed at her cheek. She must be crying. He felt in his own pocket and took out the clean square of a folded linen handkerchief and, as unobtrusively as he could, held it out to her in the upturned palm of his left hand. He looked away to his right. Suddenly, with ferocity, she brought down her clenched fist hard on his wrist. Pain burnt; the white square dropped to the dirty road. He stopped in shock, turned and picked up the mud-wet linen. As he began to walk forward he refolded the handkerchief so that he could replace it in his pocket. Then three sharp strides placed him alongside Harriet. He did not

184

look at her, but thought he saw her dab again at her right eye.

A tall, middle-aged man caught them from behind. 'Well,' he said, 'enjoying it?'

Harriet said nothing. This was the man Tim had catalogued in his mind as the leader's second-in-command. Perhaps he'd lost his position of honour in the hierarchy to Henry Meades. Here was another disappointed human, speeding up to regain his status, his self-regard, swinging his arms.

'Yes,' Tim said. 'The weather's just a bit dull, but it hasn't rained yet.' He felt he had done his bit towards the sanity of the nation.

'There was no rain mentioned in the forecast,' the man said with confidence.

'You never know,' Tim added his mite of wisdom, as the other forged ahead.

From the back of the party there came, vaguely, the sounds of disturbance, and then a clear baritone voice, 'Edgar,' and again, more agitated, 'Edgar.'

People behind were slowing down or stopping. A third shout for Edgar reached the front, halted the leaders. The tall man had turned and was powering back down the road, elbows meaning business. One or two others fell out and followed Edgar. No one else from the front of the party made any attempt to pass Tim. Harriet ventured no more. Tim stepped up to the roadside, mounted the raised verge to look down the lane. A woman was lying on the grass, with a man kneeling beside her; Edgar reached the two figures. The whole party had now stopped and the leaders were straggling back a few steps in the direction of the accident. The leader broke away from the rest and marched down the road.

Tim stepped down from his perch to stand near Harriet, who had not left her original position. Her face was pale, but without trace of tears. The tip of her nose was red.

'An accident,' he said to her. He would be polite. She turned away slightly from him and did not answer. A moment later she moved over to her father. They exchanged a few words; the professor looked up hard at the sky, which had now darkened.

'Will it rain?' Tim heard her ask.

'It's a possibility.'

The air seemed colder, with a chill breeze chipping at their faces. One or two stamped their feet on the road to keep warm or slapped hips with crossed arms.

Adelaide appeared next to Tim. 'Where's Madam?' she asked.

'Gone over to talk to her father.'

'Have you sorted it out between you?' Adelaide asked.

'No. Afraid not.'

Adelaide waited for his explanation, but he gave none. Instead, after an awkward interval he asked about the accident at the back of the party.

'It's a Mrs Gill. She had a fall. Her husband was with her and he's a doctor so she should be all right. And the man who came down from the front, Edgar Somebody-or-Other, they called his name out, he's a charge nurse in the orthopaedic department at the hospital. So she's in good hands. She tripped over the edge of the bank and fell on to the grass and so she shouldn't be too badly damaged.'

'How old is she?'

'Fifties, perhaps. I've no idea.' She breathed in deeply. 'I don't know them. They had her sitting up and had slipped a ground-sheet under her and a blanket round her shoulders.'

Adelaide backed away and dived immediately into conversation with another woman, and then both set off in the direction of the accident. Twenty yards away, Harriet and her father seemed to have parted company.

Tim opened his anorak and retrieved a small bar of chocolate. He went across towards Harriet; there were quite a few place shiftings and shufflings amongst the rest. He opened the outer cover and divided the chocolate, six squares and four. He held the larger part out to her. 'Chocolate?' he said.

'No, thanks.'

'It won't bite you.'

She looked down at the silver-wrapped, neat confection as if he'd picked it up from the mud on the road. A car passed, but did not stop. The party cleared the road untidily. Harriet assumed the attitude of one who had much to talk about. Tim, fuming, decided this was no time for peace negotiations, ate chocolate. He worked his way ostentatiously down the bar, hoping she regretted her refusal to join him.

Adelaide returned. She seemed everywhere, marching, talking. 'Hello, there,' she said, almost shouting. Tim fished another bar from his pocket and offered it to her. She broke a piece and he signalled her to try with Harriet. The girl deliberately paid no attention, but this did not do. 'Hi. Chocolate,' she said and roughly shook the sleeve of the daughter's anorak. Harriet looked this time as if they had suddenly begun to speak a language she understood. She broke off two small squares and handed it back to her mother, who held it out to Tim.

'You have it,' he said. 'I've just finished a whole bar.'

'No, thanks. A little goes a long way with me.'

He signalled her to give it to Harriet.

'More chocky?' Adelaide barked.

Harriet looked at it, with its torn-edged red and silver wrappings, and shook her head. The bar was returned to Tim, who rewrapped it carefully and returned it to his pocket.

'How are they doing back there?' he asked.

'They've decided that there are no breakages, though she went down a hell of a wallop. She'll wait there with her husband, and Edgar will set off and pick up his car and then collect them. People are handing over scarves and shawls and flasks of coffee. There you are. Edgar's off. He doesn't hang about.'

'They'll have quite a wait,' Tim said.

'They might well. That's why they're trying to keep them warm. But out here at this time in the afternoon it's more sensible than hoping for a passing car. All three, Edgar, Jack up front and the Gills have mobiles so they can keep in touch.'

Jack, the leader, returned and spoke to the fast men. 'That's the most sensible thing,' he said. 'It means a bit of a wait for them, I'm afraid, but we can always hope somebody somewhere will help them out. That's the advantage of phones. She couldn't have chosen a worse place to have an accident. So far from anywhere. They may try to ring their son, if he's at home. We have to set a foolproof scheme up. They seem sensible. You never know with some people. In half an hour she might feel better and they start to wander back, and get lost. Are we all ready?'

He waved them on cheerfully.

The remainder of the walk proved barren to Tim. He walked with Harriet but she maintained the two dismissive yards between them. Once or twice he produced a question, but she vouchsafed no reply. When they finally arrived at the field where they had parked, the sky was quite overcast. They changed their boots and Tim handed round the rest of his chocolate. Henry Meades seemed cheerful, once calling out to Jack to ask how long Edgar would be before he'd return with the injured Gills.

'Shouldn't be long. His car's not here. He's not rung so I take it there's no further emergency.' Jack walked over. 'The Blacks have come and gone,' he said, 'so they must have made a fair pace back.'

'They might have cadged a lift,' Henry said.

'I don't know', said Jack, who shifted his cloth cap and scratched his scalp with the same hand, 'why some people come out.'

'Enjoyment,' the professor answered. 'And something unusual.'

'Uh. I come to see the changes in the land.'

'Do you go walking abroad?'

'Once a year.'

'And this year?' Adelaide pursued him.

'Northern Spain.'

Jack moved on, checking health and spirits. He took his responsibilities seriously.

When they were ready to drive off Adelaide asked Tim if he'd like to stay for dinner. He thanked her politely, but claimed that he had some school work to complete. He watched Harriet's face, but she showed no sign of emotion.

'I'll run you home,' Adelaide said, scowling at her daughter.

'No thank you. It'll be fine if you drop me at the top of Merton Avenue.'

Their journey was quiet. The young people sat in unproductive silence on the back seat. The adults discussed in a desultory way what they should eat for dinner. They stopped exactly where Tim would have wished. He thanked them, but Harriet said not a word. Tim guessed that as soon as she set off Adelaide would tongue-lash her daughter. Angry as he was, he wondered what attitude the father would adopt, what interruptions he would make. The boy could not guess. Their journey would not last more than five minutes, but Adelaide would waste none of them.

XVI

Tim did not sleep well. For the three days after his quarrel with Harriet his appetite disappeared. He did his best to seem normal, but one evening after doing his utmost with the large helping his mother served he was violently sick.

'What have you been eating?' his mother enquired when he returned to the room and announced the reason for his sudden departure.

'Nothing,' he said.

'You look awful. Pasty and with rings round your eyes.'

'Drink plenty of water. Wash yourself out,' his father advised.

'I can't think of what you've eaten that we haven't,' his mother declared.

Neither parent connected his nausea and lassitude with disprized love, though that came out a day or two later after his mother had met Adelaide.

'I hear you've given up Harriet?' Melissa asked cheerfully.

'That's about it.' He spoke amiably.

'Why was that?'

'She thought I liked somebody else better than her.'

'And are we allowed to know the name of this paragon?'

'Katherine Riddell.'

'No.' Melissa shook her head. 'Unknown to me.'

To his own surprise he gave a brief account of the lift back from Arnold.

His mother listened, grinning. 'You're too handsome by half, young man,' she said.

Tim stood unmoved. He had lost strength of feeling. Sore and sorry he might be whenever Harriet's pale beauty touched his memory, but he was not without admiration for his own nonchalant performance. Neither he nor his mother was in the habit of exchanging confidences of this nature, though his mother's easy way with the facts he'd given her, and her lack of moral judgement, settled pleasantly, smoothly, unexpectedly to his mood. He had imagined that one day when she asked why he saw nothing of Harriet, his excuses would be blocked with a review of the girl's qualities and a condemnation of his behaviour, lack of discrimination on finding such perfection in a girl and then almost immediately throwing it away.

'So there's no chance of a reconciliation?' she asked.

'I wouldn't think so.'

There followed a flurry of housewifely chores from his mother before she spoke again. 'Adelaide said that old Mr Meades is back at home, but he's not very well. Now it seemed to her that the old man set considerable store by the affection between you and his granddaughter. It gave him great pleasure to talk to the pair of you, to look at you both. Or so she says. And now he's not very well, he'd like you and Harriet to go round together to visit him.'

'She won't speak a word to me. That won't do the invalid much good.'

'Adelaide will try to convince her otherwise. She says that Mr Meades will probably make a quite considerable bequest to the girl if she's in favour.'

'When he dies?'

'Of course. But she thinks he might change his mind if he's crossed.'

'Won't he leave the major part of his estate to his son?'

'She doesn't know that. And neither does her husband. But he's on a high just now. After years of struggling on with not much chance of promotion, this curious line of mathematics that he's been slaving on for so long has suddenly become important so that now he's considered one of the glories of the university. And Henry can't help but be pleased when all these Americans and mid-Europeans come flocking to his door. He says he never expected it, that the best he could hope for would be that somebody in a hundred years would not only find it right, but would make use of it. He said to Adelaide, "I've never been lucky so it wasn't likely I'd be discovered." I don't know whether that's right. She says now it's happened she often asks him why he stuck by his precious theories, when anybody who was anybody just said he was blowing soap bubbles.'

'Why did he go on?'

'She says it is because he's basically awkward. Just like his father. That's why she doesn't want Harriet to get across the old man.'

'What will he do with his money if he doesn't leave it to Henry?'

'Battersea Dogs' Home.' Melissa laughed. 'The Conservative Party.'

'Not Mrs Smith?'

'Now why do you say that?'

'Well, she's lived in his house for long enough. She may have her own expectations.'

'They don't seem very friendly. What bit I've seen.'

'Oh.'

'I don't think he's friendly with anybody very much. And now Henry's becoming so famous, at least in academic circles, his father's jealous. So Adelaide says. When he was struggling along, as a plain lecturer, the old man used to taunt him. "Why don't you get yourself a chair somewhere? With all these new universities about nowadays I should think it would be easy enough to get a job where you could at least call yourself 'Professor'." But Henry wouldn't budge; he got on with whatever it is he did. He didn't answer the old tyrant back, however much his father roared on about his ambition or lack of it.'

'What now, though? Now Henry's really made his mark. Does he rub his father's nose in it?'

'Not really. Not from what Adelaide says. And that makes the old man madder than ever. "Why haven't they offered you a knighthood?" "Why aren't you a Fellow of the Royal Society?" And all Henry will say is that his satisfactions lie elsewhere. And that makes the old man wilder than ever.'

'So?'

'It's a touch and go situation. Adelaide fears, and it may be the result of her own temperament, that Henry will say something, either too arrogant or humble, that will make the old man explode and he'll send for his solicitor and cut his son off with the proverbial shilling.'

'It's not Dad, is it?'

'His solicitor? No.' Melissa stood upright. 'This is all very interesting, but what about you and Harriet? Are you willing to go along with her and try to put a pleasant face on it?'

191

'Suppose so,' he said, hardly moving his lips.

'Are you sure?'

'Where are my scruples?' he asked sarcastically.

'You think she's treated you badly.' His mother spoke slowly. 'And I dare say she has, though in such cases it's usually six of one and half a dozen of the other in my experience. But you might go along for the ride, or in the hope she'll change her mind about you. I don't know.'

'If I went it would be pure altruism on my part.'

'Great.' His mother now seemed to find the whole conversation amusing. 'I'll tell Adelaide what you say and she can work on it from there. I imagine it's too much to hope that you might yourself get in touch with Harriet?'

'You're right.'

'She seems a really nice girl to me. You can borrow my car.'

He gave her no answer.

Two days later Harriet rang. Tim's mother called him down to the telephone, her face creased into lines of conspiratorial, excited joy.

'Tim Hughes,' he said formally.

'Oh, it's Harriet.'

'Yes?'

'I wondered if you'd go with me to see my grandpa? He said he'd like to see us both.'

'Yes. When do you suggest?'

'Friday evening, if that's convenient for him. And you. About seven. I'll get my mother to ring.'

'I'll see if I can borrow my mother's car. That means about quarter to seven at your house. Let me know, will you?'

'Yes, I will. And thank you very much.'

'Your grandfather's not well, I understand.'

'No, he's quite poorly.'

'And how are you?'

'I'm pretty fit, thank you.'

'Good. Good. See you Friday evening.'

'Thank you very much.'

Tim replaced the phone very slowly and quietly.

He was on time when Adelaide opened the door for him on Friday. She made her usual lively fuss of him and told him that Harriet was almost ready.

'How's Mr Meades?' he asked.

'Not very well at all. He's still in bed.'

'What's wrong with him? Do his doctors not know?'

'I'm not sure that they do. His chest is bad, his blood pressure's high and they think he's clinically depressed.'

'And his heart?' At this moment Harriet arrived.

'No. Not good. Ah, here's Harriet.'

Tim greeted the girl politely. She wore a coat and a fur-trimmed hat that he had not seen before. Its modesty suited the fragility of her beauty. In no way did she seem embarrassed. As he walked down the garden path behind her, the faint, delicate odour of her perfume sweetened the air.

'It's very kind of you,' she told him once he had driven off.

'Not at all.' He would match her in politeness.

'We mustn't stay too long. He's really ill.'

'How long would you suggest?'

'My mother thought half an hour at the outside.'

'You give the nod.'

Mrs Smith let them into the house. 'I'm glad to see you,' she said dully. 'He's been looking forward to your visit.'

'How is he?' Harriet asked.

'He's not well, but he doesn't make it any easier for himself. He's frustrated that he can't have his own way. He thought he'd feel better if he could sit for an hour in the library and he carried on with the idea for two days, to the doctor, the nurse and to me. I took the brunt of it. The doctor said "Yes" in the end as long as he didn't overdo it. The nurse and I got him out, we practically had to carry him and he's a weight, but we managed it. Inside half an hour he was complaining. It wasn't as comfortable as his bed, as I'd told him. There wasn't a light near enough to his chair. We hadn't given him the right seat, books, drinks. The nurse said, "We've got him there and we'll leave him until just before I go. It makes a change for him." It didn't suit, I can tell you.'

Mrs Smith had taken Harriet's coat and hat. 'This way, please.' She led them upstairs. Tim had no idea where Meades's bedroom was. They passed the door of the library and into a large, light room on the same level. Beatrice Smith knocked, shouted sedately and ushered the young people in. 'Here we are.'

Harald Meades was sitting propped in his bed. His discoloured, puffed hands lay on the duvet in front of him like ugly frogs. His hair had been recently combed, but his cheeks seemed unhealthy, purple-pale and deeply wrinkled. 'Welcome,' he said, eyes wide open. 'I'm pleased to see you.'

Harriet crossed to the bed, bent and kissed the mottled ear and, holding his hand, asked how he was.

He muttered some answer. As Harriet stepped back, Tim moved forward and shook the old man's hand.

Mrs Smith had now moved chairs side by side a yard or two from the bed. She signalled the visitors to sit. 'Tea or coffee?' she asked. They chose coffee and Beatrice asked Meades what he wanted.

'Whisky and water,' he said.

'Have a heart,' she begged. 'The doctor would kill me.'

'That's two of us,' he replied, screwing up his eyes. Tim considered the ambiguities. The ghost of a smile played on the shapeless face.

'Are you warm enough?' Meades asked Harriet.

'Yes, thank you.' The room stifled her.

After an awkward hiatus Meades made another effort. This time he asked about their progress at school. Harriet offered a long, lucid account of her studies. She spoke without speed, saying how many days they had before her first exam and how she, and her teachers, had planned her revision. Meades closed his eyes, but undiscouraged she continued.

When she had completed her account her grandfather shifted uncomfortably. 'And what are your favourites?'

'English, Geography, French,' she said.

'And you'll do them in the sixth form?'

'That's the idea at present. I can always change my mind.'

'You've no inclination towards maths like your father?'

'No. I quite like the subject. But no.'

'You're more like me, are you? Bookish?'

'Yes.'

'Your father reads,' Tim offered.

'Yes. He does. I don't know how much he read when he was my age.' She looked towards her grandfather for enlightenment, but he had nodded off to sleep. The visitors sat in uncomplaining silence, but this was shortly broken by the arrival of Mrs Smith with coffee. She arranged the cups, filled, then handed them, with their chocolate biscuits, first to the visitors.

Once she was certain they were provided for, she drew a chair to Mr Meades's side of the bed, and shook two tablets from a small phial. 'Tablet time,' she said in a strong voice. Meades stirred. 'Come on, now. Tablets.' She slightly shook a shoulder. 'Here they are. The life savers.' She bent back to reach a cup of coffee from a table. 'Now, Harald.' He showed signs of uncoordinated activity. She held a tablet, pushed it between his lips. He took it reluctantly in. 'Sip away,' she said. He obeyed. They followed the same drill with the second tablet. 'Well done,' she said. 'It's not always as easy as that. Is it, Harald?'

'Has he a lot of tablets to take?' Harriet asked.

'Yes. If you shook him, he'd rattle.' She repeated the old joke with a bland strength of voice, before standing and drinking her own coffee, quite upright, much in command. 'Your turn, now, Harald,' she said. 'A real drink this time.' She moved to stand over him. 'Careful, now. Don't let's spill it today. No. You keep your hands down. I'll hold it for you. You just suck it in. It won't be too hot now. I've checked it. Good. Good. Down she goes. You must be thirsty this evening. Again? Don't be in such a tearing hurry. That's better. Good.' She removed the empty cup from his mouth.

'What time is it?' he asked, the voice clear, normal.

'Getting on for seven thirty.'

'In the morning?'

She gave a small shriek of laughter. 'No, you silly boy. Evening. You've got some friends here to visit you.'

'Friends?' His voice drooped, but he looked across at the young people. 'I'm not very good company,' he added. 'I keep dropping off. But, then, so did Napoleon, and Einstein. It did them a power of good. So they say.'

'Does Professor Meades nod off?' Tim asked, looking round.

'No,' Harriet answered. 'He's a very good sleeper at night.'

'So am I,' Mrs Smith said. 'I don't need to count sheep. My head no sooner touches the pillow than I'm away.' She stood up and replenished the visitors' tiny cups. Mr Meades watched the beginning of the action as if it were in some way extraordinary, but soon his chin fell to his chest and he almost rolled over. 'Give me a hand,' she shouted to Tim. Between them they straightened the sagging body and she punched his pillows into place.

'At what time do you put him down to sleep?' Tim asked.

'Usually about nine. That gives me a bit of time on my own to clear up the day's work.'

'Do you not get any help?'

'Oh, yes. We have a nurse in twice a day. And twice a week a woman comes in to bath him. He doesn't get too dirty. He's not incontinent. Not yet. He's misbehaved once or twice. And we have a woman who sits with him through the night. He's restless then, she claims.'

'Do you think he's in pain?' Harriet asked.

'I think he is from time to time. Headaches he has for certain, and rheumatism and arthritis in the ordinary way, for some years now, but this stroke or seizure or whatever it is has left him so that to make the slightest ordinary movement, sitting or standing, takes a great deal out of him.'

Mrs Smith spoke over the top of the body as she gently fingered his shoulders and back into place. The patient became calm, in comfort, eyes shut, his mouth smiling, his breathing steady. Her movements were gentle in the extreme, as with a small child. Tim remembered the forthright man of a few months back, and he could not imagine Meades allowing Beatrice to caress him thus in private, never mind in public. Her ministrations seemed almost inhuman, like those of a machine, without violence or jerkiness, each touch exactly like the one before. Her fingers courteously explored the skin of the neck and the cloth on his back, her expression not tender but concentrated upon delicate efficiency. Tim wondered what went through her mind.

She glanced up at him and smiled. 'He likes this,' she said to the boy. 'It's his cuddle time. He'd have it all day. It takes his stress away. I'm not sure whether he's awake or half asleep, but he's comfortable, as he's not when he's reading, say, or listening.'

'Does he watch the television?' Harriet asked.

'He has a set.' She pointed at the very large showy screen beyond the bottom of the bed, out of Harriet's view. 'He was always listening to the news bulletins, so I'll switch it on for him if it's the night-time. He never puts it on for himself, though he's', she pointed, 'got a whatever-they-call-it. A long-distance control.' She sighed, stopping her movements, as if she herself had been suddenly disabled by pain. It took her a minute to

recover and begin once more. 'I don't know whether he understands what's going on.' Beatrice smiled down on him. 'I don't
know sometimes whether I understand what it's all about. I
switch the news on, radio or telly, and listen. But if you asked me
five or ten minutes later what the first news item was I often
couldn't tell you, unless it was something I was particularly
interested in.' She glanced up at Harriet. 'Hold your grandpa's
hand, darling, will you?' she asked. 'He'll like that. A touch has
more effect on him now than saying something.'

Harriet shyly took his right hand. His face retained the
expression that had accompanied Mrs Smith's massage.

'There,' Mrs Smith whispered, 'you've two ladies looking
after you this evening.'

Meades opened his eyes, stared dumbly about him, sank back
into ease.

'Have you young people finished your coffee?' Mrs Smith
asked. 'Yes? Then I think it's time to go. His night nurse will be
here at about eight thirty and we'll tuck him away. He seems very
content. Seeing you has done him good. It's all come together
and that really is as it should be.'

The young people stood. Harriet, Tim noticed, stroked her
grandfather's hand before she lifted it and laid it on the duvet.

'Your visitors are going now,' Beatrice said, without response.
'You're not thinking of waking up, that I can see. Can't you say
goodbye?' She turned to Harriet. 'Perhaps you would give your
grandpa a kiss.' The girl did as she was told. 'There, wasn't that
nice?' She turned to Tim. 'Shake hands. Not too vigorous, now.'
The boy took the old man's hand. 'Goodbye, sir,' he said. 'I hope
you'll feel better soon.'

'Not much hope,' Mrs Smith murmured.

'We'll come and see you again,' Harriet promised.

Mrs Smith made sure her patient was propped securely by his
pillows, then turned to repack and pick up her tray. 'Would you
open the door, please?' She motioned towards Tim. The two
followed her downstairs. 'Just come into the kitchen for a
second,' she ordered. She placed her tray by the sink and then
turned to them, her hands crossed in front of her. 'Thank you for
coming. He was pleased; I could tell that from his body as I
massaged him. Sometimes, if things have gone wrong, he'll fight
me with his muscles. He likes it, but on bad days he resists.'

'He doesn't talk much,' Harriet said.

'No. That's only in these last few days. It seems too much of an effort. He understands what we're saying but he can't or won't answer.'

'Does he eat at all?'

'Very little. Soup with a scrap of toast in it. A spoonful of blancmange. He's getting weaker by the hour. That's why I wanted the two of you to come. He's really fond of you, together. He often said so. And he was.'

'What does the doctor say?' Tim asked.

'What can he? He comes regularly to see him and is very nice. But there's little he can do. A week ago the nurse and I could get him into the bath between us. Not now. His legs seem to be at loggerheads with the rest of his body.'

'Is it the illness or the drugs?' Harriet asked.

'Both, I'd guess. I don't think it will be long before we have to put him into hospital. I'd like to keep him here while we can. Nobody likes hospital, but they're trained to handle people like him.'

'Is there anything we can do?' Harriet asked.

'I don't think so. Ten days ago you could have sent him a picture postcard and he'd have looked it over. But I don't think he would now. You can try.'

'We will,' Harriet said.

'You never know.' That seemed her motto.

'Will he get better?' Tim asked.

'No.' That sounded plain. 'He might hang on for a short time. He's looked after himself.'

She showed them solemnly out into the dark street. It seemed not long to Tim since he, Jules Bishop and Mr Plunkett stood at this gate in the wall while inside a robust Meades waited to employ them. Plunkett was to leave the school to be a headmaster in Lancashire in September. All change.

'He seemed so thin,' Harriet whispered. 'His pyjama jacket looked made for somebody three times his size. All his flesh has dropped away.'

'He hardly eats anything.'

'It's awful. Is he going to die?'

'It looks like it.'

'It looks like it,' she repeated.

198

Now she was weeping quite openly but without show. Tim took her hand and led her the few yards along the road to the car. He seated her comfortably and went round to his door. Now, perhaps because of the enclosed space, he could hear her cying. Uncertainly he put his left arm round her and she snuggled into his shoulder. 'Don't cry,' he said.

'It's wrong,' she said. 'He's only in his early seventies.'

'That's not too bad, even these days.' That sounded insulting, to her, to her grandfather, to himself. 'I mean. He's had an interesting life.'

'Do you think he feels so ill and helpless that he wants to die?'

'I don't know in his case. When you hear of some suicides they seem to want to be out of it all. I know some are supposed to be signalling for help, but most must be serious about it. Your grandpa has plenty to live for, especially when I think how he spent all that time and money choosing the pictures for his library. He deserves a few more months to enjoy it all.'

Harriet looked up at him. Her eyes were tearless now and the pupils dark in the lamplight of the street. She burrowed into his coat. He tightened his grip, but said nothing. He was afraid that if he spoke he'd put himself into disfavour again.

'Poor Grandpa,' she said. 'I'm his only grandchild. My parents had another child before me, but he died while he was being born. And I've done nothing much for him. It's only in these last few months that I've had anything to do with him.'

'That was your parents' fault, not yours.'

'I ought to have asked. My father visited him and made a remark or two. But I never followed it up. We saw him occasionally. This is the time he began to be jealous of Daddy.'

'And did your father resent it?'

'He never said so. I suppose he noticed it, though I'm not sure. He'd take it as a compliment, a proper reward for all his work.'

They looked round the few dark yards of the street which they could see from the front seat.

'Thank you for coming with me,' she said at last.

'Not at all.'

He could not go further than this. He felt no very great attraction towards the girl in her fur-trimmed hat, with her delicate perfume. 'Shall we go?' he asked. He withdrew his arms.

199

'No. May we sit here together for a few minutes? It was awful in there, so closed in, it made me feel quite ill.'

'I thought Mrs Smith was looking after him well, didn't you?'

'Yes, I suppose so. But she was too detached from it all for me. What she did she did as if she was being paid for it.'

'Does that make a difference?' he asked. 'Especially if she does it well. And she seemed to me to know what was best for him and to do it efficiently.'

'Yes.' She yielded and wound down her window an inch or two. A tiny blast of cold air reached him. Touched, he put an arm about her shoulders and pulled her towards him again. That he did this without undue difficulty seemed to demonstrate to him that she had no great objections to his intrusion. He waited shortly to learn if she had second thoughts, and then went to kiss her mouth turned towards him. Her lips were cold under his. She pressed harder before she snatched her face away.

'I don't want to die,' she said.

'None of us do.' He kissed her, but she jerked her head back.

'I meant my grandpa. I don't want him to die.'

'I know that. Especially when you're just beginning to know him.'

She kissed him again, with a painful awkwardness. He slipped his hand into her coat. Even from over a thickish woolly cardigan, a winter dress and a brassiere he felt her nipple grow hard. He stroked her, excitement mounting. She groaned with a polite, subdued ecstasy, dabbing furiously at his face with her wet mouth, and then sat suddenly upright. 'Oh, Tim,' she said, 'thank you.' She sighed. 'Just drive me round one or two of these roads. There'll hardly be any traffic here in the Park at this time of night.' He followed her instructions. They stopped on her orders outside a mansion with a huge gothic door which led impressively down some steps and straight on the street.

'There'll be a passage along there behind the door,' he guessed, out loud.

'There is. How did you know?'

'I didn't, but with a place that size they won't want a door from the street leading straight into their living spaces.'

'There are two corridors,' Harriet said, 'set at right angles from a kind of rounded chapel with pillars behind the door. One is straight behind this wall.' She signalled down the street. 'The other leads into the house, a bit like Grandpa's. And between the two walls is a courtyard with shrubs and trees. It's large and mostly paved, and in the summer when you can see, it's like a mediaeval church.'

'You've been there? Yourself?'

'Yes, a girl in my class, Dorothea Dacres, lives there. Her father's a top scientist at Boots. Her mother's French. We were best friends lower down the school. Not so much now. We haven't quarrelled. We became interested in different things.'

He examined, as best he could, bending, the carving round the doorway, saints and martyrs, kings and mounted knights. 'I like the idea of spending your money on this carving and these arches and pillars,' he said.

'Why?'

'It's romantic. It leads you to believe you're living, or trying to, in the transcendental.'

'Transcendental,' she said. 'Oh, above and beyond all others?' She appeared to muse on this. 'It seems a strong defence to be round poor, weak, fading old men like my grandpa.'

'No,' he said, 'it doesn't stop them dying. It keeps the rain off them. That's all.' Tim breathed deeply. 'Is your Mr Dacres an old man?'

'Not as grandpa. It's not Mr Sir Joseph. Older than my father. Dorothea was the youngest of four. By a long way.'

'Was he like your grandfather?'

'In no way. I don't suppose it crossed his mind that he was buying a beautiful, unusual, out-of-fashion house.'

'Why that one and not, let's say, two or three others?' Tim probed.

'You're argumentative. I don't know. It may not have been his choice. His wife may have liked it. Or a rival he'd want to do down had admired it, so he'd snapped it up to spite him. It may have reminded him of some place from his childhood, or a period of his life when he was doing exceptionally well. Or some combination of reasons.'

'Yes.'

'It's only you who wants the man inside to suit the outward appearance.'

'Yes,' said Tim. 'And that's because I think of Grandpa Meades dying inside a house he's made beautiful for himself.'

'And at the last it doesn't matter?'

'No. But it's mattered to him over so many years. While he was alive and fully himself.'

'That's right,' Harriet said and suddenly snapped open the door of the car, clambered out, to stand nose in air in the chill darkness of the street. She took three or four steps on the steeply sloping pavement, then stopped before windmilling her arms together backwards. Then she ventured two more short steps forwards and leaned on the bole of a lime tree.

Tim opened his door. The cold was sharply unpleasant. 'Don't stay outside there,' he called. 'It's too parky.'

She turned towards him smiling, then crossed the narrow pavement to slap at the stones of Sir Joseph Dacres's wall. She examined the surface for effect, then her hand.

'Don't knock it down,' he said. Words carried easily. 'It's expensive.'

She looked again at her hands, came uphill, threw herself into her seat while he stood in the shelter of his half-opened door.

'You have to admit it's a beautiful door.'

He asked her to repeat the remark before he reached out to slam his door shut.

'Do you think it's really mediaeval?' she asked. 'Stolen from some church they were demolishing?'

'I don't know how you'd tell. I should guess not. It's marvellous what modern craftsmen can do when they're put to it. But I just don't know. The house isn't mediaeval inside, is it?'

'Apart from that courtyard, no.'

'The rest is central heating,' he said, 'and wall-to-wall carpet?'

'As far as I can remember.'

He took her right hand, which struck cold. She sat stock still, occupied with some thought.

'What next?' he asked. 'Shall I drive round a bit more?'

She attended to his question at last. 'Back home, please,' she answered. 'They'll wonder where I am. My mother will be worrying.'

He drove slowly up the hill, crawling so that she could look about her. Tim felt bafflement. Their conversation about the Dacreses' door seemed not irrelevant, but distantly symbolic of their real concerns, the condition of the dying Mr Meades, the end of his ambitions. Neither was used to death. Harriet frowned slightly as she stared into the windscreen.

'Are you all right?' he asked.

'Yes, thank you.'

They left the Park by one of the top, narrower gates and drove down a lighted main road. They said little to each other, even when they were stopped and guided round the scene of a collision with flashing lights from police cars and an ambulance in attendance. That fitted the weakness of the boy's mood and Harriet seemed inhumanly quiet, without comfort.

Outside her house she asked him if he would like to come in for a few minutes. He refused, standing with her on the pavement. She shuffled. 'There's something,' she said, 'which I ought to tell you.'

He waited. She was in no hurry. He bit his cold bottom lip.

'I ought to have told you before I asked you to visit Grandpa with me tonight.'

He murmured exculpation wordlessly, his sounds polite.

She looked with puzzlement at his efforts, needing encouragement. 'I ought to have told you that I have been out with Julian Bishop.'

At a pang of jealousy he managed a polite noise of understanding, then forced himself into explicit speech. 'Did your mother know?' he asked.

'Yes, she did. She rather encouraged me.'

'She's changed her mind, then,' he said. 'Hasn't she?'

'Yes. She has.' She shifted from foot to foot. 'She told me at one time to go nowhere near him. But then she got to know his parents somehow. And they came over to visit us. And Mrs Bishop and my mother are thick as thieves now. And Julian came with them and asked me to go to the cinema with him.'

'To see what?'

She did not answer, did not apparently hear the question though they were two yards apart.

'He asked when his mother and mine were both there. I thought Mummy would just choke him off with some excuse about my being too busy with homework, but, no. "I'm sure Harriet would enjoy that," she said. And there it was fixed up.'

'Did you want to go?'

She gave that some consideration. 'I didn't mind. I'd sooner have gone with you. I thought you and I had finished, though. He was quite nice. A lot less pushy. We said we'd get together again and then suddenly my mother comes up out of the blue with this idea that Grandpa wanted to see you and me together. She thought it a good scheme, but she always does. I told her you and I had finished, and you'd refuse, but she said you'd do it just to please Grandpa since he was so ill. Did you mind?'

'Well,' he said, hesitating.

'You did. So should I. But what worried me most was that I ought to tell you first I'd been out with Jules and we were thinking of doing it again. But I couldn't seem to be able to start. You were quiet and buttoned up with nothing to say to me.' She smiled diffidently. 'Perhaps it was me, not you at all. I felt guilty.'

At that moment a few yards away the Meadeses' front door opened with a flash of light. Sharp steps delivered Adelaide by the front gate. 'I thought I heard you,' she said. 'Come along in.'

'No, thanks,' Tim answered. 'Harriet's asked me, but I ought to be getting back.'

'You needn't stay long.' He did not answer so that she was forced to turn her attention to her daughter. 'How was your grandfather?' she asked.

'Poorly.'

'Was he pleased to see you?'

'He was asleep a good part of the time.'

'He didn't recognise you, then?'

'I think he did. It was difficult to tell. He looked really ill.'

'Yes,' said Adelaide. 'Well, don't stand out here in the cold or you'll be ill.' She turned, shouting over her shoulder, 'Come inside.'

She left the door open for them, lights blazing outside and in.

'I hate her sometimes,' Harriet whispered.

'She means well. I'll come in for two minutes.'

He locked the car and took her hand. They stood by the closed garden gate and kissed. They experienced the coldness of lips and cheeks.

'I wish spring would come,' she said, knowing that it had touched her as they stood with their arms about each other.

Two weeks later Harald Meades died.

Another stroke had felled him in his bed and he was rushed

away to hospital where he hung on, mostly unconscious, for a few days. Adelaide went each lunchtime to see the old man, stood a minute or two by his bed staring down at the unconscious bundle. She made a search of his locker, packing into a bag any necessary washing. Occasionally she spoke briefly to other patients and invariably questioned the nurse, briefly and to the point, before rushing off to her office. Henry Meades went twice in the evening, the second time accompanied by Harriet. Neither knew what to do or say. The old man was in a private room, bare and tidy. A young nurse looked in on them. Henry asked if there was anything they could bring.

'Not really,' she said.

'Is he suffering?' Harriet asked.

'I don't think there is any pain. We see that he has enough to drink and try to give him soft foods. Not that he's interested. We haven't withdrawn his drugs.'

'Has he made any improvement in the last few days?'

'No. Not really. Your wife comes in at lunchtimes. She's very faithful. I don't think he knows.'

'How long has he to live?' Henry asked.

'I don't think anyone knows. Not the doctors. Everything is being done for him that can be.'

'I'm sure it is.'

'We'll see to it that he's comfortable for as long as it's possible.'

This last exchange, polite and subdued, between the professor of mathematics and the young nurse in her blue uniform, drew tears from Harriet when she reported it to Tim.

'It shook Daddy. He wasn't used to a mere girl comforting him in that fashion. He thinks young people don't know anything these days, and here was this nurse telling him they were doing for Grandpa all that they could.'

'What did Henry say?' Tim enquired.

'He didn't know what to say. He told me on the way out, "I don't think your grandpa would see much sense in all this. He liked to set his own course." And then he shook his head. I guess he'd have seen it as more satisfactory if Grandpa had died at once, alive one minute and dead the next, like drawing a line under some computation he'd done. He'd come round to like his father a lot more these last few months.'

'Because his father began to admire him.'

'Yes, because that made my father confident with his father. I don't know if that's the truth or something I've made up.'

The Hughes family went to Harald's funeral in the city church. The ceremony was well attended; his old school had sent a line of prefects and masters. The book trade was well represented. A whole set of men and women from London put in a well-turned-out appearance, and continued after the service to eat the fine buffet meal Mrs Smith and Adelaide's caterers had put together. The two women seemed in constant if quiet contact. Oddly, on Henry's orders, the library was kept locked. This seemed wrong to Tim, but perhaps the professor knew something the boy did not; perhaps these bibliophiles were not to be trusted.

At the reading of the will, some days after the funeral, Tim – who to his immense surprise had been invited to attend by Meade's solicitor at the funeral meal – learnt that the closing of the library was demanded in the will, as was the opening of the document on the next Saturday after the funeral. The bequests were simple: to Beatrice Smith a decent three-bedroomed house on the far side of the river together with £30,000 for its initial upkeep; to Harriet £15,000; to Timothy Christian Hughes £1500; for the rest, five valuable pieces of property, his house, the shops in Beechnall and London, and a warehouse and premises in Derby, and something over £600,000 in banks and investments, all went straight to Henry Dale Meades, professor of mathematics, his son. There were no bequests to charity and no comments on the heirs. All was simple, reduced, plain, typical. There were no arguments. Tim did not know why he received his inheritance. Meades had liked him and judged him as one of the family, his granddaughter's boyfriend and thus worthy of a small gesture. The will had been drawn up just two months before his death.

Adelaide took credit for Tim's inheritance. At first her attitude to the will was ambiguous. One minute her father-in-law had done exactly what she would have advised, and thus justly. Then the next she showed annoyance that she had not been mentioned by name. True, the bulk of the old man's fortune had gone to Henry, but a favourable note of her kindness in the last few months would have definitely shown people the part she had played in the reconciliation of father and son. Charles Hughes

206

would have none of that. The amount left to Henry would, Charles guessed from what he'd heard, be over two million pounds and the reason why the son had inherited almost all was that he had impressed his father. The professor had spent twenty years following his own devices to little effect, it appeared, and had then finally been recognised as a considerable mathematician, acknowledged by the rest of the academic world. That he had done this, against his father's expectations, stood in his favour. He had achieved what his father had never managed.

'So everybody's almost satisfied?' Melissa asked her husband.

'Nearly. Nine out of ten.'

'And Tim's fifteen hundred?'

'I don't understand that at all.'

Harriet at the gate on the chilly spring night knew nothing of this. Adelaide, the girl knew, had been uncertain, fearing the old man would do something foolish and shame her before he died, and was rarely these days in the best of tempers. Her friendship with Julian Bishop's mother was, God knew why, already floundering. Adelaide inhabited a harsh place in an unfair world.

Tim took Harriet's hand and they kissed. Lights glared still as the front door gaped open. Faintly they could hear music.

The two stepped inside. Adelaide appeared, agitated, rebuking Harriet for leaving the door open so long. 'Hang your coat up,' she ordered Tim. He wasn't wearing one. 'Go in with your father.' She pushed a door ajar, pointed the way and rushed off.

The music could now be heard plainly. Piano and orchestra.

'What is it?' Harriet asked him.

'Mozart. Slow movement K488. Unusual key. F sharp minor.'

She kissed him for his pedantry.

'Come in,' the professor said loudly, cheerfully, as they entered. A door banged out at the back. Adelaide at work. Henry sat with a writing pad on his knee.

'We're not disturbing you?' Harriet asked.

'No. Not at all. I'm delighted to see you', he searched for the word, sketching on the empty air with his biro until the cliché arrived, 'lovebirds. I've not seen or heard much of you, young man, recently.' He seemed genuinely pleased.

They both assumed expressions of satisfaction.

'What's it like out?' he asked. Adelaide had obviously told him about his father.

'Cold,' Harriet answered.

Tim nodded agreement; they sat together on the sofa, strangely pleased with each other. A screech from Adelaide from the next room for Harriet shattered the calm.

The girl rose. 'Duty calls,' she said.

'Exactly,' her father said. 'Or danger.' Neither youngster recognised his quotation.

Harriet left leisurely to help carry in the coffee. The professor glowered at his notepad for a second time before he put it to the floor. He smiled again. Mozart mused, disconcerting them, comforting them all, divinely.